Night of Fire

"TELL ME A TALE, CASSANDRA," BASILIO SAID.

"There was a woman who lived in London, who had lost her courage in a terrible marriage, and had come to believe the only good men God ever made were her brothers."

He gazed down at her, his thick-lashed eyes very sober. "What happened to her?"

"A letter arrived from a stranger in a faraway land: a letter scented with the sea and olive trees. The images and words were very beautiful, and the woman thought he must be a middle-aged scholar, balding and sincere."

Basilio's eyes crinkled. "She did not imagine him to be the most virile and handsome of all men?"

"Oh, not at all. Quite dull, really. Over the months they shared many letters, telling their deepest thoughts to one another. And when he invited her to see his country, she recklessly took his invitation."

"And then she discovered a virile stallion," he teased wickedly.

Cassandra shook her head. "She discovered a man who was beautiful inside and out, when she had despaired of ever knowing such a man."

He kissed her and she kissed him back, tenderly stroking his body. "Thank you, Basilio," she whispered.

He tugged her close to him, and exhausted, they slept.

Other **AVON ROMANCES**

BARBARA SAMUEL

Night of Fire

AVON BOOKS
An Imprint of HarperCollins*Publishers*

This is a work of fiction. Names, characters, places, and incidents are products of the author's imagination or are used fictitiously and are not to be construed as real. Any resemblance to actual events, locales, organizations, or persons, living or dead, is entirely coincidental.

AVON BOOKS
An Imprint of HarperCollins*Publishers*
10 East 53rd Street
New York, New York 10022-5299

Printed in the U.S.A.

Part One

*Ask me why I send to you
This primrose, thus bepearled with dew?
I will whisper to your ears
The sweets of love are mixed with tears.*

ROBERT HERRICK

Prologue

London
May 1788

Cassandra told herself that she had recovered. That she was a woman of the world, and did not fall to pieces over a doomed romance. But the moment she saw him, when he walked into a box across the opera hall, she knew she had lied to herself.

He was out of place, and so unexpected that she gaped for a long moment before she could fit her mind around the fact that it was him.

Basilio.

Here, at the opera.

In London.

Blackness prickled at the edges of her vision. She realized she had not breathed, and inhaled deeply, but she could not look away.

Behind him was a man she vaguely recognized, a ruddy-faced lord from a county near her estate, which only made it all the stranger. Two

3

women had settled at the front of the box, but the men continued some deep discussion, their heads bent together, one graying, the other darkest black.

A flash of memory hit her like a blow: her hand, white as moonlight against the jet of his hair, the curls leaping around the turn of her finger—

"Oh, God," Cassandra whispered.

Her brother Julian leaned closer. "I'm sorry—I didn't quite hear you."

She put her hand on his sleeve, trying to remember how to arrange her expression normally. "Nothing."

In the box across the crowded, noisy room, Basilio nodded seriously at something, and his hand settled in a quieting sort of way upon the shoulder of the small woman in front of him. She seemed hardly to notice, but even across such a distance, Cassandra read discomfort in her stiffness.

Abruptly, Cassandra stood, her limbs quaking. "Julian, I feel quite ill. I must go."

He leapt to his feet, his arm circling her shoulders. "What is it?"

She waved a hand, bent to pick up her shawl from the seat, and dropped it when her betraying fingers could not hold on to it. She stared at it, the beads glittering along one edge. It looked like water, she thought distantly, the way it shimmered in a pool on the dark floor of the box. It made her think of another shawl, on another floor, and she closed her eyes against the pain of that memory.

How could a week have changed her life so utterly? A single week, torn from the hundreds and hundreds that made up her life. Forty times that number had passed since then, and none of them had changed her, turned her inside out, made her into a woman she no longer always recognized.

Julian swept up the shawl and captured her hands, bending to frown closely. "You're shivering like a wet pup!" Bracing her elbow, he said, "Let's get you home."

"Yes." She vowed to keep her eyes lowered, but the temptation was too great. One more glance at him. Only one.

But of course it was the dangerous one. For across that distance, across the milling scores of humanity in the gallery below, Basilio chose that moment to raise his head. Their eyes locked, and Cassandra's heart was flooded with the pain of his gentleness, his passion, his words.

His love. Yes, his love, most of all.

She fancied his face went pale, and he hastily removed his hand from the woman's shoulder, as if it burned him.

It gave her courage. Tossing her bright copper head, she said calmly, "Please take me home, Julian."

Part Two

My face in thine eye, thine in mine appears,
And true plain hearts do in the faces rest.

JOHN DONNE

Chapter 1

Eighteen months earlier. . . .

Danger arrived in the form of a letter.

On that cold and rainy day, Cassandra huddled close to the fire in her sitting room. Her hands were encased in fingerless gloves, her shoulders draped in a thick woolen shawl, her legs covered with a lap robe. Even so, her nose was cold.

She was supposed to be working, but even with the gloves, her fingers had grown stiff after an hour, and it was not a particularly exciting project, anyway—a rote translation piece for a professor who would pay her well and claim the credit.

Sipping tea, she stared gloomily at the long windows streaked with a cold March rain. Rain and rain and rain. Ordinarily she didn't mind it, she found stormy weather exhilarating and stimulating. But the sun had not shown itself in nearly a month, and even Cassandra was weary of it. If it went on much longer, they would all have mold dripping from their fingernails. Society matrons would declare green hair to be the only shade for the season. She amused herself for a moment imagining a rout crowded with beauties sporting twists of mold from their coiffures.

A sniffle in the hallway shattered the amusing picture just as Cassandra was about to embroider it fully—waistcoats brocaded in silk and mildew, perhaps. She sighed and turned. Her maid, Joan, had had a cold for a week.

"Letter just come for you, my lady."

"Thank you." At least it was something to break the monotony. Cassandra hoped it might be from her sister Adriana in Ireland, who had once been a very good correspondent—love had made her neglectful. Cassandra tried not to mind.

At the sight of the thin, elegant writing on the letter, her heart jumped. Even better than Adriana! She had not dared hope for a letter from Italy yet.

As the maid left, Cassandra put aside her tea and carried the letter to the window seat. It was colder there, but the light was good. For a moment, she only held it up to look at her name written in his beautiful script, letting the simple presence of it enliven her day. Already she felt warmer, as if the paper itself carried beams of Tuscan sunlight that now leaked into the room, buttery and rich. She lifted it to her nose and inhaled the evocative scent of the faraway—sometimes she thought it was the ocean breezes she smelled, at others she thought it might be his cologne.

She ran her finger over the black ink that had written her name, *Lady Cassandra St. Ives*, feeling the faint indentation his pen had made. With her thumb, she brushed the raised letters of the words within the paper, a thick packet this time, words she would read, then read again, and put away, then take out and read again.

Count Montevarchi. She imagined him to be a stout, short-sighted man, middle aged if she were to judge by the breadth of his studies and travels. He wrote magnificently well, bringing his lovely, faraway world to her.

The correspondence had begun nearly two years before, when he'd written to praise an essay she'd written on Boccaccio. She'd been quite proud of it, thinking she had captured well the vivid, witty, even bawdy sense of the master, and Count Montevarchi's letter had commented on each of the points she'd thought particularly fine. He'd praised her mightily, which was heady enough.

Then he had confessed he'd been languishing for over a year after the death of his brothers, and her essay had "broken through the clouds of sorrow over this man's heart and allowed the fresh breeze of laughter to enter." Touched, Cassandra had written back and enclosed a new essay, which she hoped he would find as cheering as the first.

In return, he'd sent travel articles that he'd written—lush and sensual things that captured exotic and sunny places. They'd exchanged dozens of letters now, sometimes crossing in the mail in their eagerness, letters that became, somehow, very heartfelt. The Count was a thwarted scholar who'd had to don the mantle of his inheritance, returning to the provincial world where his compatriots did not care to discuss poetry. Though she already had a circle of witty and artistic friends, Cassandra had found it easy to express her deepest ambitions to him.

It was safe. She knew that was a part of the appeal. A confirmed bachelor scholar, a thousand miles or more away, who *listened*. It was so very rare. And that he should also be a man with a soul painted in the colors of poetry, who responded entirely to her mind instead of her physical presence, made him a very dear friend indeed. He also embodied some of the qualities she would most like to develop in herself. His example had made her braver these past months.

At last she turned the letter and broke the seal.

Villa de Montevarchi, Toscana
2 April 1787

My Dear Lady Cassandra,

I have had poor news and find myself driven here tonight to write to you. It is an affair of little importance, a matter of duty I must attend to which gives me no pleasure, so you need not worry it is some awful thing I dare not speak of. Only wearisome.

I am honored that you enjoyed my essay on Cypress—and will now urge you again to indulge that longing I sense in you to travel yourself. Why not begin by coming to my Tuscany? Here you would be able to test your bravery under the guidance of a friend. By your writings, I sense you are braver than you know, and since you are a widow, there is none to tell you it is not appropriate. Perhaps it is just the tonic you need to inspire your fine work even more. I will tempt you with the lure of my small collection of Boccaccio manuscripts, which I would enjoy sharing with one who appreciates their worth. Would it not be the deepest pleasure to hold them in your own hands?

And here is more temptation: I would have wine sent up from my vineyards (truly, you are deprived if you have not drunk our wines) and have my cook prepare the best of his native dishes to shock your tender English palate. Perhaps we could travel to Firenze for the opera, or picnic by the sea. My land is beautiful, inspiring—I suspect that you would find it most agreeable.

You spoke again of my poetry. I do labor poorly at the art, and find it a most frustrating pursuit. How to capture the perfection of a moment, when the sunlight falls, just so, across *the gray branch of an olive? And yet I am driven to it, again and again, like the painters who come here to revel in the light, driven to attempt to capture God in some small way. The holiness of a child's innocent smile, the way a woman bends her head and shows the soft, clean place on the back of her neck—even the burst of sweetness from a plum, plucked from the tree, its juices sweet and hot from the sun exploding from that tender layer of skin into my mouth! Even now, I hear the music from the kitchen as servants clean up the dinner they have served and make the room ready for morning, and I try to think how to snatch that sound from the air and send it to you. One man is singing, and his voice is as fine as any opera tenor, and now another joins, and another, and there are four of them together, their hands clattering pots and clanging spoons and sweeping, and woven all through it is that song. Down the hill, on the road below the villa, there is a woman laughing, and in my imagination I see her as a gypsy, wild dark hair falling from a fine white face, about to make love to her husband, and I smile that my thoughts should go in such a direction. On my table, a breath of sea-scented wind flutters over the candle and threatens to put me in the dark, and still I labor to capture the music of the night. Imperfectly. Always imperfectly.*

And, as my father always said, to what purpose?

*Ah, you see how melancholy lies upon me
tonight. Let me banish it now by saying yes, you
are brave, dear lady. Brave enough to carve that
life you envisioned, brave enough to hold salons
and gather like minds to you—as you have gathered mine. It is a gift, and I thank you for sharing it with me.*

*Come to Tuscany, my lady. Breathe new
winds.*

*Your humble servant,
Basilio*

Cassandra's eyes were inexplicably damp as
she finished reading. She held the letter in her
lap and looked out at the gray, wet world
beyond.

Test your bravery.

Did she dare?

Chapter 2

Tuscany
August 1787

The sound of the horses clopping—tick tock, tick tock—along with the warm sunshine pouring on her head, had lulled Cassandra into a drowsy state of delirious contentment. She smiled at the novelty of the moment—the wagon itself, and her skirts spread over the bench seat; the wagon-master in shirt sleeves, a battered hat on his head, singing as they rolled down the road. The grim horsemen to either side, so dashing that they'd widened the eyes of Cassandra's maid. The tall dark trees she couldn't name that stood sentry between the road and the fields beyond.

Cassandra closed her eyes, shutting out the sights to only listen. The melancholy minor tune sung so cheerfully, sometimes whistled, the buzzing of a fly that had chosen to accompany them on the journey. It brushed around her cheek and she waved it away lazily. Shouts came from some field, and the wagon rattled.

Such music!

She wondered if this might be the road upon which the gypsy woman had walked, her laughter sailing up to where he sat writing, where he captured the sound and sent it to her.

"You are happy, no?" the driver asked. He wore a thick black mustache over his lip, and his eyes danced when they lit upon her. "You like our country?"

"Oh, yes! It's even more beautiful than I had imagined."

"Ah, and the villa is the most beautiful of all." He winked. "You will like it very much."

"I expect I will." Cassandra wanted to ask about the villa owner, about Count Montevarchi. Was he short and stout, like the wagon-master, or tall and severe, like some of the guards posted to ride with them? How old? Could he possibly have eyes as kind as the heart that showed in his letters?

Until yesterday, she'd managed to keep most of these questions at bay. It had seemed enough that she'd left her dull, dull world, that he'd somehow given her courage enough to venture out of that safe world to discover what she might truly be made of.

She had blended the general attributes of many of her scholarly acquaintances and come up with a patchwork vision of a middle-aged man, his hair graying a little at the temples. A man unhappy with his lot in life, but given to wild bursts of joy—maybe a severe expression balanced by eyes of great depth.

Now she couldn't remember why she'd formed that picture. He could be anything. Anyone.

The wagon rounded a turn and before them rose the villa, high on a hill, the walls pale gold. Suddenly, it was no longer an abstract adventure. A bolt of giddy terror filled her. What had possessed her?

At the unexpected airlessness of her lungs, she pressed a hand to her ribs, and the letter she had tucked into her bodice crackled against her hand.

It brought back the steadying sense of the Count himself, and her panic ebbed as quickly as it had arrived.

It did not matter how he looked—if he were old or young or stout or lean or even as fat as a little troll. She had come because she had never felt such an affinity with another mind in all her life. She wanted to sit and talk with him in perfect freedom—her Basilio, her dearest friend.

Her spirits soared once again. She had done it!

A long stone stairway cut into the hillside led down from a gate in the villa walls to the road. A figure emerged from the gate and began to descend, his figure casting a sharp shadow against the gold walls. "Is that him?" Cassandra asked her companion. "Is that the Count?"

He looked at her, the large dark eyes dancing mischievously, as if he knew a secret. "*Si.*" He pulled the wagon to a halt and nimbly got out, circling quickly to assist Cassandra. She put her hands in his and jumped down in the dust, then looked up to see if she might catch another glimpse of her friend.

The sun was in her eyes, and even when she raised her hand to shade her view, she could only make out the vaguest details. Tall, moving with a limber, eager step down the stairs, his boots tapping quickly on stone.

In excitement, she moved forward, smiling. "My dear Count, is that you?" she cried.

"Lady Cassandra?" He took another step, hesitated, and then slowly took the next one, and the next, moving into the shadows only ten feet above her, where she could see him. There he paused, staring down at her with the same shock that must have showed on her own face.

A hundred times over the long journey, Cassandra had imagined this moment. She had imagined laughing, running to greet him, perhaps even sharing a quick, proper embrace.

Instead, they were both immobile. Her smile faded, and the airlessness of moments before returned. Whatever she had imagined, she had never, ever dreamed that he would be the physical personification of those beautiful, sensual words.

But he stood there, young—no more than

thirty—and tall, with a lean, limber sort of grace
that made her remember the lyric turn of phrase
that was so much a part of him. His hair, thick
and black, tumbled in loose, glossy circlets to his
shoulders. His face was sculpted by the hand of
Michelangelo himself—that wide white brow
and aggressive nose, the sensual mouth—but
statues she thought a little wildly, were always
pale gray. Basilio was color itself. His lips deep
wine, his cheeks rosy, his eyes and lashes and
brows as black as that hair.

In that single, stunned moment, a wave of
foreboding washed through her, so violent that it
nearly made her ill, and she felt she must dis-
solve now into weeping for all that could have
been and could not be. Would not be.

He stared back at her, then they both moved at
once, she racing upward, he down. They met,
hands outstretched, then tangled. Cassandra felt
the power of those long, white hands capturing
her own, and closed her eyes.

"Basilio," she whispered, a little dizzy, then
opened her eyes again and saw that she had been
right: her friend of the wild and gentle and
unhappy heart was there in the depths of his
eyes.

And she saw that he was deeply, deeply dismayed.

Torn, too, for his hands were tight on her
hands, his fingers moving over hers as if to
absorb their shape and size and texture immedi-

ately, as if they would be stolen away. His fingers were strong, the palms calloused—she had not thought a poet could be so virile, so powerful.

Suddenly, he lifted her hands to his lips and kissed them, one and then the other. His eyes closed as he did it, and then, at last, he spoke.

"I thought . . . you are a widow . . . I thought you would be older." His voice was musical, haunting like a cello. He lifted a shoulder and gave a little laugh. "Instead, here you are—so beautiful, you stole my words right out of my mouth."

"I did not mean to mislead you," she said. "If you would like me to find other accommodations, I will do so."

She expected him to laugh at that, to brush it away, but the wide mouth sobered and she saw he seriously considered the possibility. "No," he said, almost sadly. "I have waited too long for my good friend to come to me here. Please stay."

"I thought you would be a middle aged man, graying and beyond . . ." She lowered her head, hiding what she had nearly blurted out. "I thought we would meet—" she put a hand to her brow—"there." She closed her eyes at the loss of that small part of her dream.

He took a step down to stand level with her, and lifted her hand to his chest. "No, my friend, it is deeper still. Soul to soul, *si*?"

She raised her head. "Yes."

He smiled a little. "We are both surprised. But

we will go on now as we were. Forgive me for
seeing first your mask, not you."

Masks. Yes. He was still only her Basilio,
beneath that mask of beauty. "Only if you will
forgive me."

"Done." He stepped back and called to the
wagoner to bring her bags. "Come. You must be
dying of thirst."

Basilio led her to the courtyard, his heart
pounding in a combination of joy and dismay
that was so intense he thought the emotions
might burst from his skin. She swirled to look
over the wall in her violet traveling coat, a slim
figure as graceful as a bird. Her hair, a coppery
mass of curls, could not entirely be tamed, and
wisps fell down her white neck and over her
cheek, and he felt a clutch of pain at the impossible beauty of her. Not merely lovely, or fair and
pleasant. Not pretty in the way of some women,
given life by the joy in their eyes.

No, Cassandra was dangerously beautiful—
beauty given an edge by the soberness of her red,
red mouth, the intelligence and intensity burning
in her very dark brown eyes.

He should have sent her away immediately.
Instead, he joined her at the wall and they stood
there, side by side, looking toward the sea.

"This is what you described to me," she said.
Her voice was throaty and sure, without the

tricks of amusement and flirtatiousness he had grown to expect from women.

"Yes." He found himself at a loss again and scowled, clasping his hands behind his back. Never mind the rest: he was a gentleman, and she was a guest in his home, a guest who had come at his invitation. "Have I done it justice?"

"It is as vivid as you promised," she said and lifted her eyes to the horizon. "I did not anticipate the aroma."

He breathed in, smelling sea and the sweetish heat of sunlight on olive leaves. "What is different?"

She tilted her head toward the sky and closed her eyes, and Basilio found his gaze on her long white throat. "It smells—" she paused, then lowered her chin "—like your letters."

He imagined her on some gray English morning, lifting his letter to her nose and inhaling the scent. He always did it himself, when hers arrived. "Your letters smell of woodsmoke."

A rattling of dishes made them turn. A servant pushed a wheeled cart over the bricked courtyard. Basilio gestured to the table covered with a white cloth, set beneath the spreading branches of a tree where the shade would protect her from the bright Tuscan sun. "Would you like some refreshment?"

"So formal," she murmured and nodded. "Yes, thank you."

There was a bowl of fresh ripe olives, glistening with washing, bread and oil and soft white cheese in a crock, tea and wine, and water in a jug cooled in the well. "I did not know if you would drink a hot beverage on a hot day, or if wine so early would shock you." He poured a glass of water first, and she accepted it gratefully.

After drinking deeply, she gasped in pleasure. "That's marvelous!"

"We have a good mountain well. More?"

She drank another straight down, and he found himself looking at that throat again. He looked away, busying himself with cutting the bread. "Do you remember when you said your salon might shock me?"

"Yes, I do. And you promised to shock my English palate. Will this do it?"

He laughed softly. "No. It is only delicious." He plucked an olive out of the bowl and gave it to her, watching in pleasure as she popped it in her mouth and tested it. The dark eyes widened in approval. "My pride was wounded when you wrote that," he continued, and dipped bread into the pool of herbed olive oil on the plate.

"Was it?" She smiled. "Is that why you returned the challenge?"

"Yes. And why I sent the postcard from Venice. I hoped it would scandalize you." He bit into his bread. "Did it?"

Cassandra laughed, pulled off her hat, and

flung it into a chair. "I am not easily shocked, sir."

"Ah. Pity." He put a hand over his heart. "I had hoped I'd redeemed myself."

"However"—she plucked an olive from the bowl—"even I was a bit flushed over that artwork."

He laughed, and it shook loose the sense of doom that had stolen his joy over her arrival. Impulsively, he reached over the table and took her hand. "I am very glad to have you here, my friend."

Her smile was as easy and relaxed as his own when she tightened her fingers around his hand. A sharp heat, sweet and dangerous, sparked through him, but he pushed it away.

She said, "And I am so glad you invited me, Basilio. It is all right if I call you Basilio?"

He smiled. "Of course."

A sense of alignment came to him, a sense of rightness. Whatever else transpired, it was good that he had written, that day so many months before, to this woman.

After lunch, Basilio excused himself to tend to some business brought to him by his steward, and Cassandra was led to her room. She thanked the woman who had shown her there, and with relief closed the door. She felt a faint headache at the base of her skull, brought about by overstimulation of her senses. Never had she experienced such a battering of sensuality, not even in Martinique.

The room was both a continuation of that splendor and, in its silence, a relief from it. The bed was a variation of a four-poster, the posts fashioned from iron curved into fanciful shapes and painted with gold. It was piled with pillows of red and gold and amber, the colors of fire, which matched the draperies and the coverlet. Silk fringe trimmed everything.

She smiled, brushing her hand over the fabric, and wandered to the doors which led to a small stone balcony that overlooked the same view as the courtyard. She plucked pins from her hair as she admired it: green hills close in that faded to high blue mountains, and a snippet of endless sea to the horizon. She had never seen anything so lovely.

Basilio.

His name whispered down her spine, a name that was as lovely as his words. She closed her eyes with a little shudder, thinking again of his mouth, the tumble of curls, his graceful hands, the flash of his eyes when he laughed.

She should leave. He had clearly been dismayed at the sight of her, and she'd sensed his hesitation when she offered to stay elsewhere, as if he, too, felt the danger of this meeting.

Rubbing her hands through her hair to free it, she turned and dropped the pins on a little table, then began removing her clothes, managing to strip down to her chemise with a bit of wiggling. From a jug, she poured water into a porcelain basin and washed her face and arms and neck, puzzling about that odd sense of warning.

The only threat she could imagine was if Basilio's beautiful face hid twisted hungers or brute violence. It seemed highly unlikely, but even if it were true, she was no innocent in such matters, thanks to that husband who had made her a happy widow. She was perfectly able to take care of herself.

A bitterness that never entirely disappeared drew up her mouth as she blotted her face dry. She had been foolish indeed in her choice of husband. It had not been a romantic joining; she did not trust love. After observing her older sister's romantic excesses, Cassandra had decided women should never allow emotion to rule their lives: it was a sure path to ruin. A woman's lot was difficult enough without adding that complication, so she relied on wit and reason.

George had seemed the ideal husband: an earl from an old, old family, with fortune and fine manners and an agreeable countenance.

She rubbed her neck. The fortune had been an illusion, for he'd gambled a good half of it away before their marriage, and managed to lose the rest in the year before his death. The manners had only been a pretty game. But the worst of it had been the perversity of his sexual appetites—

something she could not have foreseen or avoided in her virginal ignorance. Only the old family had proved to be true at all.

Ah, well. She had learned more than she wished of men's abuses, but he'd kindly died and left her free. There were worse fates—and look where it had led her.

Tugging back the coverlet, she slid into the silky, fragrant bed and settled into the pillows. Such luxury, she thought sleepily, the headache receding as she let go of the long days of travel and sank into the soft feather mattress. Behind her closed lids, images flickered—the Tuscan sky, the ripe olives between Basilio's fingers, the wagon-master singing. The images moved slower and slower, like the swing of a pendulum, until they ceased their flashing and burned on one clean, perfect image: Basilio's curls tumbling forward as he bent to kiss her hand. The image slid with her into sleep.

When she awakened much later, Cassandra called her maid, who was full of complaints and dire warnings as she dressed Cassandra's hair and helped her don a gown of green brocade she'd brought specifically for this night. Cassandra only half-listened, her gaze captured by the haze of light falling on the hills beyond her balcony.

The long gold fingers pointed out valleys and

crags and high outcroppings of white rock that had been hidden earlier, and she felt a stab of excitement over what else might be revealed in another hour or another day. In the middle of Joan's complaint about the servants who'd slept all afternoon, she said, "Joan, look there. Have you ever seen anything so beautiful in your life?"

"I like the view out my mum's window better."

Cassandra brushed the girl's hands from her and moved to pull the drapes aside. A soft wind, considerably cooler than it had been earlier, touched her face. "I shall need my shawl, I believe. The gold." When Joan fetched it, Cassandra tossed it over her arm and slipped out, a quick eagerness in her step that she'd not felt in years.

With a sense of wonder, she realized she was as close to giddy as she ever allowed herself to be. It was a surprisingly pleasant sensation, and as she walked down the cool hallway to the main salon, she hummed lightly under her breath. The strange foreboding of earlier seemed as distant as England itself, made of old fears and lingering guilts, no more.

Though she heard servants about, Cassandra did not see anyone else as she made her way through the rooms, poking her head into a salon, then a library which tempted her mightily—did he keep the manuscripts here?—but she forced herself to keep going. The rooms were arranged around the gardens and courtyard, every window open to the astonishing view of fields and groves falling away to the sea.

She emerged into that courtyard. The paving stones were warm beneath her slippers, even as shadows crept out from the building from the westering sun. With a rush of anticipation, she realized that not only the moon would slide into the sea, as Basilio had promised, but the sun as well. It was a sight she had not seen in many years.

There was no one here, and Cassandra wondered if she ought to go back to her room until Basilio had returned. But she was too restless to be able to tolerate the slow quiet of that view. She would explore the gardens instead.

But just as she turned for the path, she heard a burst of laughter and Basilio himself came through the break in the trees, his hands filled with some ruby-colored fruit. A man walked with him, perhaps the steward, but Cassandra could only stare at Basilio. His coat and waistcoat were gone, leaving his simple shirt to blow against his body the tie loose enough she could glimpse his chest and part of a sculpted shoulder at the opening. The thin fabric of his sleeves billowed white and full against his forearms.

She wanted to run to him, run and greet him with the fullness of her pleasure. Instead, she forced herself to remain still by the wall, as if she were captured once more by the glory of colors drenching the landscape—but it was Basilio who filled her vision, who made her chest hurt. Words from his letters spilled through her mind, now lent richness because they echoed in his physical voice: *I labor to capture the music of the night. Imperfectly. Always imperfectly.*

When he saw her, his unguarded face blazed with light. He called out happily, "Cassandra! Come see what I have brought you!"

Unable to quell a smile of happiness, she moved toward him, unable, too, to keep her feet from flying over the bricks. He hurried toward her, lifting his hands with his prize, his laughter spilling out into the late gold day.

The perfection of moments, Cassandra thought, and then saw what he carried in his long-fingered hand. "Plums!" she cried happily, and took one from the many.

"Take more! They came just this minute from the trees. I picked them for you."

She gathered more out of his palms and held one in her fingers. "It's warm!"

He laughed and bit into one, those white teeth splitting the skin, juice spilling on his lip. "Taste it!"

Cassandra stared at him for a moment, overtaken by a vivid, intense wish to lick that syrup from his lip. She brought a plum to her own mouth, and bit into it. It exploded against her teeth, spilling hot dark juice into her mouth, as warm as sunlight, sweeter than sugar. "Oh!" she cried.

Trying to keep it from dripping down her chin, she bent over, laughing, and sucked from her fingers. "Wonderful!" she cried, and tossed the pit aside to devour another greedily. A tiny stream of juice trailed down her hand and she laughed again. "Messy!"

His eyes glittered. "This is why we are alive. Plums!" He extended his hand, and she saw that his fingers were also juice stained. "Come. Let's gather more for the others. You will like even more taking them off the tree."

There was no way to resist him, and though it was utterly unlike her, Cassandra tossed her shawl over one shoulder and reached out to allow him to grasp her sticky hand with his own.

Only then, when he halted for the tiniest span of time, enclosing her hand tightly in his, as she drew close to his body and smelled the sunlight in his hair, and saw his chest moving with a breath that seemed too fast, when she caught the soberness beneath his laughter, only then did she feel again the foreboding, mixed with sharp yearning.

In him. In her.

But then he tugged her hand and they tumbled down the hill to the orchard, laughing and free and young under the gold sun of Tuscany, so far away from all she had known or would ever know again.

For this time, she would live only in the moments he offered in their perfection.

Chapter 3

Basilio washed and dressed for dinner with all his nerves burning. His cologne stung the newly shaved rawness of his jaw. His scalp tingled with the bristles of his brush, his legs prickled at the touch of his breeches; even his feet in their boots were more aware than usual of the feeling of stockings, leather, a hard heel.

Dangerous. When he had finished, he went to stand in the doorway that looked down to the courtyard and paused. There below stood the reason for his distress: Cassandra, cloaked in that uncommon stillness. She looked out toward the valley, only the bright tendrils of loose hair moving. He wanted to touch that stillness, as a man would put his hand in the water to make it shimmer.

What made her so watchful? With a catch in his throat, he thought of the way her eyes—so distrustful!—had shifted to joy when he made his simple offering of plums. It made him feel protective, that distrust and the vulnerability below it. Her letters had hinted of dark times, but he did not know what they had been.

He did not know her at all. How much of a life could one pour into a few lines on a page?

She raised her face to the breeze and he found himself breathing in with her, filling his lungs with the air she took in.

How much of one's life could go into those lines? Very little. But his soul had gone into his, into the letters and the poetry and essays he'd dared to send her. In some matters, she held more knowledge of him than any person on earth. And while there had been more reserve in her words, he believed she had given the same to him: knowledge of her secret wishes for herself, for her work, for the world.

And if she had been the woman he'd imagined, his Cassandra-of-the-Letters, who wrote such earthy and witty essays, there would have been no trouble. Cassandra-of-the-Letters was middle aged and barrel-bosomed, bawdy of tongue and quick of gibe. She had carved by her will a place in a world that did not wish to make room for her.

The image made him smile. He would have loved her in that form. He would have taken joy in showing her his world, lighting her laughter, feeding her, and giving her adventures to write about. He did not know how she had so captured him, but Cassandra-of-the-Letters had made him more himself than he had been in five

years, ever since his father had insisted that
Basilio leave his studies and travel on behalf of
his business. Neither of his brothers had the
command of languages that Basilio claimed, so
he'd had no choice.

In those years he'd discovered new wonders
about the world and had uncovered a gift for
travel writings, but his poetry had languished,
frivolous, forgotten.

Until he began corresponding with Cassandra-
of-the-Letters. He couldn't say why it returned to
him then—could not have pointed to a particular
word of encouragement she'd offered, or a
moment he had decided it was time to see again
what he might write. It had simply trickled back
to him, a word here, an image there, until the
music of poetry ran again beneath every moment
of every day, as it had when he was a boy, giving
a sheen to ordinary moments, a polish to painful
duties.

Yes, Cassandra-of-the-Letters had given him
that.

The real woman was so much more astonishing. Not merely her beauty, which pierced him as
it must most men. But the poise that was so rare
in one so young; a protective bearing that spoke
of disappointments, and hidden away somewhere deep, fear.

Her youth and beauty dismayed him. Even
without the letters, he would have been drawn to
such a woman. That his beloved friend's soul

and mind should be so enclosed was a greater danger than any he could have imagined for himself. Had he known, he would never have issued his invitation. He wasn't sure how he would resist the temptation of devouring her, of nibbling through that thin skin to let the passion flow into him. He did not know how he could stop himself from that, from making love to the woman who had captured his mind, and now would snare his soul if he could not find some way to resist the lure.

But resist he would. For honor, he must.

Resentment burned in him. Resentment at God, and his father, who had put him here where he did not belong, shouldering a mantle meant for his brother. Resentment that it would now steal from him the one happiness he might have claimed.

For he did not lie to himself in this. He would have moved the earth to claim her.

But because his freedom had been stolen, he would instead spend his life married to the woman his father had betrothed him to. A political marriage, uniting two families, a marriage to continue the proud and ancient Tuscan line to which he belonged. A marriage that would take place in one month.

In spite of his resentment, he knew he must do as he was bid. Not for his father, whom he had always hated, but for his mother—who had loved the girl, Analise, and had always been protective of her. A strange, otherworldly child who had seen visions before she was six, and who was too beautiful to be allowed to be a nun when her father could gain so much from her marriage, Analise had been in need of a champion. Basilio's mother had nearly badgered his father to make the betrothal between Giovanni, his oldest brother, and Analise. When his brothers died, the obligation fell to Basilio.

Though he was not a religious man, he crossed himself and asked for assistance from the Virgin Mother, to resist the woman of his heart, to be strong in the face of temptation. To go and laugh, and give all of his mind and all of his soul if he wished, but no more.

No more.

They dined alone in the courtyard, not even servants to disturb them except to be sure there was wine enough, and bread enough, and a soft musky cheese, and delicately shredded meat. It was food they ate with their fingers, lazily.

Cassandra marveled at all of it—the simple pleasure of the food, the warm scent of the air, Basilio himself. As they sat there the sun dropped toward the sea, a blazing violet and yellow ball sinking lower and lower into the distant water.

She realized, in a slow way that seemed to go with the way the air hung in rose gauze around them, that she had not fidgeted. She felt no need to leap up or move a foot or tap her fingers on the glass. It was enough to sit here, listening to birds and drinking her wine, and grazing on the feast Basilio had ordered for them.

"Look at the birds," he said, pointing. "They're busy drawing the curtain of night."

"Ah, the poet emerges!"

His eyes glittered. "Perhaps." Pushing away his plate, he leaned back comfortably, crossing one ankle over his knee. "But I was thinking, it is our first day, and perhaps we should begin with why we have gathered here to tell our tales."

"Mmm," she said, pleased at the reference to Boccaccio. "I am afraid I have no entertainment to offer, sir. I came only out of greed, because I was promised a glimpse of rare manuscript pages."

"No tale at all from a woman who makes her life with her pen? How did she come to love the feel of that pen in her hand, I wonder?"

She smiled at his challenge, then sipped her wine, peering out to sea. "I have not seen the sun disappear that way, swallowed by Neptune, since I was a child." She cut a glance at him to see if he noticed she, too, could capture an image.

The wide dark eyes tilted up at the corners a little in acknowledgement. "And why not?" He picked up his own glass and settled back.

"When I was a girl, my mother died in the islands, in Martinique. My father did not want to return to England, where he had been happy with her, so he sent for us: my brother and my two sisters, and my cousin who lived with us."

"So many of you!"

"And we added two sisters and a brother before we finished." She lifted her brows. "It's a great blessing that we all lived, in spite of the fevers and the travel."

That soberness, that hint of deepest sorrow, moved over his dark eyes. "Yes."

Too late, Cassandra remembered he had lost his brothers and mother to fevers only a short time before. She put her hand on his sleeve without thinking. "Oh, I have been thoughtless! Forgive me."

He looked at her hand and Cassandra wondered if she ought remove it, if it was too familiar. But selfishly, she wanted to touch him, feel the shape of his forearm beneath the fabric of his coat. A small, guilty pleasure.

And because he seemed captured by the sight of her hand against his sleeve, she was free to drink in his face without fear of giving the wrong impression. Each time she was caught by some new detail. It was his lashes now, not long, but very lush and thick and black. When he abruptly lifted those lashes, they trimmed the depth of darkest irises with a kind of extravagance that made her unwilling to shift her gaze.

He put his hand over hers. "It should not be only sorrow that comes when I remember them," he said quietly, "for while they walked here, they gave me great joy. There is where my heart should go when I think of them."

Such large eyes for a man, so expressive and deep. Cassandra peered into them, feeling no oddity in her need to see within, no need to turn away even when the moment stretched to two and three and four, the world quiet but for the simplicity of looking directly into his eyes—and allowing him to look back into hers. His index finger traced the shape of her thumbnail.

Then—she was aware of the shift, a flicker, perhaps, in those eyes—it seemed they drew a little closer, then apart again at nearly the same instant. She took her hand away and put it in her lap.

"Tell me your tale, Cassandra. And then I will tell you mine."

So she told him of the long, terrifying journey to Martinique when she was six and believed in sea monsters. They'd been caught in a terrible storm for three days, where the ship pitched and rocked dangerously, threatening hourly to spill them into the hungry waves. But they had survived and gone on to the island, where they discovered the rest of her father's family—Monique, the slave who had been his mistress before he returned to England and married, and then again when his heart was shredded in grief over the loss of his wife in childbirth, and Monique's children: Gabriel, the eldest of all of them, and Cleopatra, the youngest.

In Martinique, Cassandra had discovered books and words and writing, and the pleasure of her own company. Away from the strictures of English country life, Cassandra had made up her mind that she, too, would be a writer.

"So, you see, I have good memories of myself when I see the sun sink into the sea. Memories of what I saw before the world saw something else."

"Ah, bravo! That's a very good story to begin. Thank you."

"And now yours, sir." She allowed him to pour another splash of wine into her glass, though she knew she should halt it soon. It was heady wine, musky and rich, and she could feel it tingling in her blood. "How came you to be sitting here tonight? How came the poet to his words?"

He let go of a humorless laugh. "I am no poet, madam."

She regarded him steadily. "Ah. I see I am to protest and insist you do not know the worth of your own talents. Shall I beg for a couplet?"

A hand flew to his chest. "The lady's tongue is sharp!" That glitter returned to his eyes. "As sharp as a hidden dagger."

"Sharp as the knock of a creditor on a poet's door."

"Sharp"—he paused, eyes shining—"as the blue edge of lightning on a summer's eve."

Cassandra laughed, and it felt as if something

were breaking free within her, as if the laughter were washing away some barely acknowledged miasma. "Your story, braggart!"

"It is only very simple. And sad, too."

"Melancholy makes a story sweet."

"So it does. I am the third of three brothers. Giovanni was the oldest, five years more than me. Then Teodoro, my father's favorite. Then me, the favorite of my mother."

"Poor Giovanni!" she said. "Left out."

"Oh, no. Because he was the favorite of the ladies."

"Ah! I see."

"We grew up very rich, very happy. Giovanni was glad to be the heir, for he loved figures and counting and playing Count in his cape. Teo, though, he was very smart. With my father, he doubled our fortune, in times that were not good." He frowned. "He had no compassion, I fear, but he was a very good businessman."

"A common coupling."

"It is true of my father, as well." A quick, dismissing lift of a shoulder. "The first thing I remember is lying in a bed, listening as my mother read poetry to me by the light of a candle. Every night, she allowed me to open her book to any page I wished, then she would read aloud that poem." He spared a glance at her. "It was her intent to lull me to sleep, but often, she read three or four or five poems."

Cassandra imagined him as a small boy, those

dark eyes even more enormous in a child's soft face, the tumble of curls in disarray, and understood how a mother would find her favorite in such a boy.

"This did not please my father. I do not know why he hated me, but I felt it even when I was small."

"Hate?" Cassandra echoed. "Surely that is too strong a word.

A slow shake of his head, a small frown. "No. It is true." A brush of his hand. "It did not wound me, I did not like him."

Cassandra smiled. "You had your mother."

"I did. She did not like to leave me in his care when she traveled, and since their marriage was not a happy one, she often traveled to Florence and Milan, and took me with her. We went to the opera and to the playhouse and lectures, and when it came time to decide what profession I should take, it was my mother who fought for me to go to university. I was very happy there, but my father wished for me to work with him, traveling for his interests." He gave her a bland look. "You do see where my story goes?"

She nodded sadly.

"The fever swept through the countryside like a scythe. My father fell ill with it first. Then Giovanni, then my mother, then Teo. My father was out of his wits for days and days, and could not think for a long time after. And when he awoke, all that was left of his family was the son he loathed."

"Did you sicken?"

He bowed his head a moment and sighed. "No. I had been in Venice on my father's business." He straightened, signaling an end to the tale. "It was a year after those terrible days that I read your essay and found there was laughter in me still." He smiled. "And I wrote that letter, so now I sit in the dark with you."

"Have you mended matters with your father?"

He stood to light a brace of candles in an iron candelabra. "We do not speak unless we are required. He must have an heir, after all, and there is no other but me." With a hand he encompassed the villa and courtyard. "This place he saved for Teo, and it burns that he was forced to give it to me, and that eventually I will also hold his other properties. But what can he do?"

Cassandra remembered his bitterness in one of his letters, his rejection of his riches and the position of a noble. "Do you still loathe it so much?"

Candlelight flickered over his brow, sharpened his nose as he looked toward the horizon, lost now in the darkness. "This land belonged to my mother. It was her dowry, so I am glad to keep it safe for her. And I loved my brothers. If I do not keep the trust, their lives will have had no meaning." He sighed and waved both hands in a gesture that brushed it all away. "Enough! I have no wish to think of sorrowful things this night. In payment for your good story, allow me to show you one of the Boccaccio manuscripts."

Moving on an instinct she did not question, Cassandra rose and went to him, putting a hand on his chest. "They would be proud of you, Basilio."

He pressed her palm close to his heart, and a button on his waistcoat made an imprint on her flesh. He made a soft pained noise; touched a wisp of hair with his other hand. "You are far too rich a temptation, my Cassandra," he said softly. "I am trying to think of only what lies behind this mask of beauty, but the mask is a wonder."

She wanted to kiss him. The desire came to her suddenly, fiercely, and with such power that it made her momentarily dizzy.

No. She could not bear to discover that Basilio was like all men in his baseness. Better to preserve the illusion that he was honorable and beautiful of spirit. Closing her eyes, she swallowed and stepped away, taking her hand back.

Quietly, he said, "Friends to lovers is an easy leap. Lovers back to friends—" he lifted a shoulder. "Not always so simple."

In a voice that held more betraying breath, she said, "Yes." She swallowed and looked up at him. "Forgive me." She paused, wondering at her own boldness—but this was Basilio, the friend of her heart, and if she could not be honest with him, there was no truth in the world at all.

"You are too rare to be lost to me. A friend is so much more precious than a lover."

His face broke in a brilliant smile. "Yes!" He captured her hands and kissed them happily. "Friends we began; friends we will remain." With a light flirtatiousness, he inclined his head. "Though I hope you do not expect me to ignore the pleasure of attempting to capture your beauty in my poetry."

"I suppose I shall simply have to make peace with immortality."

He laughed and took her hand. "Come. Boccaccio awaits us."

In the broad, cool room, lined with shelves full of books and furnished only with a large heavy desk and two chairs, Basilio kept his treasures in a locked trunk. Along one wall hung his collection of rapiers, and Cassandra moved to them. "Are you a swordsman?"

He lighted a brace of tallows from the candle he'd brought with him. "I am."

"My brother Gabriel is a master—some have said he's one of the greatest swordsmen in Europe."

"Perhaps one day I will meet him—I should enjoy such a challenge." He gestured for Cassandra to take the heavy chair that sat before his desk. With a quirk of her lips, she settled, like a queen awaiting her subjects. Her gown, green and gold, glittered in the light, and her breasts and throat were white as cream. Tendrils of that bright hair sprang free of the rest, more and more with each passing hour—a lock over her brow, down her cheek, across the straight white shelf of shoulder. He captured it all in his imagination so he could recreate it another day. What hue was that white? What tone, the red of her hair?

He set aside such thoughts and opened the trunk, then took out a small, cloth-wrapped bundle and untied it as he carried it over to Cassandra, putting it down before her and pulling back the cloth with a flourish.

Her reaction was all he could have asked for. A small intake of breath, a hand over her lips. Eyes to his face, hesitant, bright with excitement. "May I touch them? Or will it hurt them?"

"I would not ask you to only look at them."

Gingerly, she put two fingers on the top page, almost but not quite touching the words penned in ink. The parchment had darkened a little, and some of the edges were brittle and crumbling, but the fine strong hand remained, clearly readable. "Oh, imagine," she said softly. "His own hand, on this page."

"Yes."

She picked up the first and held it lightly between her fingers, careful to avoid the edges, and put it to her nose as if to inhale the essence. A prickle moved down his spine as he watched her; his breath caught high in his throat. Light edged her straight, sharp nose and the thin, fine eyelids, and he imagined pressing his lips to them, even imagined the jittery movements of her eye below, the bristle of lashes against his mouth.

He stepped away and pretended to be looking in the trunk, but a ghost of himself stood yet with her, putting a hand lightly on her shoulder, a finger into an escaped lock of hair. His ghost did what he dared not.

Cassandra began to read aloud in Italian, her throaty voice cascading over the syllables expertly, the sound soft and unimaginably sensual. He closed his eyes and listened, letting just that part of her come into his mind—the sound of her reading a passage about a wife kissing her lover, Anichino. When the story progressed, to Anichino creeping into the wife's room, he thought she would halt in feminine reserve, for the lover awakened his woman by putting his hands on her breasts.

But she did not stop. She read it all, with no shift in her tone to speak of either coquetry or embarrassment, and he was surprised by her again. He turned.

She raised her eyes. "It is so much more beautiful in Italian. The translations are often dry. I would like to convey the spirit of this, the . . ." She narrowed her eyes, not seeing him. ". . . the lushness. I love the bawdiness so much," she said. A smile, thoughtful and distant, touched her lips.

More than the world, he wanted to fling himself across the small distance between them and bring to fruit another kiss, like that of the wife and her lover. His flaw had ever been his own delight in his senses, and they roared now with a clamoring unlike any he had known, for she offered a feast for eyes and mouth and hand and ear.

But if he allowed indulgence in this moment, he would mortally offend her, offend the freedom she felt in speaking to him thus. So he considered his reply, taking something blindly from the trunk, then dropping casually into the other chair.

"Yes," he said, "I like his passion—the passion to affirm life, after so much death from the plague. It is the most natural thing—to celebrate that which brings new life."

Her smile of connection and happiness was gratification enough, that she was truly free with him, to discuss even that forbidden topic. "Exactly! It must have seemed the world had nearly ended. I cannot even imagine." She picked up the next page and grinned, for it was part of the Third Day's stories—the subject of her essay that had made him laugh. She read it aloud, and again shook her head. "It cries for better translation! Don't you agree?"

"I have not read English translations," he admitted.

"Oh, of course not. Well, I can give you an example." She took the page and began to read in very stilted English that captured little of the flow of the Italian. " 'And then, and then, and then . . . ' " She sighed. "Terrible. You would be far better."

He gave a mock shudder. "I intensely dislike translation work."

"Ah, but you'd bring poetry to it."

"So will you."

She shook her head, smiling as she touched the words on the page again, her eyes following the path of her finger. "I am only clever, Basilio. I have not the fire of a poet, that gift of song."

"There is more poetry in you than you recognize."

She rose impatiently, restlessly. "No. I am gifted enough to earn my way in the world with my pen, but my passion has ever been for study." She shook her head, a quizzical expression in her eyes. "There is a moment, when one has been steadfast in piecing together some subject, that a single detail falls into place, and there is suddenly a whole picture, an understanding. Enlightenment. Do you know what I mean?"

His heart swelled—God! Such an intelligent woman—what a rarity! He leaned forward, putting his elbows on his knees. "I wanted to be a great scholar," he said. "But I can never stand far enough from the work, from my own thoughts on it, to make that picture you speak of. But sometimes, when I am writing, I feel something similar."

"Yes? What brings it?"

He narrowed his eyes, thinking. "I am not certain. It is in part what you say—one must be persistent, dedicated, through all the frustrating moments when it all seems a hopeless endeavor." He looked at her intently. "Perhaps it is a matter of detail. The single small word or phrase that pulls it into focus."

"And do you see the whole in those moments? Or something else?"

"Joy," he said, surprising himself, and laughed. "I see joy." He lifted rueful brows. "For me, it *is* the moments—suddenly I have captured one moment, and whatever is there on the page is not only for me, but for whatever reader comes."

"Like your letters." Her skirts rustled as she moved toward him. A hint of a smile. "They brought Tuscan sun to my cold winter days."

He smiled at her. "I was hoping I had done that."

She sank to the floor by his knee in a puddle of green and gold, her head titled up to him. "You are very good at it."

She was so close, so relaxed and natural. In his imagination, he put his forehead on her neck, breathed the scent from her skin. "What do you wish most to do?" he asked, then answered himself. "Ah, I know it already: you burn to translate Boccaccio."

"I do," she admitted, and laughed a little breathlessly. "I am only terrified that I could not do it justice—and that even if I did, it would be scorned as the work of a woman."

Basilio hesitated, then gave in to his impulse and brushed one finger over her cheek. Just once, then away. "Do it," he said softly. "I will slay your detractors for you when you have finished."

There was a danger in her eyes, suddenly. A heat turning their brown liquid, like chocolate left in the sun. He looked away and caught on her shoulders, an endless span of warm flesh he could kiss for hours. His blood stirred, and he raised his hand again to her face.

Her cheek was small against his palm, the cheekbone and jaw as fragile as the bones of a bird, and that evidence of her mortality pained him. She blinked, slowly, like a cat, and turned her face ever so slightly into his palm.

He suddenly felt he should confess to her that he was betrothed, that he could not give himself to her even though he wished it more than breath. Perhaps if she knew, they could steal this small time, seal their hearts, one to the other. Perhaps she would not mind, if he explained that his duty required his marriage.

But just as swiftly, he knew she would mind

very much—that at heart, she was honor-bound to the plight of women, as he was bound to the duty of land and family. He could not ask her to make that choice.

As she leaned softly into his palm, as he took that small offering with the same inner trembling as that of a boy touching his first breast, he regretted bitterly that life had brought his love to him only when he could not claim her.

If he had been a stronger man, he would have lightened the moment with a jest or a smile. Instead, he lifted his other hand, to put it on her other cheek so he could touch her whole face. "Thank you, Cassandra," he whispered. "You have blessed me by coming."

She put her hand over his. "As I have been blessed by coming."

In silent agreement, they only smiled, like the most beloved of friends, then stood up.

"I am suddenly quite fatigued," she said, smoothing her skirts. "I must retire."

"Of course. We have much to see tomorrow."

"Is it terribly far to the sea?"

"You would like to go?"

"Very much."

"Consider it done." He gave her his arm and they walked, each in their own thoughts, to her chamber.

There she paused, then stood on her toes, and pressed a chaste kiss to his cheek. "Thank you,

Basilio, for sharing all of this with me. I had a glorious day."

He forced himself to pat her hand and step away, bowing courteously. "My pleasure, dear lady."

Chapter 4

Cassandra rose early the next morning, excited by the promise of a ride to the seaside. Beyond her balcony the light was gray, and she was ready to be disappointed, but when she flung open the doors, she halted in stunned delight. Rushing out on to the balcony in her nightrail, she leaned on the thick stone balustrade, inhaling the soft air, scented with new, exotic things.

She had never seen fog like this. It was thin and silvery, draped around the tree limbs in wisps. Mufflers hid the tops of the mountains and the greens and blues of the landscape were deepened, intensified. But what made it so beautiful was the promise that it would not last. The heated, buttery sun pressed down upon that mist, breaking through here and there in soft pillars that illumined a tree or a hidden valley or the path to the sea, glittering in full sunlight between the breaks in hills.

A noise from below caught her attention and

she looked down to the courtyard to see Basilio come out, wearing only a simple white shirt with those extravagantly full sleeves and a pair of breeches. In her excitement, she cried, "Good morning!"

He lifted that extraordinary face, and Cassandra saw his startlement, his pleasure, before he smiled and waved. "Come down! Have breakfast with me."

She felt like Juliet, daring and wild and free in her sleeping attire, with her hair uncombed on her shoulders. She leaned on the rail, feeling her hair tumble over the edge. "Will you feed me more of your plums?"

He laughed. "Yes! And more besides. Hurry!"

She raced inside, splashing water on her face, tossing off the nightrail as she searched for some easy thing to don. She tugged a chemise over her head, and a simply cut shepherdess's gown over that. Later she would call her maid to help her into all the proper accoutrements of a lady, the corsets and stockings and other fripperies.

For now, she brushed her hair and left it loose, stuck her bare feet into her slippers, grabbed a shawl against the chill, and hurried down to join him.

The sensation of her unconstrained breasts moving inside her chemise as she raced down the stairs made her feel deliciously free. She embraced the slightly wicked pleasure of her loose hair on her arms, and her skirts swishing around her bare ankles. When she sailed through the glass doors into the courtyard, breathless and happy, a burst of sunlight suddenly cut through the mist to fill the square with a golden wash—a beneficent approval of this new lightness in her, this new spirit of joy. She halted and tilted her face into it.

"Open your mouth," Basilio said, close to her ear.

She startled, dropping her shawl as she spun to look at him. He stood close, a hint of a smile on his lips, and appreciation in his eyes as his gaze brushed over her face and throat and even her breasts. She realized suddenly that she had wanted to see that look in his eye, that darkening, that faint flare of the nostrils.

I want him.

She didn't even question that fierce whisper in her mind, only gazed at him for a long moment, letting him see that she wished to put her hands in that glossy tumble of black curls, wanted to taste his lips. Then she closed her eyes and opened her mouth. She hoped it would be his tongue she tasted, and the thought sent shocked but delicious anticipation through her.

Instead he pressed a supple roundness against her lips, and she bit into a plum with a happy laugh, sucking on it for a moment before she opened her eyes.

He wants me.

It was there in the piercing focus of his attention, a naked expression of longing as he looked at her mouth. With a little shake of his head, he said, "You must have left a path of shattered men in your wake."

A ripple of disappointment touched her, but she could not have said why. Because he had allowed his desire to show, when she just had done the very same thing? Unsettled, she bent to capture her shawl and moved away, speaking over her shoulder. "To the contrary. They're quite terrified of me." She bit again into the plum she'd taken from him. "Men do not like a woman who is smarter than they are."

His hands settled on his hips. "You are not smarter than me."

She grinned. "We shall see, won't we?"

He inclined his head with measuring eyes and a hint of a smile. "So we shall."

After breakfast, they rode down a narrow track to the sea. The sun had burned through the mist, and Basilio insisted she wear a hat to protect her fair skin, and a shawl over her shoulders. Sweat prickled on her brow and under the shawl, but she endured it for the promise of the beach.

When they rode beneath a stand of trees to come out on an endless, white stretch of sand, when the sound of the waves first struck her ear, Cassandra dismounted in a rush and ran across the soft sand to the water. She just stood there, smelling it, listening to it.

"It's so empty!" she said. "Why are there no villages along the beach? Are there terrible storms?"

A lift of a shoulder. "Sometimes. But this land belongs to the princes, for their hunting and such things."

"Are we being wicked, then?"

That glitter in his eyes as he looked down at her. "Very."

"Good." She turned and sat down in the sand, reaching for her shoes. "You won't be tiresome then, and be shocked if I take off my stockings and shoes?" Even as she spoke, she was stripping them away. "If I'm going to be wicked, I'd like to fully enjoy the experience."

He reached for his neckcloth and untied it, tossing it down beside her pile of shoes and stockings, then took off his coat. "We could be very, very wicked and simply swim naked."

"I'm afraid I'd rather not burn all those tender parts." She did, however, take off the offending hat and shawl. "Though you certainly may frolic nude if it pleases you."

He sat down beside her, grinning wickedly. "I certainly will if it would please you, my lady."

"What an astonishingly generous offer!"

A purely Mediterranean shrug. "I wish only your pleasure."

Smiling wryly, Cassandra stood, brushing sand from her skirts.

"A moment, if you please," he said, lifting his

foot. "One would hate to ruin a good pair of boots."

"Oh, indeed." Expertly, she grasped his heel and toe and slid the boot off, then the other, and tossed them in the unruly pile growing in the sand.

He took off his stockings and Cassandra was very nearly felled by an inexplicable fist of desire, triggered by his naked feet and shins. While they were quite beautifully shaped, with high arches and silky dark hair on the straight line of shin, she had seen quite a number of ankles and toes. None of them had ever made her want to have sex. Bemused, she shook her head. "I suspect you do your share of shattering, Count."

Perplexed, he lifted his head, and saw her admiring his feet. "Ah! You like them?" He wiggled his toes and admired them himself, then plucked at his shirt. "I would be happy to take off the rest. Only in the interest of pleasing a guest, of course."

She laughed, and if it was throatier than ordinary, so what? She stretched out her hand. "Come, my wicked Basilio. Let's put our naked feet in the water."

He took her hand and allowed her to help him up, then dashed toward the water with a cry. Cassandra ran after him, lifting her skirts, gasping with pleasure as the first ripples washed over her ankles. She halted, entranced, and looked

down at the foam. Through the water, she saw
her feet, tinted a pale greenish-brown. Sand
sucked and shifted and rearranged itself in a
thousand ways, and memories came tumbling
from a thousand hiding places in her mind.

She was seven and eight and nine, and heard
the sharp shouts of her brothers and Adriana in
the distance as they shimmied up trees and
played pirate. She heard the low murmur of her
nanny and Monique, just behind them, and the
baby laughter of the little girls.

"Tell me," Basilio said, wading toward her.
"What puts that look on your face?"

It was so easy to smile with him. She kicked a
little water his direction, though it wouldn't
make much difference. Unlike Cassandra, he had
not cautiously tiptoed into the surf but waded in
with gusto, and his breeches were wet to mid-
thigh. The damp cloth clung to his body, showing him to be surprisingly strong and muscular.
Tiny silver beads caught in the extravagant curls
around his face.

"I was thinking of being seven," she said. "I
was very brave at seven."

"Too serious. Big eyes."

She nodded. "I liked to stand like this, right on
the edge of the water, and imagine I was at the
edge of the world. I tried to see those lands—
what sounds they would have and what the people
would wear and what strange creatures I would
see."

"What did you imagine?"

"Elephants. India. Spices and glitter." She smiled.

"Yes, that seems right." He reached down and snared a pretty pink shell, holding it out to her in his wet hand. "No pretty rocks and bangles?"

"Oh, yes. I had many. Boxes full of them." She examined the spiral shape of the shell, and as if he were a ghost within the shell, her father appeared in her mind, not as he had been in his last, consumptive days, but as he had been then, when she was small. "My father used to bring them to me specially. We catalogued them together."

"He was a scientist, then?"

"Not really, only concerned for me. The others, my siblings, paired off, you know. The three oldest, then the two baby girls, and my cousin with Phoebe, who is just younger than me. No one enjoyed the same things I did."

"Were you lonely?" Wind tossed his hair in his eyes and he shook it free.

"Not at all." Around them the sea rushed and rustled, eternal and somehow reassuring. "I enjoyed my own company, but he worried that I spent so much time alone."

"And he took time with you." A prompt, and an obvious one, but she gave him a brilliant smile for it, touched. What a good listener he was.

"Yes. He did. He took time for all of us, really. He was a very indulgent father."

"Is it from him you get your red hair?" He touched it idly. Casually.

"No one knows where I get this hair. I'm the only one." She tucked the shell into her palm and looked down again at her feet. "No, he was an ordinary looking man, in many ways."

"And you are not."

She chuckled. "That was rather vain, wasn't it? He had beautiful blue eyes, and a wonderful laugh. Women always loved him because he was good to his children. He was good to women, too, I suppose."

"I wish my mother had found such a man." He tossed a rock into the sea.

"So do I," she said, and he turned back to her, his hair blowing on the wind into his face, his sleeves rippling, his legs in water to his knees. Behind him, the sky cast a backdrop of vivid blue. For a long dangerous moment, it seemed that they might kiss, but the sound of a dog barking interrupted. They turned together to look for it.

It was a brown and white creature, with ragged fur and an exuberant nature. It carried a stick in its mouth and brought it hopefully to them. Gladly distracted, they played and ran with the mutt, splashing in the water, dancing in the surf, laughing and crying out jokes and warnings.

At last, pleasantly spent, Cassandra collapsed in the sand and begged for the cheese and wine he had brought. While he fetched it, the dog came and fell down beside her, panting cheerfully as she stroked his ears. She had not been so relaxed, so at ease with herself and her surroundings, in a very long time. Maybe even since those long-ago days in Martinique.

"I love the outdoors," she said. "I always forget how it makes me feel."

Basilio collapsed beside her, dropping the saddlebag without ceremony. "So do I." He tipped up his face to the sun, closing his eyes. "The world as God made it."

"Yes." His hair lured her, and that flush on his cheeks. She itched to touch the arch of his foot, and the chest she could glimpse at the opening of his shirt. Touch him. Kiss him. Lie with him, her Basilio, who was so unexpectedly beautiful—and so much more besides.

Man as God had made him.

Torture, Basilio thought. From the moment Cassandra had appeared this morning on her balcony, her hair loose and brilliant, her body clothed in only that whisper of gauze, the day had been torture. When he'd come upon her standing in the courtyard, her arms flung back, her breasts uplifted and delectably natural in their shape, she had stolen his breath. Laughing as they ate breakfast, then playing in the surf with the dog, he had seen a girlish side of her, one he suspected had been set free by his homeland.

Now they devoured hunks of bread torn from

a fresh loaf, and chunks of white cheese, all washed down with wine he'd brought in a skin. She showed herself adept at the process once she learned it, though it squirted first across her cheek and down her neck in a red trickle. She wiped it away with a laugh.

The air, salty and heavy, clung to his skin and the flavors burst on his tongue. Sun burned down on his head, and he wanted to shed all of his clothes and all of hers and lie here with her, flesh to flesh. He felt the want at the back of his neck, and in his mouth which he filled with cheese instead of her breasts, felt it in his thumbs and his knees and the primal base of his spine. Everywhere.

And though it was torture, it was very pleasant, too. After all, she was here now, before him. It would not always be so. He sighed and leaned back on one elbow. "Here is a moment I would capture."

She tore into a crispy crust of bread and seemed to care little that crumbs had fallen into her lap. "Are you going to give me a couplet now, Sir Poet?"

"Not today." He lay back and closed his eyes. "When you are back in your cold room, huddled next to the fire, then you shall have a letter from me, and there will be a poem about the sun and the sea and a Siren."

"Oh, I am to be a Siren?"

He opened one eye. "Not you. The dog."

She laughed. "I shall enjoy it."

Taking her shawl from the pile of discarded clothing, she spread it over the sand to protect her hair when she lay down. Her hand found his and he took it as easily, pleased when he felt her relax beside him.

Her fingers were slender and graceful, and he resisted the wish to stroke the length of them. Instead he only let her palm fall across his own, feeling heat and moisture build between their fingers. He drifted drowsily in the warm sun, listening to the cry of gulls and the patterns of the waves moving close and far, now whispering, now breathing, now and then crashing.

Behind his eyelids, he saw the shape of colors he would capture for that distant winter day, for Cassandra—the blue of the hills in the distance, the pale sand, the brightness of her hair. Copper? Too pedestrian. Titian? Too obscure. Idly, he tried a dozen possibilities. None quite captured the sense of that color, not truly. Thinking he had forgotten, he turned to look at it again, and narrowed his eyes so it was all that he saw, only the brightness of Cassandra's hair. There were gold strands glittering among some of a very deep red, and still others of a kind of sienna shade. Some vivid orange, others a soft carrot. The whole together was impossible to name.

He smiled, noticing she had drifted off, and he slipped his hand from her grasp to brace himself on one elbow. The lips in repose were full and not so reserved, and the aloof dignity that marked her eyes disappeared. He skirted her torso and hips and gazed at her feet, akimbo and sandy. Long, very white feet. Like her hands. He touched a nail, oval and arched.

Then he did allow himself to look at her throat, and the dip at the base, and lower, to the soft rise of breasts above her bodice, and lower to the plane of her belly. Unbidden came a vision of that skin uncovered, and a vision of his mouth at her throat, making a mark.

She turned her head and he found himself looking down into her steady, sober eyes. "I felt you looking at me," she said quietly, and lifted one hand to his hair, a gesture of invitation and permission. So natural and simple, that invitation. Basilio found himself leaning close, thinking of her mouth.

Just in time, he remembered he could not and merely put his nose against her cheek. He closed his eyes, narrowing the moment to the smell of her—faint perspiration and soap and sea air. Her hand moved, combing through his hair loosely, then again.

He wanted her in a way he had never wanted another woman. The purity and fierceness of it felt like poetry in his blood, weighted with that same magic, the promise of perfect beauty. The force of it made his breath catch, warred with his duty.

Duty. Always duty.

With graceless and urgent will, he pushed away from her and clambered to his feet. Hurt crossed her face. But better this hurt now, than the hurt that would come if he deceived her. He turned to the sea and bent his head against the brilliance of sunlight glittering on the waves.

When his voice could be calm, he turned back and smiled brightly as if there was nothing at all wrong. "Come," he said, extending his hand. "We must return to the villa." Impulsively, afraid to lose control if they spent the evening as he had originally planned, he said, "There is a feast in the village tonight, honoring Saint Catherine and her special blessing on the town, and we must rest and restore our strength before we go."

The flood of words did not take the reserve from her stiff chin, and he saw measuring in the very dark eyes. Wind tossed a long curl of hair around her throat, and he thought of a painting. Her mouth was a red bow that he wanted to taste. Suck. The vividness of his desire made him step back as she stood, brushing sand from her skirts.

But even as he put distance between them, his ghostly self was hurtling forward, tumbling her to the sand, covering her with his body, with his mouth, with his hands. He made a sound, soft and frustrated, and turned to the water once more, imagining the salty waves cooling the heat in him. In he breathed, then out, his hands on his hips, inhaling the air, the salty scent that might make him brave enough to make his confession.

"Basilio, forgive my boldness. I am a widow—I did not think it would offend you."

"Offend?" He turned to her shaking his head. "I am not offended." Honor lay on him like shroud. "But I must tell you something."

She nodded soberly, as if she expected it.

"Do you remember the night I wrote to you of the gypsy on the road, when I was in despair and said there was some matter of duty that caused me some sorrow?"

"Yes. It is my favorite letter."

"My father had come to see me that day." Words stuck in his throat. "To tell me my duty—to tell me . . ." He halted, shook his head, then blurted it out. "Cassandra, I am betrothed. I am to be married in a month's time."

Her features might have been made of wax and her eyes of glass, for nothing flickered, nothing shifted. "Oh," she said. "I see."

"It is entirely political. She is very young, in a convent all her life." He took a breath. "It is only that it would not be right for us, when there is nothing I can offer."

"Sssh. How rare for a man to resist physical pleasure in favor of honor." A faint smile bent her mouth. "I find I like you all the more for it."

Honor. It tasted like the grave.

Chapter 5

On a tiny island off the coast of Italy, a young woman knelt by her cot. Against the graying stillness of evening the song of the nuns at vespers rung out, a sound Analise diCanio found heart wrenchingly sweet. It was the sound of peace and joy, and she longed to add her own voice to their number, singing praises to God. It was all she had ever wanted.

But it was not to be. In the morning her father would come for her, and spirit her away to their villa in Firenze, where she would begin preparations for her marriage to Count Montevarchi. She did not remember him, but her mother had written a witless letter about the young count's beauty, and the great fortune Analise had found in union with such a charming, good-looking, young, rich man. She'd blathered for so long that Analise had given up and burned the parchment in despair.

She did not wish to be wed. Ever. To anyone. From the time she was a tiny girl, she had only wanted one thing: to be a nun. To serve God as truly and honorably as she was able.

Her father said that her beauty would be wasted in a convent. Her mother said Analise could serve God as a good wife and a good mother, as Mary herself had done. Analise clutched her hands tighter and raised her eyes to the small, plain crucifix that adorned the plain white wall. She knew it was true; that she could serve in marriage, serve by mothering fine children. And if God did not take this cup from her, she would serve where she was placed.

But her heart lived here, on this island, within the cloistering walls where she had discovered the pure, simple joy of morning dew on the herb gardens she helped Sister Maria tend, where the days never varied, where the song of prayers raised in purest harmony pierced her with a joy so deep she sometimes halted, stuck dumb and dizzy by the power of it, her eyes running with tears of perfect happiness.

She did not speak aloud her certainty that she had been born to take her place in this cloister, for that was prideful and a sin, to think she knew more of her heart and her place in the world than her father. She dared not even speak her passion aloud to the other sisters, though she suspected they knew, suspected they wished they had the power to assist her. A hand to her shoulder when her despair grew so large she could not keep it from her face; the sweet, jaunty whistle that Sister Katarina sometimes chirped for her in the gardens. They knew.

And God knew. He knew her pride and desire and therefore could not be surprised when she whispered, "I belong here. Please allow me to stay." The song of the sisters at vespers floated around her, embraced her like warm arms. "Help me."

Cassandra, made sleepy by the ocean air, retired to her chamber for a nap when they returned to the villa. Lying on her bed, she gazed through the open doors to a small balcony, admiring soft green hills like breasts against the hand of the sky. The smell of the sea came from her clothes and hair. Her limbs were lax from exercise. Sand clung to her feet, though she'd tried to brush them off before she'd climbed on to the bed. Later she would regret the grit, but now she was held by a thick inertia to her spot, head propped on a great pile of gold-fringed pillows.

There was only Basilio in her mind. Basilio laughing, so full of energy and simple happiness as he ran in the surf with a stray dog. Basilio, looking so gravely and hungrily at her when he thought she was asleep. Basilio, bending close to put his nose against her face.

And he was betrothed. Betrothed.

It startled her how much she wanted to—what? She thought of her hands in his glossy hair, the black curling around her white fingers;

thought of the shape of his head in her hands; of the way his face had looked in that moment, thick black lashes downcast, the bridge of his nose red from the sun.

She shifted, her gown swishing over the satin coverlet as she turned on her side. Until now, she'd had little understanding of desire. Perhaps it was because of her husband. Perhaps because she'd heard too much gossip, too many confessions of petty, changeable, and shallow longings. She'd watched her sister Adriana's fall to scandal in bewilderment, unable to fathom why she would risk so much for a man. Any man.

Lying now in a wash of sensory abandon, it seemed impossible that she had not felt it before, not even a tiny spark of it. She had seen it in men's eyes for her. She'd always enjoyed flirtations, finding them flattering and stimulating, especially with clever men.

But she had escaped lust till now.

Her female friends said it was because her brothers and father had set such an impossibly high standard that no other man would ever measure up. Perhaps that was true.

It was also true that she had been introduced to the physical side of love by a man with unnatural and sometimes even brutal tastes. Those memories had cured her of any leanings she might have had toward passion, any temptation she might have felt to take a lover after his death.

And today, even as she'd lifted her hand to put

it in Basilio's hair, she'd known a mingling of fear and longing. How ironic that she should discover her passion with a man who was not free to help her explore it.

With a restless feeling, she got up and walked to the balcony. Leaning on the stone railing, she suddenly wished for her old Basilio back again—the lonely, middle-aged poet who'd sent Tuscan sunlight and ocean winds to her cold townhouse in London, who'd brought such music and pleasure to her unchanging world. If she had not come to Tuscany, she might have put her newly discovered bravery to another challenge: maybe written something that tested her, or taken up a new course of study. And she would still have the old Basilio.

With a hollow feeling, she rested her forehead on the backs of her hands, awash with loss.

How could she miss a man who had never existed?

But he did exist. That was the trouble. She thought of his honest eyes, the look of his teeth when he laughed, the control he exercised with her—he was all she had imagined and more.

With a start she remembered the sense of warning, of dread, she'd felt upon seeing him the first time. Perhaps this entire journey had been a mistake for both of them. Perhaps some danger lurked in their meeting, a danger that could be avoided if she cut the visit short. Perhaps she ought to go away.

Not home—the idea of her staid little garden and staid little life and the same conversations made her shudder. Perhaps she could go on to Venice. She had come so far already—why not?

Urgently, she straightened and went back into the room and began to pull her things out. The trunk could be shipped later—for now she would bring only what she most required. The pile of his letters, bound in ribbon, her comb and brush; she tossed things into a pile, scarcely allowing herself to think, to breathe.

A knock came at the door, and inexplicably, Cassandra felt herself begin to tremble. She folded her hands and stared at the panel of oak that kept danger out, but did not answer. Perhaps whoever it was would think her sleeping and go away.

Another knock. Her fingers twisted tightly.

A letter slid under the door, making a soft swoosh. Unfrozen, Cassandra rushed to pick it up, and her hands trembled so in yearning and fear and despair that she could barely unseal the still-warm wax, marked by his ring.

His familiar elegant hand hurried across the page.

Cassandra,

It is still only you and I, here on the page. Because I know you, and your honor, I know you are thinking now that you must leave my house.

I beg you: do not go. Stay only a day or two, as you see fit, but do not go now, before I have been able to show you the basket of little memories I wanted to give you to take back—I have given only plums and the sea. There is still the moon, and the festival in the village tonight, and the opera, which I saved for last, a rich treat for your imagination. There is more wine to drink, Cassandra, and laughter to share.

Please, my friend, stay a little. We are adults of honor, and our meeting was of the minds, yes? We shall let nothing steal that from us . . .

B.

She opened the door, her heart pounding, and he stood there, waiting. Even the simple sight of him, his hair tamed now, pulled away from that sculpted face, his dark eyes grave and luminous, had the power to arouse her.

She wanted to kiss him, violently. The baldness of the thought made her ears hot and she spun away toward the bed, bending jerkily to rearrange things. It made her say, "Basilio, I have enjoyed your hospitality very much, but I think it best if I go now."

He rounded the great bed and reached out, capturing the fluttering of her hand in his own. "Tomorrow is soon enough, if you must," he said. "Tonight, let me show you the village and the feast." His smile held edges of melancholy, and Cassandra was pierced that she should have put that in his heart.

Even now, when calm surrounded him like a cloak, when whatever he'd felt on the beach was carefully hidden, Cassandra felt some invisible part of herself flow forward and put ghostly hands on his cheeks, a ghostly mouth against his lips, her breasts against his chest.

Oh, this was impossible! Impossible. She swallowed, blinked the vision away. "Basilio, I—"

"Shh." Slowly, he opened his hand and flattened his palm against hers. Oddly moved by the formality of it, Cassandra met it. A promise. His palm was strong and flat, her own soft and giving, and it seemed to her that the flesh between them began to heat, to burn, as they stood there.

"Only for tonight, Cassandra," he said quietly. "A few hours more, that is all."

In his face she saw goodness and passion, intelligence and laughter. A traitorous thought flashed through her: she did not wish for marriage. She only wanted a lover. Why could she not take this one, where she found him, and leave before their sin could lead to pain?

Afraid to look at him and show what was in her immoral heart, she only looked at his hand, a shimmering hunger pulsing through her bones. The air around them burned. It was dangerous. There was some portent in it for them both, but she found herself nodding. "All right. I will stay another day or two."

His hand slid against hers. "You will not be sorry, my Cassandra. I promise."

She took her hand away and met his gaze soberly. "Do not promise what you cannot deliver, sir. You cannot ever know the truth in another's heart. Only your own."

"So it is," he said. Tucking his hands behind his back, he gave a short bow, and left her.

Cassandra sank down to the bed, her hands loose on her lap. Her palm burned oddly and she lifted it, expecting to see some imprint left from his flesh, but there was nothing. Only the pale white flesh of her hand, as it had always been. She closed her fingers over her palm as if to save the impression, and thought again she should have not been swayed.

Then, with the same sturdy practicality that had marked her life, she scowled. Such drama! What could happen in a day or two to unravel anything at all?

At dusk, they rode the short distance down the hill into the village. Tall narrow trees made sharp shadows against the sky, and a breeze swept off the heat of the day. Birds whistled evensong, and from some hidden place, a cow lowed. Cassandra breathed it in with pleasure, feeling the strain between them ease under the soft force of that peace. "And here is the wonder of travel, right in this moment," she said.

"Tell me."

"I do not know the name of those birds who make that song. And I have no idea what I'll see when we round that bend. And I lift my nose to the air and smell things I've never smelled on the wind."

He gave her a swift, bright smile. "Yes. But those are the very things that frighten many people away. It could be a band of robbers around that bend. Or an ugly little town. The food might be very strange and you won't like it."

"But it might be something so delicious I would want to cook it myself forever and ever."

"Always the same choice in life: fear or joy? Do we awaken worrying, or ready to embrace? Do we fret or celebrate?"

"I think," Cassandra said slowly, "that I have done my share of fretting and worrying. It was your letters that showed me that fear was not the only way."

"My letters might have reminded you, but the gift was there in you all along." He raised his head. "That child on the edge of the world dreamed of beauty, yes?"

"Beauty, yes," she replied. "But not particularly as a source of joy."

"How could beauty not give joy?"

"It frightened me," she said honestly. "At times when I ventured out at evening in Martinique, and there was some blooming crimson, and the air blazed with the sound of birds and insects and the sea, and there was so much life, so much intensity, I would run back in my room and cover my head."

"You?"

Suddenly embarrassed at revealing so much, she lifted a shoulder. "Only sometimes."

"No, no—you mustn't run from this. What did you fear?"

"Oh, I don't know, Basilio," she answered in discomfort. "Perhaps I was only frightened because my mother died there."

"Perhaps." He rode a moment in silence, and Cassandra hoped the subject now closed. He knew too much of her already. "But let me ask you—what did that little girl see, truly?"

She would not escape, and with a little roll of her eyes, she confessed. "I saw monsters in everything in those days. Everywhere. The flowers sometimes looked like they could house evil fairies. And the birds were telling them I was there."

His laughter, soft and warm, held no note of mockery. "Ah! It is as I thought—it was only that writer's imagination in you."

"Did you have such imaginings?" she asked in surprise.

"Not so many frightening ones. I believed a chair was alive for a long time, however."

"A chair?"

"It was a big chair, with thick arms. I liked to sit there and read, and I pretended it was a very kind grandfather who let me sit on his lap."

"I see." And she did.

"And there was door in our house in Firenze that I could not bear to pass at night, for fear that some evil creature would come out and pull me inside of it." He made a roaring sound.

She laughed. "I do wish I had not been so serious all the time. Very, very serious." She mockingly assumed an expression of deepest concentration. "I had no time for frivolity. I meant to accomplish things, work hard. Study."

"Not I," he said with a chuckle. "From the time I was very small, I wandered, exploring, hoping for some new wonder around every turn."

"Did you find them, the wonders?"

"Often." He looked at her. "When you go, you should take time to visit Venice. She will please you."

"Oh?" Odd how he'd plucked her thoughts that way. "Why?"

"Venice—she is a goddess of love, adorned in the richest of fabrics and earthiest scents; she is a gypsy, taking lovers as she wishes, seducing all who breathe her perfumes." He tucked his tongue in his cheek and waited for her reaction.

She laughed lightly to cover the quick catch of her breath. "A very dangerous place, then!"

"Very dangerous. And very exciting." His attention was snared by something. "Ah, listen! Do you hear that?"

Music, exuberant and bright, reached them. "The festival?"

"Yes. You will like this very much, I promise."

They rounded the last bend, and the village bloomed below them. They stopped on the street for a moment beneath the setting sun, a light that competed with the dozens of lanterns and torches lining the square. Little shops and houses rounded three sides of the broad area, paved with golden stone. On the fourth side was a beautiful church, ablaze with hundreds of candles that made the stained glass windows seem alive with brilliant shards of color. The villagers were out en mass. Little girls had laced red ribbons through their hair, and some of the women wore red skirts. They all rushed toward the center of the square, where a great bonfire had been laid.

Cassandra was enchanted. "It's beautiful!" she cried. "What are they honoring?"

"Fire night," he said. "Long ago, the villagers were dying of plague, and in great distress they prayed to the patron saint of the village—St. Catherine of Siena. Do you know her?"

"A little. She wrote." Cassandra smiled. "I've made it my business to know the women in history who put pen to paper."

"I see. Well, St. Catherine is a local legend, for she visited our humble little village and washed her feet in the spring, and it is said to be blessed by her. So when the plague came, the villagers prayed and prayed in the church they had built in honor of her."

"And there was a miracle."

"Of course. But not quite the one you would imagine. Do you see how this village is not so old as the ones you saw as you came through the countryside?"

Cassandra had not noticed till now, but it was true. Many of the villages boasted medieval towers and ancient houses. Many of these were old, but only a century or two. "Yes. Why?"

"Because St. Catherine brought a fire to the village. It destroyed everything in its path, eating up the buildings and the surrounding trees. The people who were well enough fled to the fields and could do nothing to stop it—they stood and watched it burn for two full days. It ate the bodies of the plague dead, and it ate the hay and grass, and even the sick they had left behind."

"How terrible!"

He lifted a finger with a smile. "No, no. It was a miracle. Because the fields were not touched, so there was food for harvest. And plague never came again to our little village—St. Catherine saved it by letting it burn."

Cassandra looked back to the square, where the fire was lit with a great cry, and the music started up again. Red ribbons fluttered against dark hair, and the flames shot up into the sky, and she thought of the villagers watching the whole town burn to the ground.

It moved her deeply. "Thank you, Basilio."

He smiled gently. "I knew it would please you. Come—there is not only fire, but piles of food baked in honor of that harvest that was spared, and it is our duty to eat it."

All through the evening, Basilio ached with pride and desire. Cassandra dove into the festival with gusto—sampling every tidbit offered to her, and praising it wildly. She danced with the women, and listened to the long, rambling story of a very, very old man who was captured by the fire of her hair. They all loved that hair, and the little girls coaxed her into letting it down. "For St. Catherine!" they cried. It burned his eyes, that glittering fire.

He drank very little, fearing he could not control his hunger if wine seeped into his blood. Even so, he was drunk on her. Drunk when she rushed up to him and took his hand and dragged him into the peasant dance, drunk when a tendril of bright hair trailed over his coat sleeve, drunk when she threw back her head and laughed and her throat, white and smooth in the night, was exposed to his gaze. He loved that long neck.

She was swept away by the dance, into the embrace of the peasants. Stung by the loss, Basilio retreated to a bench in a dark corner, watching her. How could he return to his old life, take up the press of honor and the weight of his duties, and leave her here, dancing in his memory forever? He drank the sight of her, freed by night and the festival and the delight of the villagers. She seemed the embodiment of all the poetry he'd ever heard, every sonnet he longed to write, every beautiful word and syllable ever uttered.

She laughed, and the sound seemed to ring out above the tumult, though he knew it was only his imagination that he could hear it. He wanted to reach out and capture it, hold it in his hand, in his heart, forever, and it burned in him that he could not.

Why not?

The traitorous thought rose through his brain, clear and pure. Why not? She was nobly born, a suitable wife. She was beautiful and cultured, and even spoke Italian. Why couldn't he simply chose her over the wife his father had chosen for him?

Madness lay in that direction—he knew very well why not. However much he loathed his duty, he would do it. This marriage would align the two families and create a powerful, prosperous union for them all. Already rich, they would become richer. Already powerful, they would near equal the princes.

But more than that, Basilio could not dishonor the wishes of his mother. She had loved Analise, had championed her, and upon her death bed had reminded Basilio's father to protect her.

Had either of Basilio's brothers lived, one of them would be making this marriage. Because he had been spared, Basilio had to fulfill the promise that had been cut short. A sacrifice, he thought with pain, looking at Cassandra, but not the same as death. For Giovanni, for Teo, for his mother, Basilio had to resist her.

A gray-haired woman with a red skirt plopped down beside him, breathing hard. "I am not so young as I was," she said, laughing, a hand to her chest. "But you, my handsome lord, you are young! What are you doing, sitting here in the dark, brooding? Go dance!"

He shook his head. "I am content to watch."

"She is beautiful, your woman."

"She is not my woman," he said more harshly than he intended, and gentled it. "Only my good friend."

The old woman's eyes shined, dark and wide, and Basilio saw the beauty she'd once been. "Friend!" she cried with the frankness of the elderly. "Pah!"

He smiled reluctantly, trying to remember her name. "Yes, friend. We have written letters for a long time. She only came to visit, to see the countryside. Next, she goes to Venice."

Just then, a little boy with a headful of thick black curls tugged at Cassandra's skirts. She swooped down and picked him up, swinging him around, her hair and skirts swirling out around her. The boy laughed and put his hands on her face. She kissed the fingers lightly, easily, and that single gesture slayed him.

Basilio put his head in his hands. "She is only my friend," he said.

The old woman—her name suddenly came to him, Lucia—put her hand softly on his back and said nothing.

Dawn hovered at the horizon before they made their way back. Despite his best intentions Basilio had drunk a lot of wine, as had Cassandra, but there was no danger. The horses knew the way, and ambled up the road in the damp. Fog wisped around their feet and tangled in the forest branches.

"Should we have stayed out so long?" Cassandra whispered as the villa came into view. "Will bandits leap from the trees and slit our throats?" She rode close, challenge and mischief on her mouth, a boldness he had not seen before lighting her eyes.

He laughed. "They are all asleep!"

"I love your village, Basilio," she said with a happy sigh. "I plan to write a lovely essay about the festival."

"You must send it to me."

"Will you write about it, too? Oh, how could you resist it? All those little girls with red ribbons!"

And a boy whose fingers she'd kissed. "I am so pleased you enjoyed it."

"I think," she said with that exaggerated tilt of the head that spoke of a little too much wine, "that it was the best night I've ever known."

"The best ever?"

"Yes." She met his gaze, and he wondered which of them was the more reckless now.

Wickedly, he tested that recklessness. "Better than a wedding night?"

"Oh, that!" She waved her hand. "No, I did not care for that."

She had never written or spoken one word of her husband, and Basilio suddenly wondered why. "You do not speak of your husband. Are you so sorrowful that he died?"

She made an unladylike noise. "No! He was awful. I hated him."

He was glad, and then, conversely, jealous. "You're a woman now, and can choose the next one freely. It will be better."

"Are you fishing, sir?"

"Fishing?"

She smiled, a sly glitter in her eyes. "Asking if I have one in mind."

"Oh. No." He frowned. "Do you?"

She laughed. "No. I'm a most happy widow, and will never marry. Not ever. Marriage, for women, is a prison."

"Not all marriages."

"Well, my sister is content, I admit. But I do not value contentment." There was a stubborn set to her mouth. "I value freedom. And bravery. And tonight, I have both!"

"Are you drunk, Cassandra?"

"A little. Enough that I will have a headache tomorrow, I think." She inclined her head. "Are you shocked?"

"No." He was besotted.

"I do not allow it very often. But it seems to me that wine was invented so that we might put away all the dark things, all the sad things, all the worrisome things, just for a night. Tonight we all drank too much and danced and laughed too hard. Your villagers have the way of it. In my world, drunkenness is common, but offers no relief."

"I think you are right, my Cassandra. Perhaps I should order an evening of drunken revelry once every six months."

She laughed. "Perhaps I should order it as well—insist my sisters join me once a year for a great feast and dancing. My brother Julian needs to get drunk, I think," she added. "He has a heart that needs mending."

They were suddenly at the stables. "Here we are," Basilio said. He quickly dismounted and went to Cassandra's side. "Allow me to assist you, my lady."

"Assist me?" she echoed softly, and put out her hand. He put his hand on her waist as she swung free, and felt the muscles of her side move, beneath flesh, beneath silken fabric. He closed his eyes.

She slid down, very close, closer than she needed to be, and instead of alarm, he felt the world align itself. Of course it would be this way, with dawn hovering on the edges of the landscape, with fog-muffled silence deep around them, her hair the only brightness in the world. He felt her against him, her breasts, her shoulders; her breath on his neck, her hair fluttering loose over his hand. Next to him, she felt very small. Her hand slid from his shoulder to his neck, her palm open against his throat, then against his jaw.

He looked down, dizzy with wine and with passion, and saw the white oval of her face in the night, her eyes large and dark and sober. He raised a finger and touched her red, red lips, helpless to resist.

"Do not say a word, Basilio," she said, her voice throaty. "This moment, this instant, I choose joy. I choose bravery." He felt the press of her breasts, the stiffness of her bodice, against his chest, as she lifted on her toes and put her hands on his face. "I choose one memory," she whispered, and pressed her mouth against his. Just once, very lightly and chastely—and all the sweeter for it.

He'd only begun to smell her hair when she pulled away, smiling. "In the morning I will regret my boldness, and will be very angry with you if you remind me of my rashness."

Holding himself very carefully, he said, "Not a whisper." Pulling away to ease the temptation, he took her hand and tugged her toward the villa. "But in return, you must promise not to be a blushing Englishwoman about it and want to hide your face."

She laughed. "A fair arrangement."

At the courtyard she paused, looking toward the orchard. Sunlight now leaked quiet softness into the stirring day. "I think, for a little while, I would like to be alone."

He let her hand go. "Of course."

She took a step, then looked back. "Thank you, Basilio, so much."

Her hair trailed in a tangle of curls over her silk-clad arm, and her mouth was pleased but serious, and Basilio felt the hardest, deepest catch in his chest that he'd ever known.

"It was my honor," he said softly. Before he could act, before he shamed both of them, he whirled and left her.

Finally, his heart was clear. With wild haste, he broke for his chamber, shedding his hat and cloak as he took the stairs.

Of course. The answer was so very plain.

Chapter 6

Basilio bolted up the steps two at time. Tossing his coat on the bed, he sat at his desk, dipped his quill and wrote:

Father,

> *I cannot marry Analise.*
>
> *I know how you will receive this news, and be sure that I mean what I say. I will not marry her. It is a choice of honor that I must make.*
>
> *Please inform her father, and know that I will gladly arrange any compensation he feels is required. As she is a young and by all accounts beautiful girl, there should be no difficulty in finding her another husband.*

> *Basilio*

His breath was hurried and his hand shook as he sealed the letter. He took out a second sheet.

My dear Analise,

You must take your vows at the cloister immediately. I cannot marry you, but I know your true wish has always been the life of a nun, and you should have that. Not even your father can break the vows you give to God. Do it immediately, Analise, for your safety and protection. When all is settled and clear, I will visit and we can speak of this at length.

Your servant,
Basilio, Count Montevarchi

He sealed that, then ran from the room to find a servant. He pressed the notes into a footman's hand. "Post these immediately," he said. His father was in Genoa and would not receive the letter for perhaps a week or two, but Basilio could not act until he had absolved the duty. His mother had only wished the girl to be protected—she had not said how.

Then, his heart pounding, his blood sizzling and burning in his body, he went in search of Cassandra. She was not in her chamber, where he had expected to find her. Nor in the courtyard, though he found his gardener there, walking through. "Have you seen the Lady Cassandra?" Basilio asked.

The old man grinned and dipped his head toward the orchard. Basilio clapped him on the back and ran, his heart in his throat, ducking branches and leaping over roots and rocks.

Then he saw her, reaching for a plum in a tree, her hair unruly from dancing and the hands of little girls. She saw him and must have sensed his intensity. In concern, she took a step toward him. "Basilio, what is it?"

He had thought that a poet in love should deliver the most beautiful of first kisses. But there was no grace in him now.

Without speaking, he moved to her, a sense of something beyond heat, beyond desire, rushing through him. It seemed as if the air crackled, as if she glowed. He reached for her, and putting his hands on her face, bent and kissed her.

Kissed her full on the mouth, with all the longing he'd hidden. A roar came into his ears, the hugeness of his need for her, for the taste of those lips, and the smell of her and the feeling of her hands flying up around his neck.

He wanted to be skilled and patient and kind, but it was impossible. The kiss blazed, igniting him and her, and they kissed with hungry, open-mouthed need, inexact and brilliant.

When dizziness overwhelmed him and he had to breathe, he pulled back and put his forehead against hers. Her hands fell to his wrists and he heard her breathing, felt it on his chin.

He closed his eyes and opened them and she still stood there, and he was flooded with a sense of deepest gratitude, a sense of relief so vast it nearly buckled his knees. He had very nearly let her go.

"I am not married yet," he said, thinking of her vehement feelings about husbands. "And we have this little time, yes? None will be harmed if we are lovers." He pressed his mouth to hers again. "I cannot bear to let you go so easily."

She pressed back, making a soft cry. "Basilio, there are things you should know of me, if we are to take this path."

"No. This is all I need to know." He bent to capture her mouth again, softer this time. "That I have been looking for you all of my life, and God brought you to me." Swaying with relief and passion, he kissed her again, slowly, inviting her to meet him. He put his hands in her hair, breathed her breath. It was too deep for words, so he said none, only kissed her, and kissed her, and she kissed him back, there under the pale silver dawn.

And then, suddenly, he felt her drawing away. "Basilio," she whispered, a protest. She stepped completely out of his embrace and backed away from him. A hand fluttered to her chest. She stared at him, her eyes unreadable, a flush high on her cheekbones. "I . . . this . . ." She shook her head. "This is rash. We should sleep."

Basilio swallowed, reining in his sense of urgency. "Of course," he managed. "Forgive me. I lost my head."

"No forgiveness," she whispered. "I . . . only . . . I must sleep just now."

Before he could speak again, she fled, disappearing into the fog. He watched until the last of her hem swept over the lawn, disappearing beneath a shrub.

Had he been too rash? It was a failing of his, as his mother had often told him. He wandered through the trees, plucking leaves like a lost boy. Did she not return his feelings? Perhaps wine and passion had made him a fool.

Head down, he came into the courtyard and looked up to the balcony of her room.

Where she stood, her hair loose over the arms of her dressing gown, looking down at him. She was as straight and slim and pale as a candle. He stopped, stricken. She gazed at him for a long, long moment, then bent over the balustrade and held out a hand to him, a gesture of invitation.

He had frightened her! So simple. What grown man rushed like that to kiss a woman, after all?

He would wait. Let sleep cool his ardor a little. Putting his hand over his heart, he put his other to his lips and sent the kiss flying up to her. She kissed her own hand and sent one back to him. And still he only stood there, drinking in the sight of her until she drifted in, to that gold embroidered bed where he wished to be.

* * *

A bird, whistling from the balcony, woke Cassandra. The sight of it, pretty and small and black, singing on the stone rail, a backdrop of greens behind it, seemed so much an image from a dream that for a long time she only blinked at it, lazy and comfortable on her stomach in the big bed.

She did not move so much as a toe, letting everything slide slowly back into her head. A head, she noticed with some pleasure, that did not hurt at all, but only danced with vivid images from the festival.

Basilio.

A ripple went through her, an echo of the fierce, startled hunger she'd felt, seeing him hurtle down the hill so intent on her, his hair and sleeves flying behind him. And then his strong hands with their calloused palms hard on her face, and his mouth urgent and hot and tasting of woodsmoke from the bonfire. Never in all of her life had a man looked at her that way, as if he would die if he did not kiss her.

Shifting in the nest of covers that were as rumpled as if she'd had a lover in her restless bed with her, she reveled in the strange stinging sensation the memory brought with it, living it over and over in her imagination.

After a time, she washed and called for breakfast. A servant brought chocolate in a silver pot and fresh bread, which she carried to the little table by the window.

It was very warm, despite the breeze coming through the open French doors. Feeling wickedly free, she shed her dressing gown and sat eating, clad in only her nightrail. Through the windows she could see the hills, and a thick, hazy light hanging over them. She thought of the festival last night, and Basilio kissing her in the orchard, and the plums he carried to her from those trees . . . and suddenly felt the most glorious sense of happiness that she wanted to laugh out loud. Or dance. It was a pure, uncomplicated happiness, asking only to be embraced, today.

Humming under her breath, she found her box of writing materials and cut a fresh point on her pen. Sipping chocolate, nibbling on the rich, crusty bread, she began to write, intending at first only to capture her impressions, so she might collect the notes later into something more coherent. She couldn't even think what, just now—perhaps a letter or an article, or even a simple journal.

But as she jotted notes about this thing and that, she lost herself in each one. The sea water swirling over her toes, and how close she'd felt to her father, the delightful food Basilio kept feeding her, and then the festival last night, which had been one of the most beautiful, stimulating things she'd ever seen.

I feel quite unlike myself, she wrote, *and the change is quite exciting. I feel I can do anything, be anyone I chose to be. Or perhaps it is only that I feel fully myself for the first time in many years, as if that brave child I once was, who did not mind her own company, and crept through the forest to watch slaves dancing, has returned, stretching her limbs in readiness for anything, anything, that might occur. She embraces strangeness, the girl in me, embraces beauty and light and even the possibility of love and even sex. Sex as I dreamed it might once be, not as it was revealed.*

She paused and touched her mouth, wondered if she were brave enough to even write about that kiss. Tossing back a heavy handful of hair, she dipped her pen.

And now, Basilio. What will I remember of him when I must leave this enchanted place? His beautiful hair, tumbling free around his face as he played with the dog on the beach. The white arch of his bare foot. The taste of his kiss, like plums, like morning, like all the magic that has ever been in the world. I had not known a kiss could be like that.

It is Basilio, born of this golden light and the sensual feast that is his country, who has freed me, introduced me to this new side of myself. How did he know she lurked all this time within me, when I did not know myself?

She smiled, so very, very pleased, and scattered sand over the ink, put down her pen, and stretched luxuriously in the warm room. Suddenly aware that she felt damp and sticky, she called for a bath.

And even that was a wondrous discovery, a discovery of her own body. She grew aware of it in a way she had not been since earliest adolescence had turned her scrawny scarecrow of a body into something softer and amazingly more interesting. As she bathed, she was aware of the whiteness of her thighs and the weight of breasts bumping her arms; she noticed the crook of her elbows and the joints in her toes. A queer, sinuous something kept moving under her skin, making her feel both exhilarated and uncomfortable.

As she sat letting Kate put up her hair, she looked at her own mouth in the mirror and saw that it seemed very red. That brought a shocking and heady vision of a naked Basilio to her mind——those strong shoulders and his naked ankles, and everything in between. It made the restlessness under her skin tremble, and she shifted irritably, making Kate pull her hair. "Sorry," she muttered.

As a widow, Cassandra could have taken a dozen lovers by now and no one would have blinked. She'd certainly had her fair share of aspirants for the position, some of them quite handsome and witty. She had never wanted any of them. Didn't want their hands on her, their wet lips soiling her, their grunts in her ears.

But when Basilio had kissed her the way she'd longed to kiss him, there had been no reserve in her—only a rushing need to join to him, to press herself as close as possible, to *inhale* him. His tongue had thrust inside and her knees had nearly buckled with desire. His breath and her own had grown harsh and needy, and it had only seemed natural.

But he'd clasped her closer and closer, and she'd suddenly become aware of the rigidness of his sex jutting into her belly, and a cold, tight terror had closed her throat, choking off her joy. She had run away, bewildering him, she knew.

But when he'd wandered into the courtyard below the balcony, she'd been awash again with heat, longing for him, especially because of the despondent look on his face.

Hot and cold. But at least the heat held promise. A promise of healing.

The maid finished with her hair and Cassandra dismissed her. With a pounding heart, she went to peek over the balcony and see if Basilio awaited her, or if he still slept. When she saw that the courtyard was empty, her disappointment was sharp and deep.

She backed away from the balustrade, putting a hand to that erratic beat of her heart. Wanting him, not wanting him, delirious one moment, terrified the next. Was she falling in love with him?

The answer was absurdly obvious: of course she was. She had been in love with him long before they ever met. He'd engaged her heart and soul with a rare beauty of spirit. Long before she had heard his voice, long before she'd ached to touch his hair, she had loved the man she'd grown to know in those letters.

And even had she not known him before, was it not de rigueur to fall in love in Italy?

Where would it lead? He was betrothed. She felt a pinch of guilt over that, but only a little one. If he had already been married she would not have considered a dalliance, but if she were gone before his bride arrived, there was no wrong on his part—not in a political alliance. And in truth, the very fact of his looming marriage made it safer.

Freedom! A widowed young woman on holiday, a sophisticated and learned woman, might take a lover and merely count it as one of the great pleasures of travel.

If, indeed, she could follow through on her wish to take a lover.

Thoughtfully, she pulled the shawl into points at her belly, realizing for the first time how many scars her husband had left on her, left in dark places where they would never show. What if they were permanent scars? What if he had ruined her forever?

All she had with Basilio was this small, golden space of weeks, here in this magic and beautiful world. The thought gave her a soft swell of melancholy. It was hard to imagine, even now, what it would be like to return to her old life. She felt much changed in the space of a few days. How much more change would be wrought in weeks? And how much more by a lover's hands?

Moments, Basilio said. She would take them with her, safely tucked into the folds of her mind, where no one could ever touch them.

Moments. She would enjoy what *this* moment, this very night, would bring. She would not allow memories of her husband to steal her joy in Basilio's touch. She would not let fear of her own shifting perspective sully the beauty of this place. For now, she would think only as a poet, alive to her senses and the beauty of moments.

When she arrived downstairs, she smelled freshly baked bread and roasted meat, and it made her mouth water. Peeking outside to the courtyard, she saw with disappointment that it was still empty. From a room to the left came the sound of servants and glassware tinkling. She drifted in that direction, trailing her shawl, peeking into rooms as she went.

A woman came from the room at the end of the hall. "Good evening!" she said to Cassandra. "I am to bring you to the library, he said."

Basilio came out then, calling an order over his shoulder. He wore a dark coat and waistcoat, breeches and tall boots. His hair was caught back from his face, brushed into submission. He looked every inch the Count, powerful, controlled, serious—all but the betraying smears of ink on his fingers. She grinned.

When he spied her his expression changed, going swiftly between joy and consternation. "Ah good! You are awake."

Some current pulled her to him, but another held her where she stood. The servant, perhaps sensing the tension, scurried away, shaking her head. Cassandra looked up at him, wondering what to say. "Good evening."

He put his hand on his chest. "I—this—" He shook his head, and she would have vowed there was a flush on his face, making his lashes seem even thicker, darker. "I hope you will forgive me, Cassandra, for my heedlessness last night. This morning."

"Forgive you? No, I cannot do that."

His head came up abruptly. "No?"

"That would mean confessing how wicked I was, and you made me promise I would not."

A smile broke his soberness, a smile of relief and pleasure. "Then we are again in good accord. I worried all night that you would run away."

She could only look at his mouth, at the movement of his finely cut lips against the whiteness of teeth, at the glimpse of his tongue, forming the words. "No," she said softly.

"I thought we might eat in the house tonight." An soft incline of his head. "Not alone."

"The servants as chaperones?"

He clasped his hands behind his back. "It seemed wiser."

His eyes held earnestness mixed with sensuality, a combination that made Cassandra feel oddly weak. "What a good man you are, my Basilio," she said quietly. "I felt it in your letters, but I have not known a man with so much kindness."

"It is not kindness," he said, and there was a hint of darkness in those words. "I do not wish to frighten you, not ever." He bowed with exaggerated manners over her hand. "Come! You must be very hungry indeed."

"Oh, yes! And it smells magnificent."

"No pain in the head?"

She slapped his arm lightly with her fan. "You were not to mention my indiscretion, sir."

"But where is that bold woman who said we should be drunk sometimes? I liked her. Send her back to me, immediately."

Cassandra chuckled as they entered the grand room, heavily ornate with dark woods and heavy hangings and an enormous chandelier dripping with crystal. "Oh, my! You could entertain all of Tuscany in this room."

"Yes," he said with a weary sigh. "I have never liked it. We came here sometimes when I was a child, and it always seemed strange to me that a feast and ball should begin in a dark room with no view of the mountains or the sea."

"And yet here we are."

"It will do."

The servants laid the meal, tender broiled fish cooked in a broth she did not recognize but thought delicious. For a little while neither of them spoke very much, absorbed in the food and their hunger. "You have a very fine cook, Basilio," she commented. "When I leave, I'm going to bribe her to come with me."

He raised his eyes, smiling. "She will not go. She adores me alone." And there, she saw the wickedness he might contain, knowledge of women, and the things that pleased them.

"Tonight," Basilio said "we should tell a story of happy endings after adventures."

Cassandra grinned. "But that is the second day. This is our third."

"But we told no stories yesterday."

"Yes, we did! You told me of St. Catherine."

"I told a story, true. But you did not tell me one, so it is still second day."

Inclining her head, she said, "Will we have ten days, then?"

"It will need to be eleven now. Unless we miss stories another day, in which case it will have to be twelve."

She laughed and plucked a handful of berries

from a glass dish. "I will think of a story of adventure with a happy ending. Ah! I know one."

His eyes glittered. She tried not to look at his mouth, but it drew her eye, and she remembered the lush pleasure it had delivered. Seeing her gaze, he blinked slowly, touched her hand. "Tell me."

"It is the tale of my brothers, who killed a man in a duel over my sister's honor, and fled England, fearing for their lives."

"A duel! Really?"

"I did not write of it in my letters?"

"No. You only spoke a little of your family, now and again."

She almost spoke her first thought aloud: *because I wanted to keep you to myself.* Instead, she said, "Perhaps I was afraid I would look very dull by comparison."

"Never!"

"You have not heard the tale, sir."

He laughed. "So I have not. Please continue."

So Cassandra told him about her sister Adriana, who had been very wicked as a young girl and taken a lover and scandalized all of polite society, and of her brothers, who had called the lover to a duel, and killed him, then fled for five years, fearing the gallows. She told what she knew of their adventures, surviving an uprising in the islands, and plagued by slavers who had nearly stolen Gabriel, and living with Indians. "And then they came home again, whole and well, to try to rescue my sister again, but she was already married."

"Rescued from marriage? Did she not want him?"

"Not at first. She lives now with him in Ireland."

"And your brothers?"

"Oh, Julian has become quite the English gentleman. Gabriel—" she hesitated. "He has marked his own path, always." Pleased and full, she sighed and leaned back. "How is it that I tell stories of my life and you tell stories of the world? I think I need one from your life, sir."

He tsked, pursed his lips. "Perhaps I do not know one."

"No happy ending at all, ever?"

He raised his brows, his mouth rueful. "That is a very sad thing, is it not?"

"Yes," she said. "Very."

He rose. "Come. This room oppresses me. Let's retire to the library and look through the manuscripts. Would you enjoy that?"

Oddly, it held no appeal. She looked toward the garden. "Can we not walk, instead? I love the light."

"Of course." It was smoothly said, the liquid voice of an accommodating host.

"Have I offended you, Basilio?"

He let go of a breath, gave a soft laugh. "No, Cassandra. It is only that I am trying so very hard to be civilized."

"Must you be?" She frowned. "I do weary of civilization. Perhaps we should run to wildest Africa and shed our clothes and titles and live like natives."

That made him laugh, without that edge of restraint. This was the Basilio she knew, robust and full-throated. "I believe I would enjoy that."

He held out his arm and she lightly clasped his elbow, and they wandered through a set of doors to the broad courtyard. "But I have heard there are very large insects in Africa. Perhaps we'd wish to keep a few of our clothes."

"All right. But only a very few." She looked to both sides of the wall and thought it wiser to stay away from the orchard. Pointing in the other direction, she said, "Where does that path go?"

"To olive groves, and then to the garden. There is a fountain. Would you like to see?"

"I would." The light was softer than it had been the evening before, dusty, perhaps, or heavy with coming rain. "Is it going to rain?"

"I think it may. Will you mind terribly?"

She shook her head. *She would not mind anything as long as he was with her.* They walked down the hill, following a path that wound around an impressive stand of olive trees that was ringed with the same tall, dark fingers of trees she had seen everywhere.

With every step, Cassandra grew more aware of her wish to have him kiss her again. A scent of soap came from his skin, and it whispered over her senses, enticingly spicy. She found her gaze on his feet in the boots and remembered the sight of his toes and feet, and a pulse, low in her groin, shocked her. She looked away and took a breath. He felt a little stiff beside her, a little formal, and she wondered if the same sort of thoughts were in his mind.

She wished she had the courage to ask, but she found herself prattling instead, asking the name of this grass and that tree, and that flower, growing wild in an outcropping of stone. He answered with polite enthusiasm, and when they came to the garden he released her to the fountain, which shot from a mirroring pool contained in a great granite bed. Around it grew banks of lavender whose leaves cast off an alluring perfume.

"So much beauty," she said musingly, breaking off a twig of the herb to smell. "And it is all so peaceful."

He stood where he'd let her go, looking around him as if he had never seen it. "I suppose it is."

A tall corner, lined with stone, was cut into the side of the hill, creating a private and sheltered area for a pair of stone benches. Cassandra, too restless to sit, leaned on the wall and reached out to brush her fingers over the vine trailing down it. "Does this place, too, hold memories you would rather not think on?"

"My brother Teo."

"The businessman."

A distracted smile. "Yes. This was his doing, this garden. He made it for my mother. She loved to come here, and her friends brought her flowers to have the gardeners put in—all of these. But it's Teo I think of."

There it was, quick as nightfall, that dark well of emotion he hid, the grief that still lingered. A poet born to pain and joy, she thought. "What do you think of?" she asked.

He turned toward her. "I do not think, Cassandra," he said, and flung up his arms. "Not tonight. I only feel." He closed his eyes and lifted his head, a gesture of supplication. Did he pray for strength?

Cassandra smiled at the thought. A brightness moved through her, a sense of light, as she looked at him against the backdrop of the water and the sky and the lush greenery. She thought of Pan, of Boccaccio, of moments stolen from a long life.

"Feel," he repeated, and moved toward her, his eyes luminous. "I will not kiss you again if you do not wish it, but it is the only thing in me tonight."

She swayed toward him, her breath fluttering like a candle flame, and he caught her with a low, throaty sound, bending her into the hard crook of his elbow. He stared at her and opened his free hand on her face, his fingers touching her eyelids, her nose, her cheek, her mouth. Instinctively, she pressed her lips to his thumb as it passed over her lips.

He made a soft, low noise and kissed her. Cassandra circled his neck with her arm, feeling a breast crushed into his chest, her head tight in the crook of his arm, and she tilted her head to accommodate his thrusting tongue with an instinct she had not known she had. The tingling restlessness in her body expanded, rushing over her arms and spine, rippling over her buttocks and the backs of her knees, shimmering through her hands that curved to fit the shape of his shoulders.

They gasped together, then fell again into the heat of it. The force made them stumble, and he braced himself on the wall, pressing hard into her. And even then, even then, Cassandra only wanted more. Only wanted Basilio, the feeling of him like the gilded light falling on her eyelids. She touched him eagerly, his arms and face and hair, his back. He slid down a little, lifting her so he could kiss her throat.

"This place draws my eye," he murmured, and kissed it, chin to collarbone, lingering, tasting, his tongue drawing a line across that and back. Her breasts felt heavy and thick, and in a gesture she would have thought beyond her, she grabbed his hand and settled it, over her breast.

His hand moved gently, his bare fingers brushing the flesh over her bodice, his thumb going exactly where she wanted it, over that tight, burning nipple. She could not help the small sound that came from her at that, and she closed her eyes, astoundingly dizzy. He kissed her again, his mouth soft, plying, teasing over her lips, his tongue a heated flicker at the corner, at the bow, at the very center of her lower lip, and he stroked her breast as he kissed her, kissed her and teased that place, until all at once Cassandra was aware that her thighs felt wet. "Basilio, take off your coat!"

He obliged, shucking it, dropping it to the ground, and then the waistcoat. She opened the ties at his neck, then put her hands below the shirt hem to touch his bare back, his sides. His chest. His skin was like butter beneath her fingers.

And then they were kissing again, and it grew wilder, more heated, their breath hot and hurried, their hands eager, dancing, exploring. Basilio bent with a soft moan to kiss her neck, and suckled lightly, then harder. All at once, his hand, which must have been working her skirt upward as they kissed, fell on the back of her bare thigh, and his sex aggressively pushed into her belly.

Cassandra froze. Desire gave way to panic and she struck out with her fists, cuffing his shoulders, his head. "Basilio, stop!"

He released her instantly and stood back. Cassandra stared at him as a wave of trembling overtook her, so violent she could not even stand. Her knees gave away and she sank to the ground, her shaking hands over her face. "I'm sorry," she whispered.

"My God, Cassandra!" He stepped forward, reached for her, then squatted close, not touching her. "I do not want to frighten you more. I only want to put my arms around you, to stop your trembling." He crept closer. "Will that be all right?"

Cassandra clasped her hands more tightly over her face, appalled that he should see her this way, that anyone should see her so revealed.

She did not cry. Would not. She pressed her hands close to her eyes and held the scream in her throat, and when his hand touched her shoulder, she startled so violently she scraped her elbow on the wall.

Very carefully, he touched her arm, then the other. When she didn't pull away—for she did most desperately want to lean into him—he gave a soft, mournful cry. "Oh, love," he whispered, and took her into his arms, tucking her head on to his shoulder. "He must have been very cruel. I am so sorry, Cassandra." He held her close, whispering into her hair. "So very, very sorry."

She trembled even more violently, and hated herself for it. Yet she was so weak, and he was so gentle, she could not seem to make herself stand, straighten her clothes, and forget this.

As if he understood that, he only sat on the grassy ground, holding her close, rocking her a little. "Do you want to tell me about him? Was it your husband?"

She had never spoken of it, not even to her sisters. Nor did she ever, ever allow herself to be so vulnerable as she was in this moment. Sucking in a breath of air, she told herself to be calm, to be poised. It would go away, the shaking, the upset. She struggled to erect her walls.

But in the end, she could not. His hand was too gentle, his voice too soft. Against her cheek, his shoulder curved in exactly the bowl she needed, and she could not move away from it. His hand stroked her hair, over and over, and it made her remember her mother. Her trembling eased slightly.

After a long time, she said, "It was my husband."

His fingers smoothed hair back from her temple. "He hurt you."

"Yes." Squeezing her eyes tight, she pushed away the violent feel of his hands, his unnatural tastes. "He could not . . . perform with me very often. It enraged him, so he did . . . other things."

Gentle, gentle were Basilio's hands. Across her temple, over her cheek. She had no vocabulary to describe her husband's actions, and even thinking of it caused a flutter in her throat. "It was even worse when he could perform. His imagination was cruel."

Saying it aloud brought it to her in ways she

did not allow. The bruises on her breasts and legs, the sound of a certain sort of laughter, the horror she'd felt. There had been no one to whom she could go for help. "My father was dying." Her voice was calm. Or perhaps only dull. "My sisters had no power to help, and would only have been distraught. My brothers had fled England."

"Ah, my sweet." He brushed his hands along her arm. "I am not a violent man, but this makes me feel bloodthirsty. I wish I could kill him for you."

The soothing rhythm of his hands never ceased. "I hate him for putting fear in place of love, for putting pain where pleasure should be. But more," he said quietly, leaning close to her, "I wish I could take that pain from you, so you never knew it. I am so very sorry to have brought it to you again."

She pressed her burning brow into his chest, squeezing her eyes tightly closed. "I am so ashamed of it now."

"Oh, no!" He bent close. "No, Cassandra! You did nothing wrong. He stole something very precious from you."

"I should not have let him."

He took her face in his hand, held her chin patiently until at last she had courage enough to look at him. "He stole the joy you would have found without him." His eyes were sad. "I can taste your passion when you kiss me, taste the magic that is within us, but he stole the satisfaction you would have found there, the full beauty."

"I am not wholly ignorant." She lifted her head, finding the courage now to straighten, to rely again on her poise. "I have read . . . things," she said. "Frank descriptions of sex, in books from France. And there is that happiness in Boccaccio. But I've never felt it—the passion." She bowed her head, heat on her cheeks. "Until now . . . and you see how it will be."

"He stole it, my Cassandra." He took her hand and pressed it to his mouth, his eyes intent. "It is like plums, no? Those plums, hot from the garden. Or the olives you liked so much that first day. So delicious, so rich. And I watched you in the village last night, so free and happy. And at the beach, when you let the water come over your feet, you were so happy."

She didn't understand what he was trying to tell her, and frowned. "But perhaps the pain has ruined this for me. I have never been hurt eating a plum."

"There should be no hurt in this." He lifted his chin and tossed back those wild ringlets, his eyes very dark and intense as he guided her hand to his sex, soft and unthreatening beneath his breeches, though it leapt a little under her hand. "It should bring only pleasure. More than plums, more than the ocean, more than anything." He pulled her hand away and touched her face. "Your husband took from you the greatest of all the pleasures."

Cassandra felt the sinuous swirl on her nerves as she looked at him, a swirl she could name now: desire. "Can you teach me, Basilio? Will you give that back to me?"

He closed his eyes. "I fear . . . that my ardor is too much, that my passion will wound you more." He picked up her hand and kissed it. "In truth, Cassandra, if I must be content with only kissing it would be a hardship, but I would prefer that to another wound to you."

"I trust you. Only you."

Soberly he gazed at her. "Then I will try. But here is the promise you must give to me: that you never, never go where you do not wish. No matter how deep my hunger, no matter how far we have gone, you must promise that you will tell me when you are afraid. It will not hurt me."

An ache, pride and anticipation and fear, squeezed her chest. "I promise."

"All right, then." He leaned forward, touched his lips to hers, and laughed softly. "All teachers should have such a student."

"Why are you laughing?"

He shook his head, eyes glittering. "Anticipation," he whispered, and stood, tugging her hand. "Come."

"Will we begin tonight?"

"Only the first lesson." He lifted her hands to his lips. "We shall savor the moments, yes?"

Cassandra swallowed. "Oh, yes."

Chapter 7

As they walked up the hill to the villa, Basilio held her hand and considered what to do with his beautiful pupil, who had put such deep faith in his skill as a lover.

It was her faith that had made him laugh. He was not so skilled as she imagined. At university there had been the usual whores, sometimes an affair of a month or two with some willing shop-keeper. Once he had been besotted and sick with longing over a married matron, much older than he, who kept him in her pocket for a year before moving on to her next youthful conquest. Sometimes in his travels he had taken lovers, as a man will. He quickly forgot them.

He had never known a virgin, which would have been the best preparation for a task such as this. It would also be easier if he understood the exact nature of her husband's abuse. Hatred flared again, and he quelled it instantly, for tonight he did not need hatred or anger. He needed the purity of his passion for her, and all the gentleness and control he could muster, and patience.

Inside the villa, he paused, struck with inspiration. "Wait here. I will be right back."

She nodded, slightly subdued. Nervous by the look of her mouth. He paused to brush his lips over hers. "I know you like kissing. Think of that. We can kiss for hours if you like."

"Hours?" A glitter in those eyes.

"Days, even."

She managed a smile. "I could not withstand days of kissing you, Basilio. My skin would burst into flames."

He laughed. "That is very, very good. Wait. I will be right back."

He went to the kitchen and gathered wine and cheese and olives, which he put into a basket, along with a fresh loaf of bread sitting on the heavy wooden table in the center of the room. Cook scowled at him around her smile, and he said, "What other lovely things have you to give me?"

She shook her head, but heaved herself to her feet and went to a cupboard she unlocked with a great circle of keys. From within the cavernous space came a plateful of chocolates and marzipans molded into tiny fruits. Basilio grinned his pleasure. "Very good."

As he passed the library, he suddenly knew that it did not matter if he were wildly skilled, if he were the greatest lover in the world. This was his Cassandra, who had stolen his heart from far away, and he had only to be himself and trust his instincts. He took a book from the shelf and tucked it in the basket.

She stood exactly where he'd left her, by the open glass door to the courtyard. Her spine was very straight, her poise gathered around her like a cloak, and fresh desire flooded through him. He joined her, looking over her shoulder. "I have a very fine view of the sea from my chamber," he said. On impulse, he bent and very lightly kissed the back of her neck.

"I should like to see that view," she said, her voice husky. Some of the hurt had fallen from her eyes and he saw the frank hunger in her face.

But when they had climbed the many stone stairs to his suite of rooms, and closed the door, and the bed loomed over everything, mocking and alluring at once, they both paused awkwardly. Her hands fluttered up and back down to her sides. Basilio seemed stuck where he stood, the basket in his hand, seeing his things with strange new eyes. The clutter of his desk, papers piled and messy, for he did not allow the servants to straighten it. A pile of books on a table. The things he'd collected on his travels gave a foreign cast to the room: carved elephants he'd purchased in Cypress, a beautiful wall hanging in reds that he'd found in Egypt, and brass candlesticks from India.

One side of the room boasted long windows

looking west to the sea, and a set of doors opened onto a stone balcony. Cassandra moved toward it, and relieved, Basilio put his basket down on a table and began to take things out of it. Then he joined her.

This balcony was wider and deeper than the one in her chamber, and the view was more primitive: only the hills rolling across the land like a woman, and the sea in the distance, shimmering with life.

He leaned on the rail, letting the breeze comb his hair away from his hot face and scalp. "I love this view," he said. "It inspires me, the colors and the shapes and the smell of it."

She nodded, her hands folded primly before her on the stone. "I have made you feel very awkward, haven't I?"

He shifted to lean with one elbow, so he could face her. As honestly as he was able, he said, "A little. Not for you. For me." He smiled down at her. "You must see by now that I am besotted with you, Cassandra." He reached out to touch a tendril of reddest hair. "Since you arrived on that road, I have thought of nothing but you—and now I am afraid that I cannot be wise enough, good enough for you."

A brilliance came into her expression, light and graveness at once. "It is the same for me, Basilio. I cannot even sleep for thinking of you." She clasped his palm to her face. "I feel as if I have been sleeping all my life, and have only now awakened."

"Yes," he echoed, captivated by the movement of her lips. Gently he leaned close. "You like kissing, I think. May I kiss you, my beautiful Cassandra?"

She touched his mouth. "Yes, I would like that."

He did not immediately move, letting the sight of her mouth stir his imagination. Only then did he lean close, careful to keep his body far from hers. Putting his palm against her jaw, he touched her lips lightly with his own; felt the softness and give of hers, felt the immediate opening of her mouth to him.

But he did not take the invitation. Instead, he trailed the tip of his tongue along the inner edges of her mouth, teasing—now a flutter, now a long, slow, opulent circle. Her breath quickened, and he danced within the sweet-tasting lips, slipping just past teeth to the very, very tip of her tongue. A sweep and retreat, a slight sound in her throat as she followed him out, into his mouth, and back. Only his hand on her face, and their lips and tongues. He whispered instruction and she followed, sticking out her tongue only a little, and he captured it, that small, pointed end, sucking on it. With broken breath, she said, "Now you," and came a little closer, putting her hands on his face. With one finger, she traced the shape of his mouth, and then lightly, erotically, stroked his lower lip, her eyes brilliant with fever. Gently he sucked the digit into his mouth, swirled his tongue over it. She gave a soft cry and moved within his mouth, just a little. He saw that her nipples were urgently erect, and he ached to bend and take those points into his mouth, too. But he only met her eyes and did to her finger what he wished to do to nipples—swirled and suckled and let go. "Oh," she breathed, suddenly taking her hand away, stepping back one hesitant pace. She tucked her hand behind her, in her skirts.

He laughed softly, and took her other hand. "Come, my dear," he said. "Let us read and eat and think no more of kisses tonight."

"I am not sure I can promise not to think of them." A little scowl touched her brow. "Nor am I certain I wish to promise not to do it."

He lifted a brow. "If you wish to kiss me, you have my full permission."

Sitting side by side on the divan, they read aloud from Boccaccio, nibbling from each other's hands the marzipans and chocolates he'd stolen from the kitchen. They did kiss a little more, and a little more, and when Basilio came to a point he could no longer bear it, he laughed a little at the stunned sensuality in her eyes, and sent her away. Even when she reluctantly lingered at the door, leaning back into the room to kiss him again, he did not move one more step forward.

That night, as he lay alone in his bed, the moon spilling cool and white over his restive limbs, he realized that she needed wooing, needed a man who would allow her own sensual nature to claim her. In the quiet dark, he composed a poem of revelation for his Cassandra.

In the morning when Cassandra awakened, a letter waited on her breakfast tray. She opened it eagerly, and found only a few lines in Basilio's hand:

> *The moon is the ruler of women, her round white face echoing the white round flesh of a woman's breasts. Tonight, my love, we will ride on the white sands by the sea and learn what gifts the full moon will give.*

> B.

A ripple of heat went through her, and she spent the day in a state of restless anticipation. As the sun dropped low in the sky, she dithered over her hair and clothing, over which adornments to put on her body, which to leave behind. At last she was ready to join him, and ran laughing to the stables with him, her heart pounding.

The air was warm as bathwater as they rode on the beach they had visited a few days before, and the smell of the sea charged her blood with a heightened excitement. The full moon, bright and round and high, cast pale light over the world, and Cassandra felt the strangest leap of anticipation when she looked at it. Her breasts seemed to swell against her bodice, and she wondered with amusement if she would always think of breasts now when she saw the moon.

Basilio helped her dismount, his eyes glittering with mischief. "I would be pleased to shed all these trappings of civilization for your benefit if you like," he said, gesturing to his clothes. "Or perhaps you would only like to gaze at my feet?"

She laughed. "Shed your shoes, dear sir. The rest we will leave for another time."

"And what will you shed, my Cassandra?" he asked, stepping close.

A ripple of anticipation. "What would you like me to shed?"

"Turn around," he said. "I will show you."

She hesitated. The night was bright, but they were alone. Fear mixed with desire. "That frightens me."

"I would like," he said, touching her shoulder, "to kiss your breasts, Cassandra. Only your mouth and neck and breasts." His dark eyes were clear and honest. "I think you will like it. If you do not, I give you my word that I will cease immediately."

Her heart shivered, and without a word, she turned around to let him unlace her dress a little. He kissed the back of her neck slowly as his hands pushed away her sleeves; kissed her shoulders with exquisite little moist presses of hot lips as she tugged one arm, then the other out of the confining sleeves. Her corset pushed her breasts up under the gauzy chemise with a drawstring neck, and she shivered when he untied the neckline and gently pushed that fabric away, too. He stood behind her, kissing her neck and the edge of her ears and her shoulders—patiently, as a salty sea breeze and moonlight touched her breasts, naked to the night. It was decadent and delicious, and Cassandra discovered that she loved it. She loved it more when his beautiful long hands slid up her waist and ribs and stroked the bare flesh, dancing over the aroused points, stroking the sides and delicate undercurve.

"What do you think?" he whispered. "Yes? No?"

She leaned a little into his chest, letting her head fall back to his shoulders to give him fuller access to her body. "Yes," she whispered.

He drew her down with him to the sand. "Close your eyes," he said.

She did. White moonlight burned on her eyelids and she waited, barely breathing, for the first kiss. It seemed to take a very long time for it to arrive, a time filled with the low roar of the sea and the caress of the wind and the delectable wonder of being even a little bit naked outside.

At last the kiss fell, hot and open, on her right breast. His mouth closed around the pointed tip, and she cried out at the pleasure of it, lifting her hands to his hair in encouragement. "Mmmm," he said. "I wanted to do this last night, when you had your finger in my mouth," he said, flicking his tongue over her. "That is what I was thinking of: that I was doing all those things to your breasts, to these pretty pink points"—he touched them, one at a time, with the heart of his palms— "instead of your finger." His dark eyes met hers. "Do you like it?"

She pulled him down to her, wordless in her wish to have him continue. Hands and tongue and teeth and lips—oh! She would never have dreamed there could be so much feeling in the simple attention to her breasts, but he soon had her quivering and hot, her hips restless. She nearly wanted to weep with the fullness, and when he stopped, she wanted to tell him to begin again. But she saw the effort with which he halted, and she did not think she was near ready for the rest. So she only said, "Basilio, remove your shirt, please. Do you mind?"

He scrambled to oblige her, his fingers fumbling with the ties so violently that Cassandra laughed softly and rose up to help him. He made a soft, almost amused noise, his hands in her hair. "You are a goddess, my love." He kissed her, then Cassandra tugged the shirt over his head and they faced each other, kneeling in the sand.

Surprised at her own boldness, she inched closer to him until her breasts just brushed his chest, and put her naked arms around his bare shoulders. It was extraordinarily wonderful, the feel of his skin against her own, and she said earnestly, "I think I would like kissing this way, if it is not too difficult for you."

"Nothing is too difficult," he whispered. So they kissed, and kissed, and kissed, gently brushing breast to crisp hair, belly to belly, arms and hands.

At last, with trembling hands, he took her arms from his shoulders and moved away a little. "I must halt now," he said regretfully. Without awaiting an answer, he stood and dashed for the water. Cassandra laughed when he gave a great shout and dived into the sea, coming up like an otter, his hair shining with diamonds among the curls, moonlight making of his face a work of art. Without hurry she covered herself, and allowed him, dripping and calmed, to lace up her corset. They rode back to the villa in rich silence, touching hands, and he left her at her bedroom door with a long, deep, heated kiss of promise. Feeling the pulse of her sex, Cassandra pulled him back when he would have left. "Basilio," she whispered. "Come to my bed. I am ready now."

He bent and kissed her once more. "Not yet," he said. "Good night."

Nor was it the next day, or the next. In the cool mornings they rode until the sun burned away the mist, laughing and telling stories—but

mainly just reveling in the beauty of the landscape and the pleasure of each other's company.
In the hot afternoons they lazed in the cool interior rooms of the villa, sometimes sitting for long
quiet hours reading or writing, side by side, content with the silence and the company. At such
times, Basilio felt the rarest, deepest sense of
happiness he had ever known—that a woman
could enjoy the same thoughtful silence he did,
without requiring reassurance every moment.

In the evenings, they ate the dishes he'd
ordered his cook to prepare: delicately flavored
local specialties, drawn from the sea, and rich
wines, and sinful sweets. Afterward they sat
close together on the terrace, admiring the sound
of cicadas and the scents of the olive trees breathing from their leaves. Hands entwined, they
laughed and kissed and shared bits and pieces of
their lives. Basilio told her about his student
days, and a teacher who had been a particular
encouragement. Cassandra told stories about her
siblings—Adriana, the wild one, and Ophelia, the
beauty, and Cleo, about whose fate they all worried, and Phoebe, who was simple and plain and
kind. She also spoke of her brothers, one fair, one
dark, and their unusual adventures in the new
world. It was plain she was very fond of them all.

He ached, every minute of every hour, to make
love to her. Each day, he allowed only an hour or
maybe a little more, of the kissing she so loved.
He showed her new places on her body where a

man's hand could give pleasure—the soles of her feet, the palms of her hands, the inner crook of a wrist. Slowly, he uncovered her knees and kissed the small crook below, leaving her writhing. And that time, he let his fingers stray up the insides of her thighs, stopping short of the place she wanted him.

In return, she grew bolder, less skittish. One morning, she shocked him with a quick glimpse of unrestrained breasts when she came down for breakfast, leaning over with apparent guilelessness to admire a flower. When she looked up with laughter in her eyes and danced away, he knew she was nearly ready for him, but he waited just a little longer.

When his senses, his hungers, began to overwhelm him, he always laughed a little, pulled away, breathed deeply. Every night, he went to sleep with a thick weight in his groin. Sometimes he relieved the pressure himself; sometimes his dreams did the work for him—but it allowed him great patience.

And it would be worth the wait.

Cassandra was utterly, totally besotted. She had lost reason days ago, lost it in the drunken pleasure of kissing him for such long interludes, lost it in the explosion of her physical self—a part of her that had been starved and malnourished for years, so that now it was ravenous, insatiable.

One evening he slid a note beneath her door,

asking her to meet him in his chambers for dinner, and she rushed through her preparations, arriving giddy and out of breath. The room was filled with flowers: vase after vase of them, roses and ferns and violets and everything imaginable, their perfume enriching the air, their colors adding a heady sensuality. He'd cleared his books away and had a table brought in for dinner.

"Hello," he said, gesturing her inside and seating her at the table. "Eat heartily," he said with a wicked lift of his brow.

Cassandra laughed. She ducked her head a little, then smiled. "Would you take off your shirt, sir?"

"Now, so soon?"

She met his eyes. "Now."

Basilio took a breath and reached for the hem of his shirt. "It would be my pleasure." He pulled up the hem but his hair tangled in a tie and caught, so it was stuck half on and half off until she reached out to help him, laughing. Ruefully, he smiled. "I am not usually so graceless."

She stood close, shaking her head. "Not graceless." She reached out with one hand to touch him, cupping her hand around the curve of his shoulder. "Pure beauty. I have never seen so beautiful a man as you."

He stood still as she lifted the other hand and spread her palms open on him, looking at him as she touched his chest. The dark triangle of hair, his nipples, his arms. Even so simple a thing aroused him, and he hoped that would not alarm her. He couldn't bear to close his eyes, to think of something else, because the wonder in her eyes was a deep pleasure, as if she were discovering a man's form for the first time. "Your skin is very soft," she said, looking up at him. "I like the way it feels."

"I like the way it feels when you touch it."

"So I see," she said with a flash of dry humor. "May I touch you there, too?"

He grinned. "Please, my lady, touch everything. Anything. This humble form belongs to you to do with as you wish."

Her hands ran down his belly, and then lower, tentatively. He sighed softly, and she looked up in alarm. "Is this difficult for you?"

"No."

She smiled. "Yes, it is." But she did not remove her hand, and her eyes flew down to see what she curved her palm around. "Only flesh," she said.

He nodded.

She let him go and turned around. "Please unfasten my laces, Basilio. I should like to remove my dress."

It startled him that his fingers were so clumsy, that he had so much difficulty with a task he had performed many times. He at last managed it, then unlaced the corset underneath. She wore a long, thin chemise beneath it all, and he saw her skin through it when she let the dress fall away into a heap on the floor, and the corset along with it. She stepped out of the pile and kicked it to one side, and stood there with her hair piled high, the airy chemise cloaking her, yet not.

"Now, your hair," he said, his voice rough.

She raised her arms, and he watched her breasts, loose and heavy beneath the gauzy covering, lift, too. Then her hair tumbled down, falling over her arms and shoulders and breasts.

He leaned close, keeping his body apart, and put his mouth on her nipple, sucking through the cloth very lightly. Then he raised his head. "Do you like that?"

"Yes," she said emphatically, and he bent again. Her hands fell in his hair, moving restlessly as he took the crest into his mouth and rubbed his tongue over it. The action made him dizzy, and he suckled close in deep pleasure, putting one hand on her belly to brace himself. She made a low sound of pleasure and he moved to the other breast, feeling his sex pulse in rhythm. Her hands moved to his back, stroking in a rhythm he was sure she did not recognize.

It was instinct again that made him straighten, take a breath, and look into her face. Sensation made her eyes limpid, and her mouth was parted the slightest bit, but he did not kiss her. Taking her hand, he drew her to the table. "Some wine now, I think," he said, and poured it.

"But—"

He grinned wickedly. "What?"

She looked at him, and then at herself in the gauzy covering. "Weren't we in the middle of something?"

He pressed the glass into her hand. "We still are." He drank some wine and leaned in to kiss her with that taste on his tongue, then pulled back and laughed at the astonishment on her face.

"But I liked what we were doing."

"I saw that you did." He drank a little more, plucked an olive, and chewed the fruit away from the pit. He was extraordinarily aware of his body, perhaps because of her gaze touching him everywhere. He felt the brush of his hair along his shoulders, the clasp of his boots on his feet, the air on his chest and belly, the earnest and eager thrust of his sex. He gave her a marzipan strawberry. "You will like this, too."

"Not as much."

He laughed. "Such a rebellious student."

"What are you teaching me?"

"Anticipation." He found another olive that pleased him, put it between his lips, and sucked on it. "Sensuality is everywhere, not only in sex."

She licked her bottom lip, and he had the sudden sense that it was deliberate, that gesture—and it had the effect she wished. He found his own tongue moving in his mouth, wanting to rub against hers. Her nostrils flared, in amusement and arousal.

"What is it you think when you stare at my tongue that way?" she asked.

He put his glass down, and took hers. "I'll show you." He took her hand and led her to the bed. He sat there and pulled her into his lap, her legs straddling his waist, her sex pressed close to his. He waited a moment. "Is this all right?"

Her hands were on his shoulders and he felt their faint tremble, but she wiggled a little closer. He grinned.

"Yes," she said. "I like it."

"Excellent." He brushed his mouth over hers, asking invitation, which she gave, and he parried, drew out her tongue, then brushed it with his own. He groaned softly when she followed his lead, then parried on her own, sliding her tongue along his lips, into his mouth, drawing him back into hers. For a long time it was enough, the dance of their kiss, and he felt the press of her sex into him, hotter and hotter, and even a little restless movement that took him too close to completion.

Gently, he lifted her from his lap, unable to form explanations as he pushed her backward into the pile of pillows, bending over her breasts to taste them as he untied the chemise drawstring. He tugged the fabric from her, never ceasing his ministrations until the cloth touched his mouth, and he lifted his head only long enough to uncover her before his mouth claimed the hot, pointed flesh again.

She moaned, and he raised his head. "Oh, please, Basilio," she whispered. "I do like that, very much. Don't stop."

"There is more, my sweet." He went back to it, and at the same time, slid the chemise upward as well as down, so it bunched in a pool around her waist, leaving all else bare. She shied away a little when his hand lit on her thigh, but he rolled his tongue over her nipple, fast, then slow, and she quieted again. Very gently, he curved his fingers around her thigh, feeling a loosening in her hips that let him go closer, closer—a whisper of hair on his hand, the heat below it. A brush over the dampness, a tease of his fingers, then slow fingers between her legs. She went rigid for a minute and he stilled immediately, though he did not remove his hand. He shifted to one elbow to look into her face, and she opened her eyes as he bent over her. Kissed her lightly. "You are so beautiful, Cassandra. I can barely breathe for all the beauty."

He kissed her and moved his fingers the slightest bit, feeling her tenseness give way under his mouth, under his hand. He stroked her and felt the ease more, then felt her fall into the pleasure of it. She closed her eyes and her head moved restlessly, and he kissed her throat, and her breasts, and moved his hand against her with long, lazy strokes—longer, harder, until she was quivering. "Shall I stop now?" he whispered.

"Oh, no. No. No!" Her body drew up and her

head went back, and she convulsed around him, violently. Her arms went around his shoulders, and her teeth marked his shoulder as she reared, was stolen, taken far from him. When she fell back again he fell beside her, breathing hard, and when she would have taken his hand away, he did not let her. "Not yet," he whispered, feeling the tremors still shaking her in rhythmic bursts. He knew this much, knew how to coax them along. But to his amazement, they slowed, and slowed, but then the tension was back again— and another wave shook her, almost as violently as the first time.

Her hand went around his wrist, tight as a vise. "Wait," she cried raggedly.

"If you wish," he said raggedly, his words slurred with heat. "But I will tell you that right now, in this very moment when you are so soft and shivery, you will like the way I feel inside of you. Are you ready to try that?"

"I'm not sure," she said. Then, "No." She sat up abruptly and Basilio fell on the pillows, hiding his disappointment, a disappointment that eased when she gathered the chemise from around her waist and pulled it off, throwing it carelessly behind her. Her hair tumbled in glorious disarray over her arms and shoulders and breasts, and there was no shyness as she moved close to him, bending over him as he'd bent over her. "Let me touch you first," she whispered, and kissed him. "Can you bear waiting just a little more?"

Dizzy with her beauty, with the sorcery of her hands on his body, he nodded. "Anything you like."

She touched him as she had before, running her hands over his torso, touching his neck and nipples and the length of his arms. He watched her, his hand resting lightly on the curve of her hip, and knew that this would be forever imprinted in his mind—that poetry for the rest of his life would contain the curve of her white breast, shifting softly with her movements; would be lit with the fire of her hair and the darkness of her eyes, touching him in curiosity and admiration. Her hands grew bolder, moving on his thighs, and over his sex, and finally to the fastenings of his breeches.

"Shall I help you now?" he offered.

"Yes." She rocked back on her knees, her hands folded primly on her thighs, and not over the tangle of curls higher, which he loved. He lifted his hips and quickly skimmed away the last covering he wore, and kicked them away. Then he lay back, revealed to her.

There was a little fear. More than a little.

"A fearsome thing, no?" he said, gesturing to his sex. With a grin, he winked. "We men all think so."

There was only a hint of a smile in return. Acting on instinct, he touched himself firmly. "Only silly flesh." He took her hand and pressed it there. "See?"

Their hands tangled over his organ, and Basilio's breath caught when her nipples pearled. Lifting a little, he captured one in his mouth. "We can touch together, you see?"

Her hand moved on him, hesitantly, top to bottom. "It's very hot," she whispered.

He chuckled. "Yes."

"And really—I hope you do not mind me saying—kind of silly."

He nuzzled her breast, let his hand fall on her thigh, teased close to her heat again, and she made a soft sigh. Basilio suddenly remembered that she had not been afraid when she straddled him earlier, and he sat up. "You will be the mistress, I only your servant," he said raggedly, and pulled her gently to him. "Remember, any moment, I will cease. You need only say to stop."

She nodded, her eyes very large. He felt tension in her arms as he settled her atop him as they had been before, but now with no barrier between them. Her breasts pressed into his chest, pliant and supple, as he kissed her, moving his hands over her back. Her arms softened, fell around his neck, and she breathed, "I am ready, Basilio."

He shifted then, his arms trembling with desire and the need for strength, until she lay on her back, her legs around his waist, her eyes open as he knelt over her. He kissed her, and then, with all the control he could muster, eased into her—only the smallest bit at a time, gauging her reaction at each move. It was agony. It was heaven. He died and lived at the quivering around him, the sweet slick heat.

With a low groan, Cassandra suddenly arched upward, hard, and pulled him into her, her arms and legs fierce and sure. "Oh!" she cried breathlessly, "you were right. It does feel wonderful."

Basilio finally allowed himself to move. And when she met him gladly, he managed to keep control for a little while more, just a little, till he coaxed her over the edge once more, and he was at last free himself to let go.

It was not like anything he had known, but a deep, almost agonizing pleasure that spread from his groin through his legs and up his spine, and into his arms, and his mouth. He kissed her with a kind of roar, and she took his hair in her fists and locked her arms tight around him and arched high, taking him, all of him, crying out his name.

He dropped his head into her neck, shattered, his hands trembling, his chest heaving. And not only from exertion, but from a wild burning emotion in him—a fierce and pained recognition that he had nearly let her go, his Cassandra.

Cassandra lay against him, spent and sated, a languorousness in her limbs that she had never dreamed existed. His hand covered her breast. "I have never felt this, not in all my life, Cassandra." His voice was slow, and she closed her eyes.

"Nor have I," she whispered around that thudding in her chest. She rolled to her side, and pressed a kiss to his forehead.

"Basilio—" She stopped, hardly knowing what to say. "It is a terrible thing when a writer has no words," she said at last. "But there are none for what I'm feeling now."

His hand cupped her cheek. "All the words that ever come from me hence will have Cassandra in them." His lips twitched faintly. "Cassandra's breasts and Cassandra's eyes and"—he rose to one elbow, bent over her, his hair falling around his face in that heavy extravagance— "Cassandra's legs and Cassandra's kiss . . ."

She did not trust excess, in anything. "You do love to show off."

"No," he said soberly, and he put his hand on her belly. "I am a most earnest poet who yearns to express what cannot be said. If the perfection of moments is the purpose of our lives, then I must surely be close to death, for I cannot imagine a moment more perfect than this."

"Basilio—"

"I am most sincere, Cassandra. My heart is alive with all the songs, and my soul weeps with pleasure, and my body cannot think of anything else. You are rare, and I am blessed."

Her heart, already full, burst entire at that. She put her hands in his hair and pulled him down to her, letting her lips and her hands express her feelings in the oldest way. She kissed his mouth and his brow, his chin and his eyelids. She kissed his throat, and the lobe of his ear. "There is no other man in the world but you," she said at last. "None."

"And no other woman but you."

And somehow, they were making love again, and this time Cassandra felt not even a tiny nudging of fear. In her freedom, she was wanton and drunk on him, and even screamed, which made him laugh. Then they were both laughing, and that was even better.

Spent at last, they curled amid the covers and pillows, cradled close, and shared cheese and cool well water.

"Now we shall tell stories," Basilio said.

"Stories?"

He lifted one eyebrow wickedly. "We have not got to the third day. Or is it the fourth?"

"Certainly we've made it to the fifth or sixth by now."

"Then tell me a tale, Cassandra." His hands moved on her back, easy and smooth. "I cannot remember what sort of tale is to be said for the fifth or sixth day."

Somehow she could not recall, either. She slid a little closer, pressing her hips close to his. "There was a woman who lived in London, who had lost her courage in a terrible marriage, and had come to believe the only good men God had ever made were her brothers and father."

He gazed down at her, his thick-lashed eyes very sober. "And what happened to her?"

"A letter arrived from a stranger in a faraway land: a letter that brought with it the scent of the sea and olive trees. The images and words were very beautiful, and the woman wanted to know more about any man who had such beauty in him. She thought he must be a middle aged scholar, balding and sincere."

Basilio's eyes crinkled. "She did not imagine him to be the most virile and handsome of all men?"

"Oh, not at all. Quite dull, really, since the woman's experience had taught her virile, handsome men often had little else to recommend them."

"Ah, poor thing. She should have traveled to Italy, where she could have found a fine stallion."

Cassandra laughed low in her throat. "Are you telling my story?"

"No, no. Please continue."

"So she wrote to her balding scholar and painted a picture of herself that would reassure him: a widow who'd made her own way and cared little for the conventions of society. Over the months they shared many letters, telling their deepest thoughts to one another, secrets they had not shared with any other. It was safe, you see."

"Yes." The word was a whisper.

"But all of that changed when the man challenged the woman to be brave and see his country, and she recklessly took his invitation."

He pushed against her a little, wickedly. "And then she discovered a virile stallion."

She shook her head. "She discovered a man who was beautiful inside and out, when she had despaired of ever knowing such a man."

He kissed her and she kissed him back, stroking his body, his back and arms and hips. "Thank you, Basilio," she whispered.

He tugged her close to him, and exhausted, they slept.

Chapter 8

Cassandra awakened to puddles of buttery light flooding into a room she did not quite recognize. She grew aware that she was entirely naked, and that she was not alone, and in a startled remembrance, turned over. Basilio lay on his belly, his long, vigorous body wholly revealed. One knee was cocked and his hands were flung over his head, and his hair, thick and black, fell on his sleeping face.

Such a violence of emotions rose in her that she had to close her eyes, and breathe, and then open them again. A shadow of beard had grown on his lip and chin, making him appear older, yet his luxuriant hair and lashes made her see the boy he'd been. His body was sturdy and strong, with weight across the shoulders and suppleness down his long back. He was in no way fat, but she liked the substantial look of him, his healthy robustness. The curve of buttock to thigh seemed suddenly vulnerable, and she wanted to cover him protectively, but realized with a smile that she, equally bare, was as vulnerable as he. Together they would remain revealed.

The freedom pleased her, and with an odd sense of her own self, she rose and walked to the table clothed only in her hair. She had never been naked like this in her life, simply walking from one place to another with nothing on, not even in a private room, all alone. It made her feel wild and free and brave to do it, to stand by the table in a bar of sunlight and see her own breasts touched with light, even to see the beautiful glitter in the hair on her belly and thighs, glinting red.

She poured water and drank it, resisting the voices that warned her she was a wanton, wicked thing for enjoying this, for loving the feel of her own flesh on her own bones. Defying them, she put the glass down and stretched her arms above her head, revealing even more to the kiss of sun.

When she turned back to the bed Basilio had shifted position, his head at the foot of the bed where his feet had been, his head propped on his hands. He smiled sleepily. "I cannot imagine a more dazzling sight."

Given leave, she raised her hands again and whirled in a circle for his pleasure, then dashed back to join him, tackling him happily, her arms around his shoulders, her breasts pressed into his back. "I am a goddess," she cried. "That's what you've done for me."

He laughed, wiggling a little as she brushed her fingers down his side, discovering to her delight that he was quite ticklish. "Stop that."

"Are you one of those men who awakens in an ill-temper?"

"No." He looked at her above the curve of his elbow. "I am only very ticklish." He lay his head on his arm and reached for her. "Today we travel to Firenze for the opera, and perhaps we will have time there this afternoon to work."

"Work? I have no desire to work. Especially not in Florence!"

"Ah, but we must." A lift of one dark brow. "It is my duty to see that you spend time with Boccaccio while you wander his world." He brushed hair from her face. "And I will attempt to capture the wonder that is Cassandra in my humble poetry."

"Must we sit inside? Is there not some fine piazza?" She frowned, suddenly realizing that she was perhaps indiscreet. "Oh! Do you wish for me to remain hidden? Is your betrothed there?"

A flicker of something in his eyes, then it was gone. He looked at their hands, tangled together. "She is no longer my betrothed, Cassandra."

"What?"

"I could not be so dishonorable as to give my love to you while another believed me inviolate." He raised his dark, sober eyes. "She wishes to be a nun, and I wrote and told her to take her vows, and wrote my father to break the betrothal."

Cassandra went very still. "I will not be a wife, Basilio. Only your lover."

His lips curved and he lifted her hand to kiss her palm. "I know."

But she saw that he did not believe her, that he believed she could be charmed to his view, soon or late. "Do not make me say this again, Basilio."

"I should not have told you."

She slipped her hand from his grip, frowning a little. "Perhaps not."

For long moments, there was silent awkwardness between them. Cassandra thought to pull the sheet over her shoulder, but only sat with her back to him, reluctant even now to hide her newborn freedom. She narrowed her eyes on the seductive view through the long doors, and let the breeze that lifted the curtains touch her face. Some of the sheen had burned off the moment, but she would not allow it all to be stolen. Impishly, she turned. "Do you wish to keep your lover, sir?"

He grinned and tossed hair from his face. "I do, my lady. What service may I perform to prove my word?"

"Take me to Firenze and woo me with opera and open piazzas."

"Firenze can be easily done. But there is rain coming. Perhaps we will be forced to find entertainment within my house."

"Rain? How do you know?"

He leaned back, splendidly beautiful in his nakedness. "I can smell it."

Cassandra inhaled, and there it was, soft and salty, but distinct. Letting her head drop on to his arm, she sighed. "Well, I suppose if the reward is high enough, I might be persuaded to work."

"Ah. Have you some particular thing in mind?"

She only laughed, low in her throat, the sound so wicked she could barely believe it came from her. "Oh, yes," she whispered, pressing close to kiss him. "Very particular."

His eyes turned liquid. "I shall look forward to that very much."

The drive to Florence was not long. They rode in a richly appointed carriage with those dashing horsemen alongside for protection, and Cassandra peered out the windows with a sense of enchantment. She drank in the landscape and the little villages and Gothic churches, the trees and the wildflowers she had never seen, and even the changing light as the sky grew dark and ominous with rain, the clouds squatting heavily over the rounds of the hills. "Look how far you can see into that valley," she commented, amazed at the glazing of light and shadow that could reveal the pale and paler shapes of hills beyond the first.

"You will write about that, too, someday," he said, taking her hand.

"Will you?"

He shook his head. "I will write of Cassandra's face, alight with joy over the view."

Cassandra frowned. "You're so extravagant."

He lifted a brow. "You do not like it?"

"No. Extravagance is the mark of rakes."

He laughed. "I am Italian. And a poet."

"It's too much."

"Or perhaps," he said, lifting her hand to his lips, "you need only to grow accustomed to it." His eyes glittered. "For truly, there are not enough words to do justice to your glory, my Cassandra." Only the flare of his nostrils gave away his tease.

As she did a hundred times an hour, she snared on this detail of him and shook her head, half in wonder, half in mock-despair. "I can see I will have to teach you a little English decorum."

"If you must." Something caught his eye. "Look! The spires of Firenze."

But by the time they reached his house in town, a charming Renaissance structure built around an internal piazza, the rain had begun to fall in earnest, and there was no exploring to be done. They retreated to the library, this one grand and richly appointed. "My father's," Basilio said dismissively.

"Must we work?" she asked, one last time, as

he pulled out pens to be sharpened and pots of ink. The line of his shoulders made her randy, and she did not care for the prospect of scholarly studies.

As if he knew it, he shed his coat and settled it on the back of a chair. Amusement danced in his eyes. "My wish was to give you a start to your translation. If you take something else back to England with you, all the better—but the work is what I can give most earnestly."

Back to England. A pluck of warning told her it would not be so easy to leave him as she had first imagined. To cover that faint, distant dismay, she shrugged in mock ennui. "As you wish."

He laughed, putting his hands on her shoulders and settling her in a big leather chair. He placed a sharpened quill in her hand. "You will thank me one day."

She raised her head, suddenly aware that no man in all her life had ever actively put a pen in her hand and told her to write. Swift, fierce gratitude made her take his hand and put a kiss in his palm. "I thank you now, sir." Then she dropped his hand and waved him away. "Allow me to begin."

His soft laughter was reward in itself.

Rain fell in steady gray sheets all afternoon. Basilio had accounts to go over, and it was a monumental task, yet his attention was snared over and over by the flame of Cassandra, at a table nearby the windows. She did not work neatly. The single page of original Boccaccio was put on a smaller table near the desk to keep it safe from what was to come—a scattering of books taken from his shelves as she looked up one thing and another; the messy growing pile of her own notes, brought with her from the villa in a leather case; a bound book he thought must be a journal.

It surprised him, how much he wanted to crack that book open and read what she'd written privately there. His passion, far from being even momentarily slaked, had taken a new, fierce turn. His feeling for her was so large it seemed his body could not contain it, that others looking at him must see a scarlet flame burning out from him.

Only by the greatest discipline was he able to remain silent, allowing her to immerse herself in the pleasure of her work. He had known that she was quite serious about work, about the world of letters and study, but it surprised him how deeply she concentrated once given the chance. How much pleasure she took in it. Her shoulders, ordinarily so straight, eased. Her legs beneath her skirts fell akimbo, her feet tucked together at the ankle.

Here lay Cassandra's passion. He discovered he held a little jealousy over it, that it could steal her away from him so completely.

But he'd meant what he said about wanting to

see her begin that translation she wished to write, and he tried to give her room to do it, watching her only when he thought she didn't notice.

There was great energy in her movements. Her sleeve annoyed her and she unbuttoned the cuff and shoved it carelessly up her arm. She shifted to check some note she'd made, then turned back to write quickly, decisively. Her pen scratched over the paper. Once she raised her head, a thoughtful, distant expression on her face, and asked his opinion on which of two phrases was better. "The second," he said.

"Yes." She nodded seriously. "That's what I thought, too." And away she went again, into her work.

At last he gave up any pretense of accounting and tried instead to write poetry. It was not possible, of course. His brain was gauzy, full of drifting images—all sharp and rich, but too new and hot to handle just yet.

What he could do was let the past few days fill him, allow phrases to present themselves for consideration—fragments of vividness that would one day arrange themselves into some shape. A day when he was not a single burning mass of sense and feeling, but was able to think again.

It made him smile, his chin in his hand, that Cassandra was not as lost as he in all this. But then, his capacity for love was large, larger than most. He did not begin to hope that her feeling would match his.

"Basilio," she said from her post, "if you do not cease staring at me, I shall be forced to give up all pretense of work and kiss you senseless." She looked at her books as she spoke. "And in all fairness, 'twas your idea for us to work today."

"What could I have been thinking?"

"Write me a letter and tell me—for now you must wait until I have completed this, or I shall never sleep tonight."

"Will I post my letter, too?" He lazily admired the curve of her cheek. "Or shall I read it to you . . . later?"

"That," she said, glancing at him with a brow raised in a little arch, "is entirely your choice."

Suddenly, it did seem something he could do. Dipping his pen, he paused over a fresh sheet, and then, in a rush, began to write:

My dearest Cassandra,

As I write this, you are bent over your translation, and I am besotted with the bend of your white neck, by the small curls that have escaped your attempt to tame that wild hair, by the seriousness of your brow as you bend over your work. I dare not say what is in my heart, for this is too new, and I sense that you were badly wounded and will need time to see that I am different.

But here, in this letter that I will mail to be waiting for you when you return to your house in Piccadilly Street, I will confess the truth: I broke my betrothal because there will never be another woman for me as long as you are in the world, and there is but one wish in my mind: that we shall spend our days together—all of them.

It is not a simple matter, of course. My father is going to be very, very angry with me when he hears the news. He is likely reading my letter in this moment—oh, anger is not a fine thing on his face.

No, it will not be simple. And I will not speak of this to you except in this letter, which you will not see until you return to your home—but you are my heart, my love, the very blood that runs in my veins. It was fated that we should find one another across such vast distances, fated that our hearts should become one.

I am so certain of this, that it is not merely passion that binds us—sweet though passion may be!—but a union of souls that were born to be entwined, that I am willing to let you leave me, return to your home, and see that what I say is true. No time or distance or practicalities will dim what has been born here in these precious days.

And I am so certain that naught will dim this that I say now, come, Cassandra—or if you cannot, I will come to you. Be my love, be my wife.

Let us together make a mosaic of joy from our days.

There are no words in any language to express the depth of my feeling for you, so I leave you with the simplest of them all: Li amo.

Your Basilio

Smiling, he scattered sand over the page and put down his pen. Cassandra was buried in her work and did not look up, and he left her to it, a bounce in his step as he folded and sealed the letter, then carried it out to a servant to have it posted. Only when he returned to the library did she look up, slightly dazed in that way of scholars. "Did you write a letter?"

"I did. And you shall not have it till you return home."

She inclined her head, intrigued. He loved the look of her red, red mouth turning up a little at the corners. "Will you not even hint of what it says?"

Now he saw the luminosity of her eyes, falling on his throat, his chest, his mouth. A fresh, rich thrust of desire pushed through him, and he closed the door and turned the lock. "I wrote of passion."

"Did you?" There was a breathy softness to the words.

"Yes." He bent over her, putting his mouth at the bend of her neck. "I wrote of these curls, this curve." His hand lit on her smooth shoulder, slid across the flesh above her bodice, followed the gentle swell of breasts.

Her eyes drifted closed. "What else?"

He suckled her earlobe, drawing a sigh, and slid his hand lower, just beneath the edge of her bodice. "I wrote of skin like satin."

"Satin? There is an original metaphor." Sharp words, softened by slow diction as she lifted her hands to his side.

"Perhaps it was not satin." He curled his fingers around her breast within the bodice, his thumb finding and rubbing the aroused tip. He closed his eyes. "No," he whispered. "I wrote of cloud softness and the softness of the wind, whispering through a morning, and the rich weight of—" He could not think. "I wrote," he whispered, kneeling and taking her into his arms, "of love."

She put her hands on his face and kissed him. "You have bewitched me, Basilio. I do not like such extravagant talk and excessive emotion." She kissed him again, slowly pulling away. "Yet now I cannot think how I lived without it."

Then there were no more words, only a fierce, half-clothed coupling in the gray light of a rainy afternoon.

Afternoon slid to evening. The rain did not stop, making the streets a mess of puddles and mud. Cassandra held up her skirts carefully, allowing Basilio to assist her from the carriage into the opera house. It was a grand place, and busy even in the rain. Cassandra blinked a little at the sound of an entire crowd speaking Italian, which suddenly made her aware of how far from home she was. The women were glorious, sophisticated—and unabashedly sexual beings. As they milled about the hall beneath bright chandeliers, she watched them covertly, astonished and a little shocked, but mainly dazzled, at the way they leaned close to a man, a hand sliding along his sleeve. Or a flash of a dancing eye, cutting sideways in arch knowledge. She admired the flash of their jewels and the cut of their gowns to show every inch of voluptuous or slim or even plump bodies.

Next to her, Basilio leaned close. "You see? We are all extravagant."

"My sister Adriana would love this," she said without thinking.

Basilio grinned. "The wicked sister, yes?"

Cassandra laughed. "Yes. She is . . . a very sensual person. She would be at home here." In surprise, she confessed with a little frown, "I judged her harshly, I'm afraid."

"You did not understand, that's all."

She nodded, but privately resolved to write a letter to her sister and share all of this with her. Riana would understand—all of it.

Basilio was well-known, and there were steady introductions, so many that the names blurred. They were a courtly lot, dashingly formal and somehow still extravagant. They eyed Cassandra curiously but without rancor, and many of them commented on the upcoming nuptials—which was to be an enormous social event, from what Cassandra could gather.

One matron, short and plump, heard that Cassandra was visiting Basilio, and asked pointedly, "Are you here for the wedding then?"

Amused, Cassandra said, "Yes. I am so looking forward to it."

When she departed Basilio leaned close, taking her hand behind the cover of her skirts. "I did not think how it would be, Cassandra. I am sorry."

"It's to be expected. I don't mind." It was a lie and she suspected he knew it, the way he seemed to understand everything about her. It was oddly painful to hear the girl mentioned in such glowing terms, to hear about the wedding. It was disconcerting. "We knew at the outset how our story would end."

His lashes dropped, his thumb stroked her hand. "Did we?" he asked softly.

She was spared the difficulty of a reply when another party swarmed over and Basilio stood, bowing courteously, to greet them. Cassandra smiled politely at the introductions, but behind her mask, her thoughts whirled.

She had not understood that she would fall in love with him. Not like this. It felt as if every vein in her body was connected to his heart, as if his hair grew from her scalp. Watching him laugh lightly with what appeared to be long-time friends of the family, she wondered how she would bear to live a day without him in it, after this.

But there was no other answer. He had to marry. And for all her newly discovered bravery, she could not bear to take up the place of mistress in his life, far from her home and family. She could not bear to give up her independence that way.

When he sat down again, he must have seen a hint of her disturbance. "This was a mistake," he said. "Come. Let's fly to our own world."

She smiled at him ruefully. "Perhaps I do not wish to share you, after all."

With a perplexed frown, he said, "But whatever will we do to amuse ourselves, all alone?"

"I imagine we can find some entertainment." She tucked her hand into his elbow, grateful for even that small reassurance. She was here now. In this moment.

They waited inside for the carriage to be brought around. A few latecomers dashed in from the rain, a party dressed resplendently save for a young girl who exuded misery.

"Oh, God," Basilio whispered, and Cassandra felt the rigidness of his arm beneath her fingers.

"What is it?"

One of the men, a razor-thin man with the

heavy features of a sensualist, saw Cassandra and his eyes swept her with almost insulting frankness. She narrowed her eyes at him.

"I will explain later." Basilio turned away from the small group and took Cassandra's hand, almost too tightly. Moving with an urgency she did not understand, he pushed her into the shadows and kissed her. It was a way to hide their faces, she knew, but she could also taste the despair on his mouth, could feel the fierceness in his fingers.

"Basilio, what is it?"

He closed his eyes and rested his forehead against hers. "Catastrophe, my love." He did not say it lightly.

"Why—"

"Wait." He glanced over his shoulder. The small party lingered in conversation with another acquaintance. Cassandra watched the girl resentfully be herded toward the doors, her body a straight exclamation of protest.

Basilio held her firmly, his mouth deadly serious. "Do not show your face." His arms and body held her tight against the wall.

"Who is she?" Cassandra asked, and realized at once who it must be. "Your betrothed?"

"Yes. And if she is here, she did not receive my letter." He made a harsh, pierced sound. "What have I done?"

"Basilio, it is not so tragic as that! Men take mistresses when they have already taken a wife—how much less a crime to take a lover before you have married?"

"It is dishonorable, Cassandra." The group drifted within, and Basilio at last let her go. His voice was raw as he repeated, "She did not get my letter."

A deep gulf lay between them, invisible yet as substantial as glass. Cassandra wanted to touch him, knowing her hand would be halted flat against the barrier. "Who is she?"

His hand fisted at his side and he closed his eyes momentarily, as if fighting some battle within.

"Her name is Analise." When he opened his eyes there was tragedy in them, longing and sorrow. "She is to be my wife. But her father must have heard—"

She guessed. "That you had a lover?"

"My mother was right," he said miserably. "Her father will sell her to the highest bidder."

"But you will marry her," Cassandra said, confused.

He shook his head, but before Cassandra could ask any more, the carriage arrived and they had to duck through the torrent of rain into the vehicle. Within, she said, "Tell me, Basilio."

Instead, he pulled her close, under his arm, into his kiss. "Not now. Tonight yet belongs to us."

But he pressed his face into her neck. "Oh, God."

"Basilio, I do not understand your horror in this."

Heavily, he raised his head. "I am bound to protect her, bound by a promise to my mother. If I do not marry her, her father will sell her to the highest bidder—and there is one who should not have her. He is cruel and has already had three young wives." His mouth tightened. "She cannot marry him."

Horror crawled on her skin, remembered pain and humiliation. "Basilio, you cannot allow that." Fear made her sharp. "I told you I would not marry, ever. Why did you do that?"

He took her hand and put it to his lips. She had been thinking of him as boyish in his joy, but she saw now that he was not a boy at all, but a man who lived vividly, a man bound by duty and honor. "Because I believe in love at first sight," he said quietly. "And so do you."

She fell forward against his chest. "Yes," she whispered. "I do."

His big hand curved around her neck. "In the morning, I will see what I might do to put this back the way it should go. Tonight belongs to us."

Chapter 9

Basilio made love to her slowly, lingeringly, in the cold damp night. The rain pattered steadily, slapping the windows and the roof, as he imprinted her upon his mind—the twining of their fingers, illuminated by soft candlelight; the shape of her ear against his mouth; the curve of her ribs beneath his hands.

They did not speak, for it would have broken the illusion that both of them wished to hold close: that these were not the last hours of their too-brief idyll. Afterward they lay close together, bodies pressed tight beneath a shelter of heavy quilt.

After a long time, she said quietly, "This has been so beautiful, Basilio." She raised up on one elbow, a hint of a smile turning up one side of her mouth. Her hair tumbled wildly around her face, down her back, and his heart caught at the simple beauty of her slim white shoulder. "We've been wonderfully wicked, haven't we?"

"Yes."

167

"And think of this: now I will always be perfect. And you will live like a god in my memory."

"A stallion, I think."

She laughed. "The god of stallions."

He took up the game. "And I won't have to see you throwing up when you have a belly full of baby." But when he said it, he wanted to see her then, her breasts heavy with milk. It pierced him to know how much he wanted that, and he quickly added, "Or watch you laugh when you don't have any teeth."

Her brows lifted. "And I"—she pinched his side—"won't have to see you fat as a pigeon."

"And I will never have to endure you calling for me like a shrew. 'Basilio!' " He made his voice shrill and raw. " 'Basilio.' "

"Ugh!" She slapped his arm lightly. "Not even at my worst would I sound like that."

"No? And how would you sound?"

Her tongue darted out, touched her lip, slipped back. In a throaty, sexy tone, she said, "Oh, Basilio, come here."

"Come . . . where?" he said, and slipped a hand down her back, curling around a buttock, and grinned.

She laughed and fell against him with a sigh. "It's no use, Basilio. I will miss you desperately."

"As I will miss you." He thought with regret of the letter Analise had missed, lying on a table in the cloister. An agony of missed chances. "If I ask you a question, will you promise to answer me honestly?"

She looked at him. "Yes."

"Would you have married me?"

"No," she said, but lowered her eyes. Raised them. "Oh, I lie. It would have frightened me— but yes, I believe I would have. It appears I was not meant to be a married woman." She smiled sadly.

"Perhaps now you will see there is a man who can be your husband." He swallowed, twisting a lock of her hair around his finger. "I do not like to think of you old and alone. You should have children."

A flicker crossed her eyes. She shifted, hiding her face. "My work is important to me," she said. "And no man but you has ever begun to understand that. In marriage, a woman loses herself, loses all that she has worked to gain. Why would I bind myself that way?"

He couldn't answer her.

"I am not given to extravagant words, Basilio. I cannot say it the way you do." She raised up, sitting naked with her hair as her cloak, her hands folded before her. She gazed at him with that odd composure for a very long moment, then reached out to touch his face.

She took a breath, her face sad and soft. "But I loved you before I saw you, as if we are two sides of a coin. That will not happen again, and having known it, I will not settle for less." A single tear glistened in the corner of one dark eye, and she bowed her head. "I'm glad to have known it with you. I do not regret it, not even a little."

With a violence of love, he rose and kissed her, and kissed her, and kissed her. There was nothing else.

Basilio awakened suddenly a little past dawn, woke suddenly and completely, and then lay there, not knowing what had drawn him from his sleep.

Cassandra lay in his arms, her hair scattered over his chest, and he put a an open palm over the scattered strands, bemused by the fierce pleasure it gave him. One of her legs was flung over his thighs, and her head was deeply cradled in his shoulder. He had never loved a woman like this. In gratitude, he pressed a kiss to the top of her head.

Then he heard a shout from below. No, not only a shout. A bellow, a crash. His limbs tensed, recognizing the voice before it fully penetrated his sleep-glazed mind.

He sat up urgently, bringing Cassandra with him. "Wake up," he cried, reaching for his breeches on the floor with suddenly unsteady hands.

Sleepily, she peered at him. "What is it?"

Yanking up the breeches, he heard the bellowing coming closer and looked around madly for something for her to put on. "Cassandra, take the blanket, and run to the balcony." Outside his door, he heard the rage in his father's voice, and urgently, he pushed her. "Go, Cassandra. Hide."

"I don't—"

"Go!" he cried.

Cassandra clutched the coverlet to her as the door burst open, scooting backward in the bed instinctively as a man, crimson-faced and enormous, roared into the room. "You dare!" he cried, and his great hammy fists clutched Basilio's hair. "You dare defy me?"

Basilio grabbed his father's wrists. "Father! Listen!"

The man shook free. "You cub!"

One of the enormous fists slammed into Basilio's face, and Cassandra cried out, "Stop!"

Basilio wrenched around and slammed his hands into his father's chest, shoving him back. "Listen to me!" But his father punched him hard, in the face, and Basilio reeled backward.

She saw the madness in his eyes as he rallied. "Do you still beat me like a child?" he cried in disbelief, wiping blood from his lip. "Do you not see that I am a man, and one younger and more hale than you?"

His father made a gesture that needed no translation, fingers wiggling him closer. The great jaw jutted out, and with a roar, Basilio hurtled across the room, his shoulder catching his father's chest.

"Basilio, stop!" Cassandra cried again, terrified at the difference in their sizes. His father was a bear of a man, stout and burly, and far beyond reason. He bellowed again like a baited bear, and batted Basilio with that enormous, powerful fist.

Cassandra rose in place, clutching the cover to her. Basilio saw her and held out a hand, as if to keep her in her spot as he narrowed his eyes at his father.

His voice was dead calm. "You can beat me. You can even kill me, but you cannot make me obey you. It will be my choice, Father, to marry Analise or not."

"What?" The crimson in the man's face went mottled, and Cassandra thought his head might explode. He surged toward his son, and she had never seen such pure, unadulterated hatred in her life. She had not believed Basilio when he spoke of his father's hate; now she believed. The huge fists rained down on his head, his shoulders, his face. Basilio's blows were less frequent, but landed more squarely—to his jaw, his gut— but size won out. Basilio would be beaten to death by this bear.

"Stop!" she screamed. Without thinking, she caught the blanket around her and rushed toward them, vaguely aware that two servants had crept into the room. One grabbed for her ineffectively as she moved to intervene, but she slipped free.

"Stop!" she cried again, nearly sobbing in fear that this enraged beast would kill Basilio before her eyes. She flung herself between them—

And caught an agonizingly powerful blow squarely beneath her eye. The force of it sent her sprawling, stunned and grasping madly at the blanket that barely covered her.

"Whore!" the beast cried, and made to come after her.

Basilio went mad. With a cry, he leapt on his father, shoving back at him, his fists wild and pure and strong.

"Stop them!" Cassandra cried at the servants. "They will kill each other!"

And then the room was full of people, servants drawn by the noise, men who leapt in and separated the crazed father and son. Cassandra curled close to the foot of the bed, one hand clutched to the blanket over her shoulders, the other to her face, which was already swollen and wet with tears beneath her palm.

Basilo panted in the grip of the servants, his eyes ablaze. "I defy you!" he said, and spat at his father's feet.

The elder count was also bleeding, but his rage subsided now. He narrowed eyes in a piggish face. "Why did your brothers die, and leave me with my one worthless son?" He shook off the arms of the servants. "You will marry Analise. That is my final word."

He stormed out, and the servants followed. One peered in concern at Basilio, murmuring in Italian so low that Cassandra could not catch it. Basilio shook his head and the servant left.

Then it was only the two of them, the silence echoing oddly after the roaring, screaming chaos of moments before. Basilio sagged, then fell beside her, and she cried out helplessly, weeping into his arms. She could feel trembling in his body, and clutched him more tightly. "Are you hurt badly?"

"Nothing that will not heal," he whispered, his arms tightening around her. "It is not the first time he has beaten me."

"Oh, God, Basilio, I thought he would kill you."

She trembled, too, unable to think past the immediate seconds.

"Let me see your face," he said grimly.

"It's nothing."

But his fingers slid under her chin, and she raised her head, fresh tears springing to her eyes when she saw the bruises, the split lip, the damage a father had wrought on his own child.

Basilio kissed her cheekbone very gently. "I am so sorry, Cassandra. I knew he would be angry. I did not know he would come here."

She clasped him to her, breathing against his hair, wishing with all she was that they could somehow make a happy ending from this.

Yet she could not allow Basilio to turn his back on that girl. To throw away his birthright, his place in his world. As long as their passion ruled him, he would not think of his mother, his brothers. But honor formed the heart and soul of him, was the very kernel of his being. His duty lay here—duty to his mother, whose land he held in trust, whom he had loved deeply, and to his brothers, whose untimely deaths made him feel an obligation to live in part for them. In time, guilt would eat at him, would eat at the joy they had discovered, at all that was good. Eventually, his lost honor would destroy him.

A swell of pure grief and love moved in her, making her lean close and press her face to his neck as her tears flowed hot and real and honest. "I do not cry, Basilio. Did you know that about me?" She put her hands to his face. "I never weep. And with you, I have wept for love and for joy, and now I weep in sorrow. I do not want to leave you, but I'm not selfish enough to ruin you."

He closed his eyes as she kissed his cheekbone, his brow, his mouth. "In time, my love," she whispered, "we will rediscover how to write to each other as friends."

She knew she would remember this moment

in exact detail all of her life. His shoulders, bare and hot beneath her hands, his eyes dark and full of love and pain.

"I will never love another woman as I have loved you, Cassandra."

"I know." She smiled softly, and lay against his shoulder. They clung together for long minutes, rocking and drawing comfort.

At last, Cassandra drew away. "You must have your wounds tended," she whispered. "And I must find ice." She tried to laugh a little, but it was as hollow as a rotted tree.

He swallowed, his sober, beautiful eyes troubled. "My father will not stay. Hide in your rooms until he goes." He paused, his hand lingering on her face. "I must go out this morning." They both knew why.

She nodded, then very carefully, leaned forward and gently pressed her mouth to his, imprinting it upon her mind, her heart, her soul. She wanted to spill out her love for him, wanted to thank him for all that he'd given to her, wanted to tell him that she would never regret this all-too brief idyll. Instead, she put her hand once more in the thickness of his curls. "You have changed everything about me, Basilio. Thank you."

Forcing a lightness, she added, "Now, help me to my feet and allow me some dignity so I may have a bath and renew my sense of humor, will you?

There was relief in his soft chuckle. "That

would depend on whether I am actually able to arise myself."

"Then we shall assist each other."

Cassandra washed and dressed and took time to eat. She would need the sustenance. She gave instructions to the girl who brought her breakfast, then sat down to write a letter. When the girl returned an hour later to say that Basilio had gone out, Cassandra gave her the letter and instructed her to deliver it to Basilio later.

She would have to act quickly.

It was awkward to manage the departure from Florence, when everything she had brought was at the villa. But she sent word to Joan, instructions she knew that Basilio would see were carefully followed. She had a change of clothes and her leather case of papers. Enough. She would go to Venice and recover herself before she returned to England.

Cassandra wore her violet traveling costume, an ensemble that gave her courage. She squared her shoulders and went in search of Basilio's father.

A little quake of fear struck her knees when she found him in the library. "I would like a word with you, sir," she said in Italian.

He eyed her, then lifted a chin at the servant, who scurried away. "I speak English," he said. "You think my son is the only one with an education?"

"Not at all," she replied, cloaking herself in English coolness. "I was merely being polite."

"What do you want?"

"I have come to inform you that I am leaving Tuscany."

A shrug. What else would she do?

A flicker of hot, pure anger made her stride forward. "I am leaving, sir"—the word carried great irony—"because I am in love with him, and because if I do not, his honor will destroy him. But I am leaving only with a promise from you."

He snorted. "Promise? You dare—"

"Please, do not begin blustering again. You need hear what I have to say. I do not presume to know why this marriage is so important to you, but I can see that there is more here than a wish that he do your bidding."

He threw down his papers. "Go on."

"I will leave here only if you will honor your son's gifts, and support his wish to write, as well as tend your properties. It is not a gift you respect, but it is a very great gift indeed. And I do not mean just a little nod of your head. And you will never darken his door except in the most dire of emergencies. It's quite plain you hate him."

He glanced her over, a reluctant respect in his eyes. "And if I do not?"

She raised her head and met his eyes. "Then I will return to Tuscany, and I will destroy the marriage—even if it destroys all three of us in the bargain." She paused. "If you do not think I can, you do not know your son at all."

A blink, a purse of the lips, then the slightest shrug. "How much do you want?"

"Want?" She shook her head, amazed that a man like Basilio could be the issue of such a father. "Nothing." At the door, she paused. "He had already decided to take Analise as his wife, so do not think you beat him into submission."

She went to the stables, where a carriage awaited. Cassandra allowed the sober, mustachioed driver to help her into the interior, and said in a harsh exhalation, "Go. Before his father has another reason to kill him."

He drove. Cassandra sat very still and straight in the seat, feeling as if her heart were tearing out of her body. She ached to look back yet feared it, as if she were Lot's wife and would be turned to a pillar of salt.

But she could not halt the tears that streamed down her face. In all her life, she had never wept in front of another, but now she did not care. It was real. It burned. Her life would never be the same.

Basilio walked to the villa of the Count diCanio in the hot August morning. He carried a cluster of flowers cut from the garden: late roses and some white thing, and something that smelled good to him. His head ached and his heart was heavy with dread, but he put on a cheerful visage when a servant opened the door to him. He was only an eager bridegroom, seeking to reassure his very young bride.

Analise's mother twittered and fussed over him, but Basilio read relief in her eye. Her papa was not at home, but Analise came down, dressed soberly in black, a fichu tucked into her bodice. "You did not receive my letter," he said.

"No. Was it important?"

He shook his head with a faint smile. "Only a greeting."

She was unhappy and shy, and he did not linger. What a coil! It made his headache worse, and by the time he returned to his own house his stomach was unsettled, and his heart was a dead rock in his chest. Today, he would have to bid farewell to Cassandra. He could not bear it.

A young servant girl approached him, a look of apprehension on her face. "This is for you," she said, bobbing. Quickly she put the letter in his hands and scurried away.

Seeing Cassandra's writing he tore it open, his heart pounding in dread.

Dearest Basilio,

It grieves me to leave you, but this is best—a quick, sharp parting that will heal more easily than the tearing I envision for us.

I have enclosed a list of instructions for you in

regard to my things and know you will see to them carefully.

And here is my plea: marry this girl, make a life with her—it will not change what we have known together. None can steal that from us. I want to think of you as happy.

Thank you for making me brave, for returning to me my heart and soul. I will ever remember these days in Tuscany as among the best of my life. In some ways, we have had the purest and best of love, and should respect that.

If you care for me even a little, you will not write to me again. If you do, I will burn your letters without reading them. Allow me my dignity in retreat. Allow this time to be unsullied in our memories.

I will never forget you.

Cassandra

"No!" He crumbled the letter in his fist and dashed after the maid, taking her arm too fiercely. "When did she leave? With whom?"

The girl's eyes were wide with fear. "Three hours. Guilliame drove her."

"Thank you." He turned and ran toward the doors, heading for the stables to find the wagonmaster. He would tell him where Cassandra had gone. Only three hours—he should be able to catch her.

His father emerged from the library, blocking his way. "Do not, Father," he said, his limbs jumping with the need to run after her before she could make this terrible mistake. "I have no will to tangle with you now."

The old man shook his head. "No, son," he said, and Basilio was startled at the use of the filial term.

He frowned, thrown off by this unexpected response. "Then stand aside sir, and allow me to go after her—we have unresolved matters between us."

"First you must listen to me."

"And what will you tell me?" Bitterness edged his words. "I have just come from Count diCanio's house, where I gave my bride a fistful of flowers. What more do you want me to do?"

The dark eyes were grave, and Basilio unwillingly saw that the lines on his father's face had deepened. "You have done the right thing."

"Have I?" He stepped closer. "She is a child. She does not want a husband. She wants the cloister, as she has since we were children. And I do not wish that child as my wife. It smells of disaster."

As if he had not spoken, the elder Count turned heavily to the banks of windows. "She was a great favorite of your mother's—a very pretty girl who visited you in Florence. She would have been no more than six, I suppose. You mother liked having her come to visit, for she was bright and sweet and very determined to be a nun, even when she was quite small."

A faint sense of dread moved in Basilio. He did remember the girl, tiny and laughing, with yards of black hair, sitting with his mother on summer afternoons. She had charmed them both. "I remember."

"You mother worried that she would grow to be too beautiful to be hidden in a nunnery, and her father was greedy and a gambler. The scene was set, even then, for the disaster that brews now for Analise. Your mother—" the word grew rough. He laced his hands stoically behind his back, regained control. "Your mother asked me to protect her when the time came."

Basilio made an impatient sound. "I know this! Why are you telling me all over again when I have agreed to the marriage?"

"The English woman. How did you meet her?"

He shook his head, wondering why it mattered. "She is a writer. I read some of her essays." Wearily, he sat at the table and put his head in his hands. "I thought she was a middle-aged widow."

"She threatened me."

Basilio raised his head in time to catch the quirk of his father's mouth. To his surprise, his father chuckled.

"What was her threat?"

A lift of a shoulder. "It does not matter." He

turned, his face not unkind. "Any man can understand why you fell in love with her, Basilio. Fierce, strong, beautiful."

Too much emotion. Basilio raised his hand. "No more, Father. Please."

"If you do not marry Analise, her father will give her to Tortessi."

Heavily, Basilio rose. "I know. Excuse me."

He climbed the stairs to the chamber he'd shared with Cassandra. When he opened the door, the scent of her—musk and wildflowers and cloves—enveloped him. It brought the memory of her hair, trailing over his arm.

A feeling like a knife wound seared the middle of his chest. His flesh burned with sensual memories—the smoothness of her skin, the sweetness of her kiss, the throatiness of her laughter. He thought of the long conversations they'd shared, and the simple, rare, deep pleasure he'd found in a mind that engaged his own. His heart ached with the certainty that she was his only love, would ever be the only woman his soul would even recognize. It was more than passion, more than friendship, a combination that transcended both.

How could he let her go?

But even as he stared at the blue and green of the Tuscan hills, he knew that he already had. The only thing that could destroy the beauty of what they'd shared was his guilt, and if Analise married Tortessi, his conscience would never allow him to sleep again.

So he would don this mantle. But even in his resolve, he could not halt the grief that swelled around him. He put his hand on the glass, wondering how he would bear it.

Chapter 10

Analise allowed herself to be garbed in the breathtakingly beautiful gown her mother had ordered from Rome. She did not protest, did not weep, did not smile. She lifted her arms when directed, turned her head when nudged, stood straight to let them tie her into her corsets. The voices of the women rose in waves of excitement around her, then subsided and rose again.

Beyond the windows of the villa a heavy rain fell on the green Tuscan hills, and Analise watched it, thinking fancifully that the angels were weeping with her.

In her hand, she clutched a letter that had come only this morning, a letter that had followed her from the convent to Florence to the villa, and only just arrived. It was the letter Basilio had asked her about that morning he had come to see her, demons in his eyes. Now she understood.

Analise burned with shame over her weakness. She had known she ought take her vows, but she had been too afraid to defy her father. If the letter had reached her, it would have given her courage enough.

And now she also understood that the young beautiful Count was a pawn as much as she. What hope could such a marriage have of ever bringing joy?

But it was too late. Because she had been a coward, she would be married today to a man who did not want her. She had resolved to do her duty in this marriage, but the angels knew her heart. They wept in her place, because she could not disappoint her mother and father by doing so.

A servant girl from the village, hired especially to help Analise with these preparations, whispered, *"Bellissima!"* her hands clasped under her chin.

Analise turned to the long, smoky colored mirror. Dispassionately, she viewed her beauty. Very thick dark hair and smooth olive skin, and her best feature, blue eyes, which startled against the darkness of her hair. Her figure was like her mother's, full at bust and hip, and much had been made of that bust so it flowed indecently into the square bodice of the pale gown. "A fichu," she said firmly, and held out a hand. The girl made a token protest as Analise tucked it in.

"Do you know the Count?" she asked.

"Oh, yes! You will be pleased, my lady. He is young and healthy and beautiful." She adjusted the back of the fichu carefully. "It is said he is kind, good to his servants. Such a man does not beat his wife, no?"

"Thank you." The girl had given the reassurance Analise needed.

"They're waiting."

Analise hesitated, looking over her shoulder to the dark clouds. There was still time for a miracle. "Please," she prayed silently. "Let me go back!"

The girl was young, too young. Basilio turned to her in the silence of the chamber that had been prepared for them and his wretchedness increased a hundredfold. Yet whatever he felt, there was no wretchedness in the world so deep as that of his young bride.

She stood, tiny and straight, adorned in her great cloak of dark hair, and raised her eyes to his. He had expected a virgin's terror, but in the enormous and extraordinary blue eyes, there was something else. A fire, dark and turbulent; one he would not have anticipated in a sixteen-year-old, never mind one so gently reared. "We have sinned here today, sir," she said suddenly, her chin lifting.

"Sinned?" He halted in the act of removing his neckcloth.

From her bodice she took a folded parchment. He recognized his hand on the letter. "It came too late," she said, her mouth tight. "Had it come only one day sooner, I would have heeded its message. It came to me here, following me from Corsica."

He let go a snort of humorless laughter, bowing his head. "And had I acted in true conscience and faith when I first knew my heart, you would have had the letter one day sooner." Regret knifed through him, then he raised his head. "God's will is done now, and we are bound."

"God's will?" she echoed with a fine irony. Twice today he had seen intelligence in her. But of course she would have access to knowledge in the convent that she could not have gained elsewise. "Is it?"

"That I cannot answer." In sudden decision, he turned and locked the door so no servant could disturb them. When he turned back, purpose in his step, she shrank away, and he shook his head. "Do not fear me, Analise. I had no more wish for this than did you." From the desk he took a knife and cut his finger—not so obviously that it would be noticed, but enough to bring welling drops of blood to the surface. She watched him silently as he strode to the bed and, a little to one side of the center, smeared the blood on to the sheets. "There," he said, turning back. "It is done."

She closed her eyes and covered her face with her hands, her bravado dissolving in the soft trembling of those long white fingers. Gently, Basilio led her to the bed and pulled the coverlet over her. "It would be better if you untied your gown," he said quietly. "Sleep now."

"Thank you," she whispered, reaching out a hand.

He nodded. "Sleep," he said again. Shedding his coat, he settled at the desk, looking out to the rain pouring beyond the windows. With only a single taper to cast flickering light on the page, Basilio took up his pen, and the words frozen in him for a month came pouring free. He wept as wrote, and once was so overcome that he put his head in the curve of his elbow, waiting for it to subside. But write he did. And every word held Cassandra's breath, and the curve of Cassandra's breast, and the sound of Cassandra's laughter.

He wrote until his pen fell from his fingers, leaving a small blot in the shape of a star across the page. Then he fell, exhausted, into sleep.

Chapter 11

On a cold, wet November night, Cassandra opened the door to her London house. Only then, looking at her familiar things with new eyes, did she understand how very much she had changed. The servants had lit fires and her cook had prepared a comforting English meal—roast beef and potatoes and carrots. Cassandra praised it and ate it because she was hungry, but her mouth craved olives.

In the great basket of correspondence that had collected during her travels, there were three letters from Basilio. She took them out and put them on the table, telling herself she needed to burn them. It would be cleaner.

But she was too hungry for a the sound of his voice in her head, and she opened the first.

10 August 1787

My dearest Cassandra,

As I write this, you are bent over your translation, and I am besotted with the bend of your white neck, by the small curls that have escaped your attempt to tame that wild hair, the seriousness of your brow as you bend over your work. I dare not say what is in my heart, for this is too new, and I sense that you were badly wounded and will need time to see that I am different.

But here, in this letter I will mail to be waiting for you when you return to your house in Piccadilly Street, I will confess the truth: I broke my betrothal, and there is but one wish in my mind—that we shall spend our days together, all of them.

It is not simple matter, of course. My father is going to be very, very angry with me when he hears the news. He is likely reading my letter in this moment—oh, anger is not a fine thing on his face.

No, it will not be simple. And I will not speak of this to you except in this letter, which you will not see until you return to your home, but you are my heart, my love, the very blood that runs in my veins. It was fated that we should find one another across such vast distances, fated that our hearts should become one.

I am so certain of this, that it is not merely

passion that binds us—sweet though passion may be!—but a union of souls that were born to be entwined, that I am willing to let you leave me, return to your home, and see that what I say is true. No time or distance or practicalities will dim what has been born here in these precious days.

I am so certain that naught will dim this that I say now, come, Cassandra—or if you cannot, I will come to you. Be my love, be my wife. Let us together make a mosaic of joy from our days.

There are no words in any language to express the depth of my feeling for you, so I leave you with the simplest of them all: Li amo.

Your Basilio

With a cry, Cassandra scooped them into her hands and threw them all into the flames, her hand over her mouth as she fought the swell of grief in her.

It was over. Over.

Part Three

England
May 1788

Come to me in the silence of the night;
Come in the speaking silence of a dream;
Come with soft rounded cheeks
and eyes as bright
As sunlight on a stream...

CHRISTINA ROSSETTI

Chapter 12

It was one of those early spring days that appear from nowhere, laden with the promise of what was to come. Cassandra felt the difference in the air when she awakened. Drawn by something she couldn't name, she carried a cup of chocolate with her to the newly greening garden and breathed it in with a sense of emerging from a winter cocoon. Until that moment, she had not realized how deep and long her lethargy had been.

It seemed she had barely moved in the dark, short days of winter. She had taken callers, returned to an erratic schedule of salons, and done her work, but all of it had been done mechanically while Cassandra hibernated.

Perhaps that was why, when Julian arrived late in the day, and urged her to come out with him to see a new singer at the opera, she found herself agreeing. Sitting with him in the box, waiting for the music to begin, she watched with amusement as one mama after another spied

Cassandra's imminently suitable—not to mention dashing—brother, the Earl of Albury. One by one, they found excuses to stop by to speak a word, the eligible daughter in tow, of course. Julian was unfailingly polite, often even witty and charming, but he was equally skilled at dismissing them.

After one such mama and her awkward, obviously mortified daughter left, Cassandra laughed. "Why, I believe you are the most eagerly sought bachelor in all of England, Lord Albury."

"Which is why you are here as my protection, my dear. Were you absent, I'd be forced to entertain them and listen to the silly chatter all evening." He scowled, and the expression hinted of the darkness and secrets that lurked below his elegant features. "I have no intention of taking one of these witless women to wife."

Cassandra smiled. "Eventually, I expect you will be forced to. An heir and all."

"No," he said. "I will not marry." He plucked a loose hair from his sleeve. Cassandra admired his long, graceful hands, smiling a little.

"No?" she echoed. "But who will be the next Earl, then?"

He shrugged. As if to distract her, he raised one arched brow. "Surely you understand the wish to avoid matrimony."

His pale gray eyes were too sharp by half. Cassandra turned her head. "I had one terrible husband. I'm in no hurry to hand myself over to another."

"Exactly." He smiled, that cool, aristocratic expression that would no doubt send the mamas into swoons. "Lovers are plentiful, after all."

Cassandra laughed lightly. "I wouldn't know. Is there some beauty you've been keeping?"

"Why do you think we're attending the opera?"

"Oh, Julian, what cliché! An opera singer?"

"Dancer, actually."

She inclined her head. "I'm pleased, I think. We worried about you, when you came back from your adventures."

That flicker of distance, of sorrow appeared, then was gone again. He took her head. "As we have worried since your return from abroad. Will you never speak of what happened, Cassandra?"

She managed a light, bored shrug. "Ah, only a silly love affair turned sour. No more than that."

"You are in much improved spirits this evening."

"How could I fail?" She spied another hopeful mother headed their way, and laughed, directing his attention. "I have come to the opera with the most popular gentleman in London."

With a nearly imperceptible smile, he stood to greet the newcomers.

At last the musicians began to tune their instruments and the steady stream of marriageable girls trickled off. Cassandra settled herself in readiness for the opera, which she always enjoyed.

When she looked across the opera house, there he was. Out of place, and so unexpected that she gaped for a long, silent moment before she could fit her mind around the fact that it was him.

Basilio.

Here, at the opera.

In London.

Blackness prickled at the edges of her vision. She realized she had not breathed, and sucked in a breath, but she could not look away.

Behind him was a man she vaguely recognized, a ruddy-faced lord from a county near her estate, which only made it all the stranger. Two women had settled at the front of the box, but the men continued some deep discussion, their heads bent together, one graying, the other darkest black.

A flash of memory hit her like a blow; her hand, white as moonlight against the jet of his hair, the curls leaping around the turn of her finger—

"Oh, God," Cassandra whispered.

Julian leaned closer. "I'm sorry—I didn't quite hear you."

She put her hand on his sleeve, trying to remember how to arrange her expression normally. "Nothing."

In the box across the crowded, noisy room,

Basilio nodded seriously at something, and his hand settled in a quieting sort of way upon the shoulder of the small woman in front of him. She seemed hardly to notice, but even across such a distance, Cassandra read discomfort in her stiffness.

Abruptly, Cassandra stood, her limbs quaking. "Julian, I feel quite ill. I must go."

He leapt to his feet, his arm circling her shoulders. "What is it?"

She waved a hand, bent to pick up her shawl from the seat, and dropped it when her betraying fingers could not hold on to it. She stared at it, the beads glittering along one edge. It looked like water, she thought distantly, the way it shimmered in a pool on the dark floor of the box. It made her think of another shawl, on another floor, and she closed her eyes against the pain of that memory.

How could a week have changed her life so utterly? Ten times—forty times!—that number had passed since then!

Julian swept up the shawl and captured her hands, bending to frown closely. "You're shivering like a wet puppy!" Bracing her elbow, he said, "Let's get you home."

"Yes." She vowed to keep her eyes lowered, but the temptation was too great. One more glance at him. Only one.

But of course it was the dangerous one. For across that distance, across the milling scores of humanity in the gallery below, Basilio chose that moment to raise his head. Their eyes locked, and Cassandra's heart was flooded with the pain of his gentleness, his passion, his words.

His love. Yes, his love, most of all.

She fancied his face went bloodless, though of course she could not have seen such a thing at such a distance. His hand still rested upon the shoulder of the woman, and she saw him take it away, hastily, as if it burned him.

It gave her courage. Tossing her bright copper head, she said calmly, "Please take me home, Julian."

Below, the orchestra began to play, the violins and flutes setting a soft, sorrowful introduction, and Cassandra wanted to put her hands over her ears. She bustled into the hallway behind the boxes, rushing for the stairs. If only she could get outside, all would be well.

She took the stairs at nearly a run, thinking wildly that Julian would want an explanation and she would have to think of something, but that did not slow her steps. Her skirts flew behind her, and her breath began to be rushed. She rounded the last landing and fled through the opening into the first floor hallway—

"Cassandra!"

She startled with a little yelp, and glanced over her shoulder to see him—oh, God!—so beautiful, so arrestingly himself that she felt herself dissolving. She lifted her skirts and bolted, running for her life for the last set of stairs.

"No, Cassandra, wait!" He ran behind her. She could hear him and it amazed her that she could hear anything above the soft, sobbing sound of her breath, the roaring of blood in her ears, but she could. She could hear his feet, hear—

He grabbed her arm, not gently. "Wait," he said softly. "Oh, please, Cassandra. Listen to me."

She fell against the wall in the isolated stairway, hiding her face, unable to bear looking at him. Her arm burned where his fingers touched her, and she yanked away, putting her hands over her face. They were trembling violently.

He leaned in close, and her body rippled with yearning. "Cassandra, oh, God—"

"You are married."

"Yes."

She had already known the answer. Of course that small, pale child was the woman his father had yoked him to. "Basilio, please go," she whispered. "Leave me a shred of my pride." Tears spilled from her eyes, and she could not halt them.

His hand, so gentle, so achingly familiar, fell lightly against her bare shoulder. His fingers, too, trembled. "I can only think your name, speak it," he whispered, and bent close. "Cassandra. Cassandra." His breath touched her neck.

She closed her eyes tightly, willing herself to

remain still, to resist the wish—no, the agonizing need—to turn and fling herself into his arms, to kiss his lips, to hear his voice. She had not believed it possible to miss another human so much. She had not only missed his breath in her ear, and his sweetness around her—she had also lost her friend, the friend who'd made the past winters so rich. "Stop," she whispered. "I cannot bear it, Basilio."

He dropped his hand, and her body cooled with the absence of his closeness. "Very well," he said. "I will go, if you will turn and look at me. Just let me see your face."

"No." She pressed closer into the corner. She could not look into that beloved face. Could *not*.

"Cassandra," he said quietly.

Helplessly, she dropped her hands and turned, letting him see her ravaged face, her eyes downcast.

"Look at me," he said, and she heard the raggedness there, his own sorrow.

She raised her chin, then her eyes, and embraced the rushing wish to kiss him—to kiss that mouth, those eyelids, that brow. But she saw that he, too, had suffered. In the end, she could not help raising a hand to the hollowness in his cheek. "Oh, Basilio, you should never have come. Was there not enough pain already?"

"There was joy," he said fiercely, his eyes burning.

At last there were footsteps overhead: Julian

coming to rescue her. They drew apart and Cassandra hastily wiped her face with her fingers, hoping nothing showed.

And there was Julian, concern on his face. "Are you all right?"

She managed a nod. Basilio stepped away, made a short, stiff bow. "We are only old friends, sir," he said.

Cassandra realized he thought Julian was her lover. "He is my brother," she said wearily. "Lord Albury. This is Count Montevarchi, Julian."

They nodded stiffly and Basilio backed away. "I must return to my party. Good evening." His eyes, molten with unspoken words, burned on Cassandra's face. Then he abruptly turned and moved up the stairs, and Cassandra found she could not help staring after him, watching as candlelight gilded the black curls caught in an elegant queue at his nape, admiring the breadth of his shoulders under his coat, the sturdiness of his thighs——

"Come," Julian said. "Let me take you home."

Cassandra nodded, suddenly so depleted she could barely take a breath. She was deeply grateful to him for saying not a single word as he took her arm and led her out, called for their carriage, and settled beside her in the darkness. Once the horses pulled away, he took a clean handkerchief from his pocket and handed it to her wordlessly.

Only when they were in her salon, and he had poured her a brandy—waiting as she drank a great gulp of it—did he say, "Montevarchi is his name?"

She lifted her head, frowning. "Yes. Why do you ask?"

Julian fastened his hands behind his back. "Perhaps you should know he's published a book of poetry. Gabriel spoke of it this afternoon. The name stuck with me."

She had not thought it was possible to be even more breathless. "Poetry?"

Julian nodded. "Gabriel was quite complimentary, so I purchased a copy. I'm sure that he is here on the invitation of his patron, a Mr. James."

A book of poetry. She closed her eyes. His name would be on the lips of her entire set. If it were good poetry—and if it was Basilio's, how could it be poor?—they would sing his praises endlessly. Even if it were very bad poetry, the novelty of a Tuscan count publishing poetry would make them talk. Panic made her leap to her feet. "I must go abroad."

"You will flee your entire life, if you begin to do it now."

She halted in her pacing. "But . . . I cannot face this, Julian. I am not strong enough."

"I will ask him to keep his distance if you like."

Cassandra found she had a smile. "Dear Julian, always ready to defend us." She shook her head. "He did not dishonor me, or even betray me. It would have been easier if he had."

Fresh sorrow rose in her throat. "It was only impossible." She looked at him in her misery. "Oh, Julian, how does one live this way?"

"A moment at a time," he said, and it was too much like something Basilio would have said.

She nodded.

He put his hand on her shoulder in silent comfort, and she was deeply grateful to him for his acceptance. Adriana would have insisted upon details, and Cassandra could not have borne that.

Analise washed before bed, and sent the maid away. She was relieved to be back in the tall, elegant townhouse that Basilio had procured for them, relieved to be in the quiet and stillness, away from all the confusing voices and questions she could not understand. She said her rosary, and then, clad in her wrapper, went in search of her husband.

Something had transpired at the opera tonight. He had bolted from the box without a word to anyone, and come back looking as if he'd undergone torture, his eyes shadowed with that bleakness she had come to recognize. Many times over the past months, she had seen him fall into a brooding state of mind without warning. It was a faraway place he went at such times, and she sensed great tragedy in him. Tonight, that darkness had trebled. She did not want to sleep until she made certain he did not need whatever compassion she might offer.

From the beginning, she had sensed powerful undercurrents about this journey to England. The invitation had come from a well-respected English writer who wished to introduce Basilio to his circle, and Basilio had been very pleased when he told Analise about it. It had been the first time she had seen pleasure or joy in his face, and of course she had insisted he must go.

But the elder count had roared and insisted that if Basilio was going to go to England, Analise would go with him. She had been terrified—she did not speak the language, did not understand the customs, and did not like being in the world even in her own country. How much worse could it be in England?

Very much worse, she had discovered. In three days, she had learned new depths of misery. They thought her quaint and foolish and backward. Few of them spoke Italian and she could not speak English, and although Basilio was attentive, she was still often left holding yet another saucer and cup with more tea, sitting alone while the rest of them laughed uproariously and talked earnestly of things she would not have understood even in her own language.

She was desperately homesick. Yet tonight, she wished to make certain Basilio was all right.

She found him in the library standing by the fire, his arms loose at his sides, his head bent in an eloquent posture of defeat. "Basilio, would you like me to call for something?"

He roused himself, turning. "No, thank you."

"Is there anything I might do to ease your discomfort, my husband?"

He closed his eyes briefly. Shook his head. "You are a very kind girl, Analise. And patient. That is enough."

She was not the patient one; it was he who had shown the greatest patience. "Are you certain? Perhaps a little wine, or a tea to help you sleep?"

He smiled a little. "No. Truly."

"Then I will leave you," she said. "Good night."

His attention was already back on whatever he saw in the fire. "Good night."

Analise paused, feeling a powerful sense of illumination here, hovering just on the edges of the night. "Will you not speak of your sorrow, Basilio? Perhaps I may be of some help to you."

He straightened, drew in a breath, and with great effort arranged his face into a gentle smile. "It is only the darkness of a poet's heart that plagues me. Ghosts and shadows. No more than that."

How beautiful he was! In Italy, and now in London, women eyed her husband with avaricious eyes, and Analise could see that he was all a woman could ask. The tumble of curls, that sensual mouth—and most of all, the kindness in his eyes—these things made him an object of great longing.

Why, then, did she feel nothing? He might

have been a flower, or a sunset, for all the heat he stirred in her. It was some lack in her femaleness that she did not long to lie with him, and he had thus far not pressed.

Perhaps it was her duty to make it easier for him. Folding her hands neatly before her, she said quietly, "If it would ease you, husband, you may share my bed."

Instantly, she knew it was the wrong thing to say. A shift in the air—no, more than that, a shift in her own inner sense of connection to the forces of spirit in the world—made her understand that before he even spoke.

With troubled eyes, he approached and took her hand. Planting a chaste kiss on her knuckles, he said, "A generous offer, and one a man would be mad to resist if it were truly offered." He smiled, and this time, the small spark reached his eyes. "But for now, we are chaste, and I will not ask that of you. There is time, Analise. When you are ready, you will know."

She did not deserve such consideration, but a wave of vast relief filled her. "Good night, then."

He let her go. "Good night."

Cassandra was abroad in the streets of London by ten the next morning. Walking amid the peddlers hawking everything from fruit to ribbons, and the clerks bustling on their way to offices, reminded her that life went on its way, after all. By the time she reached the rooms Gabriel kept

near St. James Street, much of her tangled sense
of tragedy had eased.

Common sense had ever been her hallmark,
and hadn't she spent those long, darkening fall
days in a state of never-ending gloom? Once was
quite enough. Reason was a woman's ally; emotion was her enemy. It appeared she had to discover that lesson again.

It was reason that led her to rap on her brother
Gabriel's blue-painted door. He said it reminded
him of Martinique, and the neighbors forgave it
because he was generous and charming and
obviously a fine gentleman, for all that he was
mixed race.

Reason had led her to his door, because she
had realized she must prepare herself for the
next weeks by taking the sting now. She would
discover where her brother had purchased the
book of Basilio's poems, and go there herself this
morning to procure a copy.

In her salon, alone, she would read his words.
His poetry. She would do it alone because reason
told her that it would upset her, and she wanted
to get it over with. She must be braced for the
discussions that would ensue. No book or painting or play or opera went undissected in her
salons. Soon or late, they would come to the new
book by that Tuscan count.

As she stood in the hallway, awaiting the servant's response to her knock, she imagined herself coolly saying to some little group gathered

around a divan in her pale blue room, "Oh, yes. Of course I've read it. Extraordinary, don't you think?" and turning to pour tea or bit of port.

Her heart skittered a little at the daydream, and Cassandra raised her head, wondering what was taking so long. Impatiently, she rapped again.

At last the door swung open, and it was no servant at all, but Gabriel himself who stood there, wearing only breeches. His astonishing hair tumbled loose over his arms and back, his pale green eyes blinking in surprise and confusion. "Cassandra!" He stepped back, gesturing for her to enter. "Has someone fallen ill?"

"Oh! No." Cassandra stood in the middle of the broad, sunny room, suddenly realizing it was quite early for Gabriel. The door to his bedchamber stood open a little, and through the gap, she spied the hair and shoulders of a sleeping woman.

Cassandra jerked her gaze away, flustered. Oh, yes. She was certainly behaving with perfect reason in this—coming to rouse her brother at what was the crack of dawn for him! "Forgive me, Gabriel—I did not think . . . I will come back."

He reached out and snared her sleeve. "Come, sister." Amusement twinkled in his eyes. "Surely you did not believe me celibate." Pushing her into a chair, he calmly crossed the room and closed the door to his chamber.

"No." She tugged on her gloves. Last night,

Julian and an opera dancer, today Gabriel and his paramour. It was more than she wished to know of her brothers' lives. "I am only embarrassed to have disturbed you so early, on so thin an errand."

"Mmm." He poured a glass of water from a pitcher and offered it to her wordlessly. She shook her head, and he drank it himself. "What errand would that be?" He reached for his shirt, hanging askew on the back of a chair.

Against the sunlight streaming through the long windows, he was a startlingly exotic sight— the pale ocher skin of his chest and arms as satiny and perfect as it had been when they were children, when he often wore only a scarf around his head, a sword belt around his waist, and a pair of aging trousers. The image made her smile. "You look exactly as you did at thirteen," she said.

He tugged his shirt over his head, then plucked an orange from a bowl and sat down, beginning to peel it. An impish grin flashed. "I don't often feel any different, either. Terrible, isn't it?"

"Not all."

"So what is this mysterious errand?"

"Oh. That." She clutched her gloves, then put them back down. "A book, actually. Julian said you praised it yesterday."

He inclined his head, his eyes sharpening. "You came to ask about a book?"

She straightened and took refuge in her poise. "Yes. A book of poetry by a man named Count Montevarchi?"

"Not Count, I don't think." He popped a section of orange in his mouth and hopped up, going to a table cluttered with books and papers and assorted debris. From a pile stacked neatly to one side, he took a cloth and wiped his fingers carefully before he took a book from the pile. "Ah. I was right. It is Basilio di Montevarchi. Is he a count?"

He had a copy here. In this room. Her palms felt suddenly damp and she clutched her cotton gloves. "I believe he is."

"I haven't read it all, but he's very good." He carried it over and put it in her hands, almost carelessly. "A little more emotional than I like, but strong images, very powerful. I'll be interested to hear what you think of it." He took up his orange again and leaned back, all ease and grace.

Cassandra only held it for a moment, touching the corners and the spine, unable to even look at it. It seemed warm to her, almost too hot to hold close. "May I borrow it, then?"

"Of course." He looked at her steadily, his thoughts hidden behind that ever pleasant expression, and Cassandra realized she ought to be flipping it open—he expected her to be eager to examine a book she had walked two miles for, very early, and awakened him in order to get.

She swallowed and bent her head, heat radiating from the book into her arms and upward. It was bound in red to go with the title *Fire Night*.

Just as she had at the opera, Cassandra forgot to breathe for so long that the edges of her vision began to blacken before she sucked in a great lungful of air. Her head spun with images, and she didn't know if she could read what he'd written after all.

She most adamantly could not read even one line of the poems while her brother watched. He would see too much.

"Have you met him?" Cassandra asked, pleased at how ordinary her voice sounded. Her fingers moved over the title, touching each letter.

"Not yet. He is to give a reading at Child's tonight. I thought I would go—would you like to go with me?"

Cassandra managed a smile. "Not yet. I'll read it first."

"As you like."

She stood. "Thank you, Gabriel." She lifted a brow. "I'll leave you in peace, and please do forgive me for waking you."

"Not at all." He walked with her to the door, waiting as she tugged on her gloves, the book tucked under her arm. "It is always my pleasure to entertain you."

She rolled her eyes, noticing the silence once more. "Where is your housekeeper?"

He crossed his arms. "Sick mother. She had to

go to Sevenoaks for the week. She'll be back Monday next."

"You're welcome to dine with me, you know, if you grow weary of the pubs before then."

"Thank you." He leaned over and kissed her head lightly. "Do take care, pretty Cassandra. You're always so careful and dignified, but the world will not gasp if you allow us to see your heart now and again."

"I don't know what you mean."

He only smiled. "I hope you enjoy the poetry."

Chapter 13

Basilio was to give his first public reading and discovered the prospect gave him an odd case of nerves. It was not the work, so much, as the idea of reading his poems to a group of Englishmen who might or might not be predisposed to liking his work. Women, yes. Men, he was not so sure.

Still, it was an honor, and he could not refuse. To give himself some courage, he paced in the room he'd taken as a study, and practiced reading aloud. His accent concerned him.

Analise appeared in the doorway, as if called by his frustration. She carried a basket of sewing with her. "Would you like an audience? I cannot understand the English, but I am at least a true presence." Her smile was kind and soft, serene.

It was something he liked about this entirely too young girl—there was a deep, wide pool of serenity that surrounded her like light. Wherever she moved, the quiet followed her, along with whatever house pets might be about. Just now there was a fat gray cat winding about her skirts, and a loose-eared hound, too old for the hunt, limped on arthritic feet to stand beside her, waiting to see where she lit.

She was very beautiful, this child. She favored simple, modest clothing that hid her voluptuous curves, and wore a cap over her dark hair at all times. He persuaded her to leave it off when they went out.

But in spite of her kind smile now, he saw the shadows beneath her eyes. She loathed London, the people and the noise and the bewildering language and customs. A prick of guilt and anger stabbed him. "What are you sewing today?" he asked politely.

"Only embroidering handkerchiefs." She plucked a square of fine linen from the basket to show him. "Violets."

"Very pretty."

"Shall I stay or go?"

He hesitated. "Please stay." He gestured toward the chair sitting by a sunny window. "Thank you."

She smiled, a somehow wise smile, for all her youth. "Of course." She put her hands in her lap.

"You may sew if you like."

"No, no. I will listen with my full attention."

He smiled, thinking he was not sure he wanted that full attention, only an audience, so that he could grow used to hearing his own voice. He opened the book and began to read the first lines, not thinking at first of the meanings of the words, only trying to hear how his accent sounded on them, concentrating on the troublesome little consonants.

Then he came to the dance, the dance around that great, leaping bonfire, and suddenly Cassandra was there in every syllable. He felt surrounded by the essence of her as she'd been that night. The feeling was so strong, so vivid he halted, unable to speak as a fresh memory came to him: her face so white and stricken when he saw her across the yawning gulf of the pit at the opera.

He had not thought, only acted in a kind of madness that frightened him now.

Nothing had changed.

And everything had.

There, in her chair, biddable and quiet, sat his wife—who was not a woman he could loathe, as he'd hoped, but a child of great innocence who roused his protectiveness. This poem was not precisely a love poem, only a tribute to that night as he'd seen it through Cassandra's eyes and his own. But he did not think it was appropriate, even if Analise did not understand the words.

He looked up from the page. "I am sorry. Perhaps I do not wish to do this."

The large blue eyes, so very still, regarded him patiently. "I was enjoying the sound of it. It was like a song in your voice. Very full of love."

Shame seared him. He bent his head and turned away.

"Basilio, do not be ashamed of love in anything. It is God's greatest blessing on us, is it not?"

"Or His curse," he muttered.

"I did not quite hear you."

He shook his head. "It was nothing." He frowned a little. "Are you absolutely sure you do not wish to accompany me this evening?"

"Do you want me to come?" Only her hands showed her agitation, twisting her sewing into a tight coil.

"Analise, you must learn to say what you are thinking with me. I will not mind, truly. If you loathe the idea, simply say you do."

She hesitated. "I wish to be there only if it will give you heart, sir. In truth, I dislike this place very much."

He nodded. "Then you shall stay here and do whatever you like. I have heart enough."

"I am not betraying you?"

"No," he said sincerely. "I would have spared you all of this."

"Yes, I know." Calm once more, she smoothed the fabric in her hands and gave him an encouraging smile. "Please," she said, "continue with your practice reading. It is the least I can do."

She thought him so very noble. Basilio felt the bitter irony of that. But because he did have to face that crowd tonight and wanted it to go well, he took a breath and began to read. This time he let the feelings spill through him fully, letting his tongue caress the syllables that contained Cassandra. It was for her that all of it had been written. And for her, he would read tonight.

Cassandra carried the book of Basilio's poems up to her sitting room, where she had so often read his letters, and called for tea.

While she waited, she stood by the long, bright window, holding the book in her hands, aching over the small intimacy of touching words he'd originally written in his elegant, slanting hand. That handwriting that had had the power to change the direction of her day. A day with a letter from Basilio could not ever be bad.

Fire Night. She took a breath and blew it out. It was an unusual phrase. An unusual celebration. He had named his poems for it.

Cassandra had named her essay the same.

Since her return, she had worked very hard. The translation of Boccaccio engaged her deeply, and she had also been exploring other forms of writing, daring to try forms she'd always thought beyond her. Some of them worked and some did not. She was feeling her way, trying to understand what elements, both in herself and in her work, had changed. There was new bravery in her when she went to the page, and she liked herself better for it. The woman she had been seemed a shadow, afraid of everything.

She had written of Italy, of course. Once she'd recovered a little of her equilibrium, it had been the very best tonic for her flagging spirits. She wrote of Venice as the seductive courtesan Basilio had described, for she'd loved the city. Even in her grief, it had proven irresistible.

She had also written an essay on that lovely, unusual festival, and titled it *Fire Night*. It had been published only last week, in a collection of essays on travel. Which her set would also read. Along with Basilio's poems.

With a soft cry of dismay, she leaned against the glass. Everyone would read the two and know. If there were love poems in his collection, all of London would look right at Cassandra and know for whom they were written.

The idea of such an enormous invasion of privacy mortified her.

Joan came in bearing a tray, and Cassandra straightened hurriedly. "Put it on the table," she said.

"You asked only for tea, but Cook sent up some scones, too. You've not been eating enough, she said."

Cassandra smiled. "I have discovered a yearning for olives," she said. "Do you not miss that food?"

Joan looked surprised. Cassandra was not known, after all, for offering or asking confidences. Warily, Joan said, "I do, every now and again."

Staring at the horizon, Cassandra said quietly, "I loved it there. I'd like to go back someday."

Joan stood by the door, shifting from foot to foot nervously.

Cassandra released her. "Thank you, Joan."

Even then, Cassandra did not open the book. She carried it to the table and poured the tea, adding lemon to the steaming cup, and sugar. She sipped a little, hoping for courage, but only burned her lip.

She had gained so much courage in her travels, yet in matters of emotion, it appeared she remained a coward. She held Basilio's collected poems in her lap, loosely clasped between her fingers, and remembered a conversation she had had with her sister in this very room. Cassandra had warned Adriana of too much feeling, the passion that had been Adriana's downfall more than once. Adriana had not listened, of course—she was likely incapable of living without passion.

But till now, Cassandra had found an intellectual base quite pleasing—and if she'd only heeded her own edict, she would not have to sit here now with this ache and this terror and this agonizing anticipation.

Yet would she trade safety for the extraordinary changes that knowing Basilio had wrought in her? Would she change one moment of time they had spent together?

No. She was honest enough to say that she would not. She had loved him in his letters, and loved him more in the flesh, and loved him still. Might always love him.

And for all those reasons, for the sake of her heart, which was raw and sorrowful today for all the right reasons, she simply could not open the book. Not yet.

She simply held it, touching the title, pleased to know that he had been as changed as she by their meeting; that this book would not exist in the world if she had not taken that trip to Tuscany. It had been born of those pure and beautiful days, and she could not regret that.

The reading went surprisingly well, Basilio thought later, slightly stunned to find himself at the center of an admiring group. George James, the writer who had invited Basilio to England, stood at the outer edges, smiling faintly. He gave Basilio a slight nod and Basilio grinned in return. The attention was heady indeed, and he answered the many questions cheerfully and with a modicum of wit that won him favor with the group.

When the well-wishers thinned, a man approached. Basilio had noticed him earlier: a tall, very fit figure in a gold-embroidered coat and spotless shirt. He had the golden skin, high cheekbones and slightly tilted eyes Basilio associated with his travels in Spain, but when the man spoke, his English was that of a born and bred London gentleman.

"Bravo," he said, smiling. "Enjoyed it very much."

Basilio inclined his head. "Thank you."

"A few of us are about to leave for a salon at my sister's house. I know she would be delighted to have you come with us." There was an odd light of—what? Curiosity, measuring?—in the long eyes. "Would you care to join us? Some of the finest talents in the city arrive there at some time or another."

Basilio measured the man in return, wondering if there were some joke afoot. "And you are?"

"Ah, forgive me. Gabriel St. Ives, sir. My sister is Lady Cassandra St. Ives, and you may ask about her salon from anyone in here. I assure you she is well known."

A roar shut out the rest of the world as Basilio looked at him. Gabriel—this would be the brother who had nearly been taken by slavers. Basilio sought some sign of resemblance between sister and brother, and with surprise saw there was quite a lot: the wide-set eyes, the cat-slant of cheekbones. And something else, too: for all that the brother was more relaxed, Basilio sensed the same alert and careful poise about Gabriel that he'd observed so often in Cassandra.

Basilio considered all the reasons he should not go, should not be tempted, but he was not strong enough to resist. He would only see her, only for a moment, then make his apologies. "I would be honored, sir. Thank you."

They got out of the carriage in Piccadilly Street, the address that had once given Basilio such pleasure when he glimpsed it on a letter. It was just going nine—a church bell chimed out the hours as St. Ives settled with the driver.

Basilio availed himself of the chance to examine the house. Tall and narrow with a small flight of steps leading to the door, it was exactly like its neighbors in the row. All were three generous stories with tall windows overlooking the street, and they struck him as exceedingly English. Proper and neat. He would have expected something else for Cassandra.

Or perhaps not. He remembered her still poise, her self containment, her distrust of extravagance. He smiled.

"Ready?" St. Ives asked, tapping his carved teak walking stick on the ground.

Basilio inclined his head and they climbed the steps. A manservant opened the door to them and took their hats and coats. The foyer smelled of cinnamon, and St. Ives said approvingly, "Ah, Mrs. Hayes has made her famous wine punch." He inhaled heartily and waved the servant away. "Thank you. I know the way."

Basilio heard voices and laughter—even music—coming from somewhere to the back. The hallway was well-lit and he captured a glimpse of an obviously ill-used room furnished with heavy dark wood. A painting of a landscape graced one wall of the hall, a very golden scene with trees and a distant castle on a hill.

Something in him eased at the sight of that painting. Her things. Her rooms. It was nearly enough to simply see the way she lived. He took pleasure in the small, startling touches of color she used—a splash of red in a glass jar, a vivid yellow painting in a dark corner.

From the back came a sudden crackle of laughter from many voices. A clutch of warning tightened around his heart. He should not have come. It was not fair. It was—

But he was swept into the salon before he could retreat, make an excuse—and what excuse would he have offered anyway? The room was brightly lit and gay, pale blue walls with white-and-gilt accents. An enormous potted plant with white flowers and dark green leaves in the shape of long hearts bloomed profusely by one window. The furnishings were covered in demure but cheerful fabrics.

He had been expecting to come into the room and see her immediately, but there were too many people. Two dozen or more filled the chairs and stood in little knots. A man smoked a pipe by a pair of glass doors propped open to the garden. When Gabriel paused by the door, evidently taking measure of the room, Basilio halted with him.

Her salon. How often had they discussed it? She wrote of the gatherings often, telling him in her wry, entertaining way of the dress a woman had worn to scandalize her lover to jealousy, or the outcry over a particular pamphlet smuggled from France. Isolated in his villa in Tuscany, far from the scholars at university, Basilio had envied her these gatherings.

On a sideboard, in a small wooden frame, he spied a painting of a courtesan with red hair sprawled over a baroque divan, her body nubile and tender in its nudeness. One long white hand touched a breast, as if in offering, and a knowing smile turned up only the edges of her lips. He grinned, remembering when he had sent it—an attempt to scandalize her. Bemused by the resemblance he now saw to Cassandra herself, he turned his attention back to the crowd, looking for her once more.

They were not the glittering set Basilio had somehow expected: fops and beauties in satin and brocade. They were rather a plain lot, most of the men in dark coats of simple cloth, with shoes worn a season too long. The women were similarly demure. No daring décolletages, no breathlessly expensive jewels, no ridiculously elaborate hair styles. These were scholars and bluestockings, and would be dependent on their own cleverness and the generosity of patrons and the vagaries of public taste for their bread.

There were a few exceptions—a tall man with

the ineffable air of nobility, a beautiful brunette in ruby-colored silk that displayed her prodigious bosom to the men clustered about the chair where she held court. St. Ives, beside him, also stood out for his elegance.

He noticed Basilio's attention to the woman in red silk. "Glorious, isn't she? An actress."

Basilio inclined his head without much interest. There was only one face he longed to see among the many. Quite suddenly, a roar of laughter broke out to one side. Basilio turned and the group parted, revealing Cassandra.

As if a horse had stepped on his chest, he froze. Engaged in light banter with a man who was reluctant to allow her to depart, she did not see Basilio. There was still time to plead the headache or some urgent stomach condition.

But he did not move. Could not. He drank the laughter on her face, the tilt of her saucy smile, the quick, impatient way she brushed away a lock of hair. The man made some jest, close to her ear, and Basilio thought it might be a little ribald—*Dio!* The jealousy bit deep!—for she lifted one arched brow and spatted him with her fan. Basilio did not miss the disappointment in the man's face as she brushed by, dismissively.

Still time to turn, to unfreeze and take his leave.

"Ah, there she is!" St. Ives said beside him. "Cassandra!" He lifted a hand toward her.

She shifted her skirts and briskly turned. A

large red jewel, a garnet by the depth of color, glittered darkly against the white slope of her breasts, acute and alluring. A drop of blood. She smiled at her brother.

Only then did she see Basilio.

He did not miss the half-second of hesitation in her body before she narrowed her eyes and drew up her head. Her mouth sobered.

Then she drifted over, cloaked in that extraordinary calm. After standing on her toes to kiss her brother's cheek, she stood back, not quite meeting Basilio's eyes.

"Cassandra," St. Ives said. "Since you could not attend the reading tonight, I've brought the poet to you. This is Count Montevarchi."

"We have met, Gabriel," she said. "As I am sure you have already surmised." Steel in those cold tones. Ice in the dark eyes. Not a whisper of warmth as inclined her head toward Basilio. "Good evening."

A small, low laugh, full of mischief and something else Basilio could not quite name—challenge?—came from St. Ives. "Have you? You did not tell me, sister."

"My brother is a jokester when it suits him," Cassandra said evenly. "I hope you were not dismayed to learn where you had arrived."

"Not at all," he said. Gravely, he inclined his head. "I had hoped for a word."

"Of course." With brisk formality, she took his arm. "Shall we walk in the garden?"

"Do not monopolize him too long," said a man at Gabriel's elbow. "You will read for us, will you not?"

Basilio looked to Cassandra for direction, but her profile was as expressionless as marble. He answered the only way he could. "Of course," he said with a little bow. "It would be my honor."

They went to the garden, silence a gulf between them. He did not know how to speak to her when he couldn't read her expression. Worse, he did not know what he intended to say.

In a silence as awkward as any he'd ever known, they moved from the house under the gossamer light of a full moon. Her skirts swished against his ankles. The light caught on her shoulders, milk white and utterly smooth, and he suddenly felt quite dizzy.

He stopped, putting a hand over her fingers where they rested on his elbow. "I wrote to you."

"I know." She could not look at him. She only stood there, her eyes fastened on something off to the left.

Abruptly she drew away, lifted her chin. Her voice was quite reasonable. "It was finished. I did not see what could be gained by our correspondence."

He made an aggrieved sound. "Cassandra—"

"No." The word was fierce. "We shall not relive the past. It is done. I have recovered, as I presume you have, and we shall simply go on from this moment."

"Recovered?" He thought of her in the stairway at the opera, falling to pieces in grief.

"Yes."

He did not know this side of her, the woman who could lie so coldly, but of course it existed. How else had she made so much progress in a world dominated by men? "Was it so simple for you, Cassandra?"

She raised her head, and for a moment he saw the wavering softness. Then she took a breath and stood straight. Her hands were balled tight in her skirts. "No," she said clearly. "It was . . . it . . . it was terrible."

"I sent a man to England to carry a letter, when you did not reply." He reached for her hand.

She slid out of his grip. "I did not go home. I went to Venice; stayed there through Christmas. By then, you were married."

Venice. A fine, swift agony went through him. "And what did you think of her?" His question, softly uttered, affected her as nothing else had. He heard the soft intake of breath even as she took another step away from him.

"She reminded me that passion can be intellectual, and that a woman must return always to reason if she is to survive."

Basilio could not halt an incredulous burst of laughter. "Venice did not teach you that!" He grinned, finding here the heart of their friendship, a place where he had sure footing. "You must have been in some other city."

A toss of that head. "We all see what we need to see."

Moonlight washed over the slope of her shoulders, and he ached to settle his hand there, feel the warmth of her flesh once more. Instead, he laced his fingers together behind his back. He had missed his friend, and it was his friend he wished to woo. With a proper lightness in his voice, he said, "Venice must have moved you deeply indeed if you will not tell me what she gave you."

She skittered away, then turned to face him decisively. "What once was between us is now dead, Basilio. I am willing to be civilized if you keep your distance, but only if you do not speak to me, or attempt to rekindle my dead feelings."

Now he could see what she had been attempting to hide—the shimmer of tears and the agitated rise of her breasts. Her fingers were knotted so tightly it was a wonder they did not break. He stared at her for a long moment, his heart, his lungs, his loins all afire with longing that made a mockery of his wish to be her friend. And yet, that was all that could be between them—and better than nothing at all.

"We are forever divided as lovers, it is true," he said. "But that does not kill the love. What was born between us is immortal."

She gave a snort of laughter he guessed was meant to be cynical. "Only a poet could believe such idiocy. There is no such thing as immortal love."

"Say what you wish. I know you, Cassandra."

"Basilio, you are married! I will not be party to a betrayal of that level."

"And I will never ask it. Never wound you in such a manner." A swell of feeling rose in him. "But I have missed my friend. Do not take that, too."

"We cannot be friends, Basilio." She closed her eyes and shook her head. He waited, knowing that she would raise her head and be stronger in a moment. And she was. Meeting his gaze directly, she said, "I'm afraid that if you wish to attend my salons in the future, as you will surely be urged to do, I must require you to bring your wife, or I cannot admit you." She moved toward the door. "For now, you must go. I'll give your excuses."

Mockingly, he bowed. "As you wish, madam."

He waited while she stalked by him. Yes, they were friends. As she and Analise would be friends. It was a poor sort of passion, but he would settle for renewing the friendship. Merely talking to her had eased the weight of sorrow in him as nothing else had since her departure.

He would come back here, with his wife, the fine, sweet Analise, who could speak no English. Cassandra, in her own kindness, would be forced to converse with her in Italian. And perhaps Cassandra would begin to see . . .

What? That the child should never have been a wife? That there must be some answer to this triangle that made them all so miserable?

Ah, no. He only liked them both, thought they would like each other. Analise would not mind a friend in this cold, confusing place.

A ripple of warning rushed over him—the same dark foreboding that had touched him upon seeing Cassandra for the first time. There was danger here, danger he did not understand.

He frowned as he made his way to the gate in the wall, trying to pinpoint the reason. What fate did he court in this? What disaster might befall them if he took this path?

On the street, he paused and looked up at the moon, like Mercutio. It only gazed impassively back at him, giving away no secrets. Did death await him in this?

He turned to look at the house one last time and saw the shape of a woman illuminated by flickering candlelight in a chamber on the second floor.

She bent her head into her hands, and Basilio did not need to see colors to know it was Cassandra. He knew the curve of that neck, the movement of those arms. He read the despair in her posture, and nearly scaled a nearby tree to climb up to her.

A bright memory flashed in his mind—the

morning she had spun around naked in his chamber, celebrating the sunlight on her skin. He wished more than life itself that he could give those moments, free of sorrow, back to her.

Abruptly, she moved, striding out to a small wrought iron balcony. Out of respect, Basilio dropped into the shadows cast by the tree. He put his hand against the trunk and looked up at her through the branches, feeling closer to her when she reached out and plucked a leaf to twirl in her fingers.

Cassandra, his dearest friend in all the world. He could not bear to live a life without her in it. Kissing his fingers with a smile, he pressed them to the tree bark, sending his affection to her. Whistling, he walked home, feeling buoyant and clear at last.

Chapter 14

Analise could not have said what awakened her. She slept well, especially in the coolness of the soft English air, which was something she found very appealing about this strange country. The climate seemed very gentle, unlike the blazing heat of Italy.

It was very late, perhaps even close to morning, for a blackbird sang from some hidden spot, its cry mournful and beautiful at once. She donned her dressing gown and opened the window that overlooked the garden to see if she could spy the bird, but it was hidden in the darkness, somewhere very close.

She did not feel tired, only surprisingly hungry, and decided she would begin her day now, whatever the time, with some chocolate—another thing she had come to enjoy in this worldly place—and the soft, fluffy rolls the cook made especially for her.

She did not bother to dress so early. Not even the staff would have awakened yet. Padding down the carpeted stairs in her slippers, she felt mildly wicked and oddly virtuous at once. The dog and cat came with her, as they always did, following her from one room to another, even when she simply had forgotten a bit of thread in one and jumped up to fetch it. They never seemed to mind when she turned around and went back to where she had been, but patiently trailed her. Sometimes she thought their devotion must be much like the devotion of humans to God. Or perhaps even God to humans. It pleased her, this gentle belief, and she always felt a faint blessing when it came to her.

From the study where Basilio spent so many of his hours, a light spilled out to the hall carpet in a pale yellow square. Quietly, not wishing to disturb him, she crept up to the door and peeked in. As she had so often, she found he'd fallen asleep over his work. With a gentle smile, she moved into the room, and plucked the pen from his ink-stained fingers. He did not stir.

Even in sleep he looked troubled, and Analise wished she could discover the source of his pain, to ease it. It had grown worse since they'd been in London, and she suspected there was a woman.

If that was so, if he was in love with another woman, their marriage was an even greater sin than she thought. She had grown fond of him these past months, but she had no carnal love for him. Such things were not part of her nature, and Basilio did not insist.

He'd been working hard, she saw, for his bold, elegant hand covered pages and pages, the shortened lines of his poetry making a beautiful wavy pattern down the paper. She wished she could read it, but he wrote only in English. Perhaps at some time she could attend a reading with him, and someone might translate to Italian for her. She was reluctant to ask Basilio himself.

So beautiful, she thought distantly. Like an archangel, with those thick black curls and the red lips and thick lashes. His hands were works of art, so elegantly lean and graceful. She briefly wished that she felt some yearning to lie with him, for his sake, to ease him. Yet she could not even think of it without shuddering.

And in truth, perhaps he did not wish it. From the first, he had never touched her in that way.

Until their wedding night, Analise had considered only her own despair. He had said nothing as he tucked her into his bed, but his sorrow was deep and clear. They had been pawns, both of them. In some terrible way, it unified them.

And now Analise ached for his despair. The despair that drove him to write, sometimes all night long, of something he could not speak of. From the corner, she took a blanket and tossed it over his shoulders, pinching out the candle and shutting the door behind her.

*   *   *

Cassandra carried her chocolate to the salon, and sat at her desk in the clean and peaceful room. Sunlight streamed through the windows, fingering the bright white flowers of a gardenia plant she'd slipped out of the conservatory at the family house. Her cousin Leander was the only one who would notice, and heaven only knew when he'd grace them with his presence.

She'd stolen the plant after her return from Italy, when winter had seemed endless and the sunshine of the land she'd fallen in love with, very far away. This morning, with the bright new sunlight illuminating the glossy darkness of the leaves, exaggerating the heavy scent of the blossoms, it made her ache in odd ways.

No matter how she tried to forget it, those days in Tuscany lingered. Which made her remember, with a little flutter of worry, the travel essay on Fire Night.

In the past she'd often taken a male pseudonym, sometimes at the insistence of a publisher, sometimes simply for the ease of it. But this essay had been published under her own name. It had never occurred to her to write so clearly as a female before, and now it amused her that she had not. The public was mad for travel essays just now, and the success of the book was assured.

What surprised Cassandra was that there was a great deal of comment on her work in particular—some of it predictable sneers from the male guardians of the literary establishment, but more of a complimentary nature. It pleased her very much, and she had begun to consider more travel to do more work in the same venue.

It was, however, appallingly precipitous of Basilio to appear just now—particularly in his incarnation as a poet. Her brother Gabriel had clearly made the connection very quickly— though not without a good deal of help from her.

A flash of memory burned across her inner eye: Basilio last night, standing in her garden, his hair caught in that elegant queue. Moonlight caught and held in the curls, and sailed along the broad brow and swooped over his aggressive nose. And his eyes, burning, burning, alive and full of determination.

"Oh, God," she whispered. Her hands had shaken for hours afterward, even after he'd left her. She wanted to be the very picture of Reason, and had failed miserably.

Narrowing her eyes, she picked up her pen and wrote forcefully in her journal:

I will not allow him to be my downfall. I have come too far, learned too much. I have made my way as a woman in a man's world, and I cannot allow a man to be my undoing. As it was, fortune smiled and I did not conceive a child in those rash days, allowing me time to regain my sensibilities.

What woman would not have fallen under such a

spell as those days cast? The sun and the lush colors of the landscape, and the sensual beauty of the man himself? I am only human. I fell to my senses.

I do not regret it. I will not. Not even now can I find it in myself to regret what he gave so freely—himself and his world. And more. So much.

When I am honest, I know it was a true and generous love we discovered there, on those magical days. Though it would be simpler to call it the magic of the country, that would be a lie. It was the harmony we discovered: a perfect melding of hearts, minds, and bodies. It grieves me that life did not allow such a perfect union to be joined in a marriage, for after all, that is what a marriage should ultimately be.

It would be different if he had been married upon our meeting, or if there had been true feeling between them. It is impossible to imagine the honorable Basilio breeching such a trust. Instead, we are all the victims of politics—Basilio and I, and the child who wished only to be a nun—a marriage of another sort.

For that reason, I will not regret and I will not forget one moment of those beautiful hours. I will gladly live every day remembering what he gave, and every day I will remember that I let him go because it was best for him. He could not have borne the ghosts of his mother and brothers.

Honor is not, after all, the sole realm of men.

She paused, feeling stronger, wiser, braver, and then continued.

Just now, in order to maintain that honor, I must keep myself very busy. Every day, every evening. Perhaps I shall write to Phoebe and ask her to come visit me. Or even speak with Julian about the possibility of bringing Ophelia and Cleo to Town to be presented at Court. 'Tis not too soon to be thinking of marriage for them.

Yes. That is a fine idea.

"My lady?" Joan put her head in the room. "There's a gentleman caller most insistent in seeing you this morning. Mr. Wicklow. Shall I bring him in?"

Robert. Cassandra hesitated. The heir to a tradesman's fortune, he had attended a salon with Julian one evening not long before. Tall, good-looking and well-spoken, for his education had been seen to very nicely by his social climbing parents, he had been an excellent addition and Cassandra urged him to return whenever he liked.

He had how established himself as a fixture. Not because he had a particular aspiration to the scholarly world, but because he'd become quite enamored with Cassandra.

She had not encouraged him, though she supposed she had not particularly discouraged him, either. His attention had been a balm to her wounded spirits. He amused her. He was kind. He had good manners. A good companion.

Just right, she realized sensibly, for a morning

like this when she was tempted to brood. "Send him in, Joan. I'm nearly finished here." Carefully, she put the pages away and stood to greet him.

Pleased with herself for allowing Reason rather than Emotion to rule this morning, Cassandra agreed to a stroll in the park. Robert entertained her with tales of a soppy and comic duel that had taken place after the opera the night before, and chatted lightly of the various people they knew in common. He had an acute and wicked tongue, and Cassandra laughed at his descriptions. "How can I ever be sorry when you do not attend my salons, sir, if you bring me such amusing tales from the world?"

"Ah, but I understand I most certainly should have been there last night, since I missed that dashing poet who has so charmed the literary set," he said. His russet eyebrows, raising in amusement, were all that gave his jibe away. "I was fair devastated to hear."

Cassandra grinned, surprised it was so easy to don a mask. Robert did not particularly care for poetry, thinking it fanciful. His was a solid world. "You missed little."

"Did he read?"

"No."

"They let him get away with that?"

"I believe he had another appointment," Cassandra said vaguely. She held his arm as they walked, enjoying the first roses of spring and the fresh green of the landscape. The pathways were busy with others drawn out by the same soft weather, and Cassandra nodded pleasantly to a matron with a young child in tow. "I do love this time of year," she commented, hoping to change the subject.

But Robert did not take the hint. "I expect he needed full props to pull it off. All that emotion. I find it too much."

"Oh." Cassandra blinked against a tic in her eye. "Have you read the work, then?"

"Of course, of course. One wouldn't want to appear the cretin." He gave her his sideways grin. "Have you not?"

"Not yet."

"Overwrought, I'd say, though I expect the ladies will like it."

"Love poetry, then?" Perhaps if she learned enough this way she would never have to actually read it. "Sonnets and the like?"

He pursed his lips in thought. "Not love poems, or not exactly, anyway. Sonnets to nature and festivals and plums."

A memory, too genuine, rushed through her. "Plums?" she echoed. It sounded passably ironic.

"I like that one, I must say. It's vivid."

Cassandra swung her reticule. "Well, I expect Fashion will find some new marvel before long. A fickle lot is the public, particularly for poets."

"Oh, yes. That Ovid fellow is simply not to be borne."

She laughed, suddenly glad she had come out with him. "I do enjoy your company, Mr. Wicklow. I always feel as if you've blown away the cobwebs in my all-too-serious brain. Thank you."

A soft pause. "I would that you enjoyed it more, Cassandra."

She looked up, hiding her alarm in a light smile. "What more could I possibly offer?" She gave the words a slightly ribald edge.

He did not smile, only turned earnest eyes to her. "I have made no secret of my attraction to you, but aside from these little crumbs you toss my way, there is little encouragement." He paused on the path. "Should I turn my attentions elsewhere?"

"My husband made me a happy widow," she said, looking at him as directly as she knew. "I am in no hurry to sacrifice myself to that altar again."

"No hurry? Or determined to do it never?"

"Once, I would have said never. But that may not be true."

He nodded seriously, his hands clasped behind his back. He stepped aside for a boy chasing a ball down the walk, then raised his head again. "I would not require a declaration of love, you know. I do not expect that."

A stab of guilt touched her. "Robert, I—"

He lifted one hand with a rueful smile. "Forgive me. Do not answer."

Troubled, she said quietly, "I did not mean to mislead you, Robert. I am very sorry if I did."

"You have never given me any indication that we were more than good friends." He offered his arm. "I hope I have not endangered that with my rashness. Perhaps that poet stirred me more than I believed."

"Poetry does have that power at times."

He smiled with his usual jovial good humor. "Come, my lady. Shall we find ourselves some refreshment?"

Cassandra plunged herself into a whirl of activity, accepting every invitation she was issued to every rout, every assembly, every dinner. More soon came her direction, more than she could begin to accept.

It seemed that she'd become something of a curiosity. Partly on her own merits, and partly thanks to her sister Adriana, who'd become a legend in their set in a duel.

But more than herself or her sister, Cassandra suspected the invitations were issued to her in hopes that her brother Julian might accompany her—which he did, but only rarely.

She even, to her astonishment, discovered the pleasures of shopping, a pursuit she'd found empty-headed in the past. But armed with a footman and her coach, she found she could avoid thinking of Basilio for entire afternoons.

It was one such day, spent in mindless amusement at the milliners, that she emerged into a bright, warm afternoon, and spying a tea shop across the street, decided to revive herself with a cup and a pastry. She deposited her packages in the carriage and sent the driver home. There was plenty of time to walk home after, and walking eased her restlessness as well or better than any other pursuit.

Inside the shop, she paused, blinking in the darkness after so bright a day. Voices rose and fell, the constrained low murmur of ladies engaged in gossip, the laughter of a young woman, and the clatter of china and silver. The air smelled of sugar and yeast.

And something more. The hairs on the back of her neck raised as she caught the scent of Basilio—a hint of sunlight, that memory of olive leaves. With a little shake of her head, she told herself she was imagining things to make up for her momentary blindness. But as her vision cleared, she saw that she was not mistaken.

Basilio sat alone at a table nearby a window. Sheaves of paper littered the space before him, and an empty cup, and the remains of a pasty. As if he had been waiting for her, one arm was flung over the back of the chair, and his dark eyes pinned her.

She froze, one part of her moving toward him, the other running away.

His smile settled it. It was that easy, nearly impish expression that she could not resist. "I will join my friend there," she said to the girl. "Bring tea and something sweet."

He rose to greet her. "Do you come here often?"

"Never."

"Nor do I." That glitter in his eyes. "It must be fate, no?"

"Or accident," she said acerbically, taking her chair. "But I am famished and it would be more pleasant to take tea with a friend than alone."

"So we are to be friends?"

"I suppose we will."

"I was not sure, last night." He sat down and gathered his papers.

"Is that more poetry?"

"Yes." He held it out to her. "Would you like to read it?" A dangerous light on his face, that faint flaring of his nostrils.

She shook her head. "No, thank you." Arching one brow, she added, "You've been very productive."

"I am inspired." He blinked, his gaze lighting on her mouth, then her brow. A mockingly innocent smile, then. "By your country."

"I see."

The girl brought a tray and Cassandra waited as she settled it: a fine feast of little cakes and jam and tiny, perfect strawberries with a pot of cream. Cassandra made a sound of approval, her stomach feeling suddenly as empty as a dry well.

"How do you find our pastries, sir?" she

asked, plucking a strawberry and dipping it in the pot.

"Very good." He watched with intense focus as she carried the strawberry to her mouth. His lips parted the slightest bit, and Cassandra saw the edge of his lower teeth. A bolt of desire raced up her spine. She felt a perverse and powerful wish to simply lick the cream from the berry, showing him her tongue.

But what would it accomplish? More thwarted desire? There had never been any question that they desired one another.

He watched her intently, leaning forward over the table, and suddenly, their eyes locked. Before she could react, she was snared in that world that only the two of them occupied. There was only Basilio's face.

And he felt it, too. Dismay and wonder warred on his mouth.

Her breath caught, and she knew what she had wanted a moment ago with her impulse. Slowly, she looked at the strawberry in her hand, and put it down with a sigh. Pushing the dish toward him, she quietly said, "You must try them. Not as lovely as your plums, but quite good nonetheless."

She watched as he plucked one from the bowl, and dipped it, and raised his eyes. The red fruit met his beautiful lips and he sucked it into his mouth, his eyes on her face, burning.

Beneath the table, their toes, safely covered in

shoes, touched, tip to tip. Sunlight streamed down between them. They ate strawberries, one by one, speaking not at all.

When there was only one left, they both reached for it and their fingers touched, nail to nail, in the shallow white bowl. As if dancing to the same strings, they turned, touched fingertips, then drew away.

A dog suddenly jumped against the window, his nails making a sharp tapping sound as he grinned at them, tongue hanging sideways out of his mouth. "It's your Siren!" Cassandra said with a laugh.

Just as quickly, the dog was distracted by some better prize and ran off down the street, but his purpose had been served—they were no longer in that dangerous, drifting world.

He smiled at her when she looked back at him. "I cannot feel tragic while I look at you. I should, perhaps. I should beat my hand against my breast and howl with sorrow. But you make my heart lift. I thought I would never look on your face again."

Cassandra smiled in return. "I dislike tragedy."

"All that excessive emotion."

She laughed. "Yes." Picking up a cake frosted with a thin layer of sugar, she said, "Did you enjoy meeting my brother?"

"Gabriel? Yes—I seem to see him quite often. He's quite interesting."

"He's the one who fences. You'd enjoy a match, I'm sure."

"So he said. Except he said he would enjoy trouncing me."

She laughed. "And he would, I'm afraid."

"Will you come and tie a ribbon around my sleeve?"

"No. That should be Analise."

His face bled of all emotion. "Yes. Analise." He stood, nodding, a tinge of anger on his jaw. "Good day, Cassandra."

She let him go; it was what she had wanted.

The last strawberry lingered in the bowl. She picked it up and examined it, but it no longer held any interest. Her fingers trembled as she held it, betraying the power of emotions he'd roused. She let it drop back in the bowl, wanting to make him ache as she had ached these last months.

It was so unlike her. Twirling the berry by its stem in the pool of thick cream, she congratulated herself on resisting the wickedness, the urge to lead him into temptation.

Friends. She snorted inwardly, dropping the berry. They could not be friends. It was absurd to even consider it, when his very nearness made her tremble, when her mind fell to dangerous visions and memories when she was with him. How cruel it was to have him here, so close, yet so completely unattainable!

She hoped his visit would not be a long one. Please, not much longer.

She redoubled her efforts to keep busy. She invited her sister Phoebe to come stay with her, and wrote piles of letters to friends and cousins, to her sisters and fellow scholars. She took brisk walks. She poured herself into the Boccaccio translation, discovering it carried her away from herself.

Phoebe sent regrets, saying she had too much to do with summer arriving. No new letters came from Leander or Adriana.

And everywhere, people spoke of Basilio: the dashing poet, the charming Count. The women fluttered and the men tried not to mind. His caricature appeared in the scandal sheets.

Desperate to keep herself distracted, Cassandra approached Julian about the possibility of bringing Ophelia and Cleo to Town for presentation at Court. He promised to consider it for the upcoming season, but failed to understand the magnitude of planning that such an event would require.

To press her case, she insisted he attend open Court with her one evening, hoping he might begin to see what was required if he saw the other marriageable women who would be vying for the same pool of husbands. Julien had agreed.

She had dressed as finely as the occasion warranted, in a deep blue silk brocade with a low cut bodice, and now sat with her shoulders covered with a towel as Kate wound her hair into an elaborate style, then powdered her face.

In a moment of whimsy, Cassandra dug out a box of rarely used patches and adorned herself with a star below one eye and a heart above her mouth. A stunning complement of sapphires—a fall of them around her throat, drops hanging from her ears, a bracelet clasped around her wrist—completed the adornment, and she stepped back to admire herself in the mirror. She would do. Very nicely, if she said so herself.

What would Basilio think of her like this? She smiled sadly at herself. Each time she left the house, she was dressed to stun him if he should appear. His name was so much on the lips of society—at formal dinners, in small clusters at routs, over cards at an assembly; even the Queen was rumored to have read the poems—that it was a miracle Cassandra did not meet him at every turn. But she had not. Which was how it should be.

A footman tapped and told her that Julian had arrived. Brushing away her foolish musings, she hurried down to join him.

Chapter 15

Analise had never seen anything so grand as the palace of the King of England and the people in it. There was so much she almost did not know where to look first. Everywhere there was color and glitter—on the walls and the tapestries, in the jewels of the women, and the brocades of the men. Their voices murmured and swelled and fell, interwoven with the music from a quartet playing on a raised dais to one side. Warm sunlight spilled through the mullioned windows, and air blew in through open doors leading to the grand gardens beyond.

Basilio held her fingers against the crook of his elbow tightly, giving her courage. When the invitation had arrived, he had sent out for a dressmaker immediately to have something made for her, and although Analise had never worn anything like it, she was glad he'd insisted.

It had seemed quite immodest at first, with the deep square neckline and the close fit that displayed her hips and breasts and waist. But she had been seduced by the bold turquoise color that reminded her of the sky over the cloisters where she'd been so happy. It suited her complexion, bringing out golden tones to her skin, exaggerating the darkness of her hair, setting her eyes afire.

Dispassionately, she had seen she was very beautiful in it, and because the summons to be presented to the queen meant so much to her husband, she was pleased. She had donned the diamonds he found for her, and let her hair be dressed in a simple way.

Next to her, Basilio was more splendid than any man at Court. He carried himself as the Count that he was, his Italian manner of dress only a little more romantic than that of the English gentlemen in the room.

But Court was more than a little terrifying. Analise had been attempting to learn a few English phrases with the help of the cook, and she'd believed she had been making progress until she entered this vast room and heard the language spinning out all around her.

Basilio looked down as they approached the monarchs. "Do not fear," he said with a smile. "We are not important enough to warrant more than a word or two."

She nodded.

And it proved to be true. They were presented to the stout king and his kind-eyed wife. Analise could understand nothing of the few sentences exchanged, though the queen had considerately greeted Analise in her own language. She smiled and curtsied deeply, as she had been instructed.

Then they were free. Basilio guided her to one side and fetched a cup of wine for her. "Now we must linger a little while, then we can depart." He squeezed her hand. "Thank you."

"Of course." Her tension easing, she looked curiously at the people, taking it all in to remember for later. "It looks like a room full of butterflies," she said. She admired a slim blond girl, not much older than herself, who moved so gracefully she nearly seemed to float. "Oh, look at her!" she said softly.

"And this one," Basilio said, nodding to a gentleman in the most outrageous suit of clothes Analise had ever seen, shiny satin in a most incredible shade of yellow-green. Acres of lace dripped from his sleeves and cravat, and he tottered dangerously on high heeled shoes.

Analise laughed, then covered her mouth. "It is sinful to laugh at the vanity of others."

His eyes twinkled. "Then I fear I'm doomed today."

Analise grinned. She wished she could love such a man, so kind and easy to be with. But she felt nothing, even when she tried. It made her a little melancholy.

To distract herself, she lifted her head and looked to the crowd. At the entrance, a footman in splendid livery announced the attendees as they arrived. Each paused at the door, though no one paid particular attention, as he called out their names in a bored voice.

A man and woman appeared at the door, and paused to wait for the footman to announce them. Analise caught her breath. The woman was breathtakingly beautiful, a beauty dependent less upon her features than her coloring. Large dark eyes in an oval face, a glory of red hair piled high. Sapphires in three tiers circled her neck. She spoke to the man at her side, gesturing with her fan. He nodded.

But for all her beauty, it was the man who captured Analise's attention. He was quite tall, and rather soberly dressed in dark green without adornment. His breeches were tucked into tall boots. He was not nearly as handsome as many in the room, but she liked the character in his face much more than the simple prettiness of many of the other men. There was living in the creases of sun lines around his eyes, and a lack of illusion in the firm mouth. "Basilio, look at this pair, with the red-headed woman. Are they not a striking couple?"

"Where?"

She looked up at him, surprised by the hint of urgency she heard in his voice. "Just there, coming in. The very tall blond man."

There was no mistaking the soft intake of breath, quickly hidden. "Ah, yes." He smiled.

"They are siblings. I am acquainted. Would you like to meet them?"

"Oh, I don't know, Basilio." Her throat went dry. "I feel so foolish."

"Lady Cassandra speaks several languages. I believe Italian is one of them." He did not give her time to object again but he hurried her over, as if he was afraid they would disappear.

Cassandra saw Basilio bearing down on them with purpose in his eyes, a tiny, very young and beautiful girl on his arm. For a moment Cassandra wanted to flee, but something in the girl's terrified expression made her hesitate. She felt a burst of sympathy, and touched Julian's arm. "Do not give me away, Julian," she said quietly.

He glanced up and assessed the situation in the blink of an eye. "Good God. She's a child."

Cassandra met Basilio's eye as he approached, and then looked at his wife. No more than five feet tall, she looked like a doll made of china. Her hair was darkest black, her skin honey, her eyes large and blue and terrified. A beauty by any standard. "Good afternoon," Cassandra said to them both, clutching Julian's arm for strength.

In Italian, Basilio said, "Lady Cassandra, I would like you to meet Countess Montevarchi, Analise. Analise, this is a friend of mine, a scholar who is very fond of Boccaccio."

The girl smiled, extending her hand, and against her will, Cassandra was captured. There was an old, old wisdom in those fine eyes, and an unmistakable sweetness in her smile. "I am so relieved to meet someone with whom I might converse," she said.

Cassandra clasped the small hand in her own. "I can imagine how bewildering it must all seem to you." She gestured to her brother, who was very still beside her. "Allow me to present my brother, Lord Albury." She switched to English. "Julien, this is the Countess of Montevarchi. The poet's wife."

With a very courtly gesture, Julian bent over her gloved hand. "Delighted."

A knot of fops descended upon them, clasping Basilio around the shoulders, noisily—and a little drunkenly—greeting him. Cassandra watched them attempt to drag him away, and he pushed back, laughing, but his face flushed with consternation. He took back his sleeve and put them off, "A moment, please."

But they were not to be so easily dissuaded.

"Everywhere we go," Analise said quietly, "this is how it is. They are all very eager to—" She frowned. "It is more than talk. I almost think they want to bite him, take away a little piece of his flesh."

Startled by the insight, Cassandra looked at her. "You are closer than you know. They cannot do what he does, but some part of them hopes they might if they tear a bit of him away."

"Yes," Analise said. "Very sad, that they do not look within."

Basilio fought his way back to them, brushing a loosened lock of hair from his face. Looking at Cassandra, he took her hand and Analise's hand, and pressed them together. Cassandra's hand was shaking slightly. She hoped neither of them noticed.

What was he *doing*? She gave him a fierce look, but he appeared not to notice. In English, he said very quietly, "They think her quaint and are unkind. Please."

The absurdity of the situation should have made her scream, but Cassandra sensed there was honor in his request. She found herself nodding, bringing the girl's tiny hand into her elbow. "We will find a quiet corner, shall we?" she said in Italian, so Analise would understand. "Go bow to your audience," she said to Basilio.

He gave a quick nod, one hand touching Analise's shoulder lightly, and rejoined the impatient group.

Julian watched the interchange without a word, his gray eyes going the silvery shade that made them unreadable. Now he looked at his sister. "Are you all right?"

She nodded. "I'm fine."

He turned his attention to Analise, a gentleness and warmth in his manner that surprised Cassandra. For a moment, he only looked at her, then abruptly said, "I must have a word with a man. Excuse me."

Which left the two women, linked more deeply than Analise could dream, standing arm in arm in the crowded room. Cassandra knew a moment of panic. What if Analise guessed that Cassandra's feelings were less than pure toward Basilio? What if Analise made some remark that roused Cassandra's well-squelched jealousy?

As if the girl sensed her discomfort, she raised her head. "It is very kind of you to take me under your wing, but if you have appointments to keep, please do not worry too much." A simple, self-mocking smile. "I have learned to be invisible in these places."

She could not be more than sixteen, Cassandra thought. There was that radiance to her skin, the unformed blankness about her mouth. "I shall consider it a pleasure to entertain you while the fops steal your husband. I can't imagine being adrift in a setting like this. It would be terrible."

"My husband allows me to avoid it most of the time," she said. "He only thought I might like coming to meet the king and queen."

"And did you?"

She laughed, bell-like and quiet. "A little, though I could not understand a word."

Out of the corner of her eye, Cassandra saw

Basilio watching them. That she could not bear. Gesturing toward the open doors, she said, "Let's walk in the garden. It is quite beautiful, though very unlike the gardens in your country."

"Have you visited?"

Cassandra frowned, berating herself for this misstep. "Only a little of it. Venice. Have you been there?"

"Yes, when I was a little girl. I thought it was beautiful, like a fairy tale. And you? Did you like it?"

"I did. I was . . ." she paused, choosing her words carefully, "grieving, and went there to forget. It reminded me of the reasons we live—how precious beauty is, and how rare, and how worth celebrating." Surprised at this sudden gush of words, she glanced at the girl. "Forgive me. That was more than I intended to say."

"No, no! Do not apologize. It was beautiful." Her head inclined softly. "You are a widow?"

"Yes." She did not say it had not been her husband she grieved in Venice. "How long have you been married?"

"Six months," she said, without elaboration.

"Ah, newlyweds." They settled on a stone bench beneath the spreading branches of an enormous oak tree. "A very blissful time."

"I suppose. He is a very kind man." Her smile was sad as she looked toward the horizon. "He—" She shook her head, raised those innocent eyes.

"Forgive me. Women talk freely in my country. I sometimes forget it is not that way here."

It was very, very wicked of her, but Cassandra could not quell her desperate wish for information. "I have four sisters," she said with a smile. "In such a world, we did not take the same vow of stoic silence as many of the women in my class."

"Four! How wonderful! That is what I liked best about the cloister—being so constantly in the company of other women. They were my sisters, and I miss them terribly."

"A cloister?"

"Yes." A soft radiance, most extraordinary, came over her face. "I went there when I was six. It was Basilio's mother, actually, who fought with my father to let me go there. I thought, all my life, that I would be a nun, you see." That sad smile. "But my father felt my beauty would bring him more in the world."

Cassandra had known these basic facts, but it pierced her to hear the story from Analise's own lips. "So you did not wish to be wed."

"No." A slight shrug. "At least the saints saw me delivered to a man who is kind enough to understand my wish to remain bound to God. It is most extraordinary."

"Remain bound to God? Do you mean you are still a virgin?"

Analise gave a bright laugh. "You are so shocked! I suppose I should not have confessed it, since my father and all believe the marriage to be consummated. But yes, I remain pure, because he has never insisted I join him in that way."

Cassandra swallowed. A queer heat crept up her cheeks to her ears, and even she heard the hush in her voice as she replied. "I had heard that he is honorable," she said. "But you are correct: that is most extraordinary. How can you help but fall in love with such a man?"

"Because I love God," she said, as if it were the most obvious thing in the world. "I do not wish to love a man."

"I see."

"No, you do not." Analise smiled, that benevolent, somehow old, smile. "But I sense you are a very passionate sort of woman, and I do not mind that you cannot understand that my passion is for God. Few do." She paused, a puzzled smile on the flawless brow. "In truth, I do not think even Basilio grasps it. He is very much of the world."

As if her speaking his name conjured him, he appeared at the doors to the garden, looking concerned. "There, see? He will not abandon us for too long."

Cassandra's heart squeezed. An unwelcome rush of memories poured through her, memories that made her feel evil as she sat next to this sweet child. How incredible that he had been so careful of her.

In despair, she realized it made her love him

even more. She held her back very straight as he approached them.

"I think," Analise confessed quietly, "that his heart belongs to another woman. He has not said, and he has never shown the slightest interest that I can see, so he is discreet. But I sometimes think he has been weeping over his poetry."

Cassandra did not trust herself to speak.

"Is it not a tragedy, that we should both be so devoted elsewhere and chained by money and family?"

"Yes," Cassandra whispered. Forcing herself to look at Analise, she took her hand. "But you must trust that all will be well. God has given you a kind, good husband. You will learn to love him, in time."

"Will I?"

Cassandra forced herself to smile. "Of course." She gestured toward his muscular figure, moving gracefully over the lawns. His hair shone in the light, and women turned to watch him. "Look at him, Analise. Every woman here is wishing she could be you."

Blinking, the girl looked around, and said, softly, "Oh!"

"Poet! Sir Poet!" The cry came from a matron, squeezed tightly into her gown, an abundance of powdered bosom spilling out above. "You must read for us!"

Cassandra automatically translated, and Analise gave a laugh. "I do not think it is exactly his poetry she is longing for, do you?"

Surprised, Cassandra laughed with her. It felt good, the shaking loose of laughter. It had been too long.

She knew she should stand, take her leave, escape while it was still possible, but something held her there. A strange protectiveness engendered by the girl's small hand in her own, perhaps. The bevy of women descending on Basilio could be a cruel lot, and Cassandra could not abandon Analise to them.

Or perhaps it was only the need, however wrong it was, that Cassandra felt to simply look at him. It amazed her, sitting there in the late warm sun, what an enormous tide of emotion he could rouse in her. It never waned, not even a little. Every detail of him seemed dear. The lobes of ears and the cut of his mouth, and his thickly fringed and beautiful eyes that fixed on her, clear and direct. *You see?* his eyes said to her.

And Cassandra nodded, as if they spoke without words.

The bevy of women surrounded him but Basilio kept walking toward Cassandra and Analise, listening, laughing, donning a charmer's guise. He knew these were the women who would increase his fame, and did not take it lightly. One pressed a copy of the book into his hands.

"Have you read it, his book?" Analise asked.

"No. I have not yet had the opportunity. Have you?"

"I have heard him read, but he composes in English."

Basilio reached the bench, the ladies in their bright gowns crying out for him to read, leaning on his arm, fawning around him.

Cassandra repressed a smile, and he caught it. "What say you, madam?" he said to her. "Shall I read?"

And it was, suddenly, impossible that she could pretend that what had passed between them had never been. She smiled, very slightly. "As you wish."

"Will you translate for my wife?" he asked in Italian.

Caught by the entreaty in his eyes, she nodded. Fear made her hands clammy. In a voice that was more breathless than she would have liked, she told Analise, "I cannot promise to make the Italian as beautiful as his English."

"At least I will understand the spirit."

Basilio opened the book, seemingly at random. The whispers and rustles settled until there was only the sound of the birds in the background, twittering and calling, and the distant sound of the musicians playing Handel.

The world narrowed for Cassandra—narrowed to his hands, loosely clasping the book, to his throat, to the place above his upper lip where he'd shaved so cleanly, to the fan of his lashes over his cheekbones.

At last he began to read, his voice lilting. Cassandra listened, unsure she could capture the rhyme scheme he used, and decided suddenly that it was not necessary.

Quietly, earnestly, she began to translate:

"How to capture the magic of moments? How to capture the perfection when the sunlight falls, just so, across the gray branch of an olive?"

He raised his eyes, speaking to Cassandra alone. Captured by his eyes, by the burning in them, she dropped her voice even lower.

"I am driven to it," she said quietly in Italian, *"again and again, like the painters who try to capture the light here, driven to the attempt to capture God in some small way. The soft brown swell of the sea swirling over bare white feet, the way a woman bends her head and shows the soft, clean place on the back of her neck . . ."*

Cassandra translated faithfully, her heart shattering a little more with each word, each image, all of it drenched with Tuscan sunlight and the taste of Basilio's kisses. He spoke of olives and plums and the smell of a woman's mouth.

Around him, the women's eyes filled with tears of appreciation, their mouths going soft in wonder and yearning. It was his passion they responded to, the reflection of a side of man they wished they could taste for more than a moment of playacting during seduction. Cassandra ached with the recognition that he was truly rare in this, that his passion was not illusion.

Cassandra closed her eyes, whispering to Analise in Italian, letting the pictures he roused float through her mind, so bittersweet and beautiful that she could do naught but let them fill her.

" 'And always,' " he finished softly, " 'I labor imperfectly. Always imperfectly.' "

Cassandra translated the last words in a whisper, feeling the tight clutch of Analise's fingers around her own. She opened her eyes and Basilio stood there, his mouth sober, his eyes fixed purely on Cassandra. "Thank you," he said, bowing, and turned away. "No more today, ladies. I have suddenly got a headache."

Without waiting for Analise or for release from the bevy of ladies, he swiftly moved away, nearly running by the time he made the doors.

The women drifted away, fans fluttering, their voices circling in sighs.

Analise and Cassandra sat without speaking for a long time. At last, Analise said, "Do you hear that music of love in his voice? I thought it was the love of a woman, but perhaps he simply loves the world and everything in it."

Cassandra's throat was tight with guilt and love and unshed tears. "Perhaps," she said quietly.

"I have never thought of the world in that way before—that it is the hand of God on everything.

It makes it far less wicked." She stood, a faint frown on her brow. "It is all God's creation."

"As you are," Cassandra said, reminding herself.

"Perhaps I should go to him now." She rose. "Many thanks, Lady Cassandra. It was a pleasure to meet you. Perhaps you will visit me."

"I would like that." She rose and kissed both cheeks in the Italian way, then stepped back. "Go to him now."

Chapter 16

Basilio burned. A good rain at suppertime had washed the air clean, leaving behind a taste of summer in the mild wind. It reminded him unbearably of Cassandra and August and plums, and he feared he might go mad within the walls of the townhouse.

So he had seen Analise home, and murmured an excuse and left again immediately. He had been walking for hours in the London streets, walking past pubs and dress shops and homes and churches, through squares and along parkways. Walking and walking and walking, to give himself what little peace there was to be found in movement.

It had been a terrible mistake to come to London, even for the benefit of his work. He had not thought what he would do when he arrived here, only let the force of his passion carry him here like a stormy sea. And now he gasped on the beach like a dying fish, unable to breathe or think or act in his own behalf.

His sin had ever been too much emotion; even his indulgent mother had worried over it. Too much love for the look and taste and feeling of things, too much sorrow for the sadness in the world, too much passion for the pleasure of food and women and drink. Excessiveness would lead to ruin, she admonished him, many times.

And what could this feeling in him be called if it not excessive? It was beyond excessive. It was the excess of excessiveness.

He had not felt like himself in weeks, his mind unbalanced by his yearning for one kiss from Cassandra's mouth, one moment in her arms. Day and night his mind was filled with a wilderness of images—her hair and her eyes and her laughter. When he slept, he dreamed of their limbs entwined; he awakened to the taste of ashes that it was not real. In the dark of night, he entertained a host of fantasies—all of them impossible. His duty, her duty, Analise, even their writing, stood between them.

Everything stood between them.

And nothing.

It did not seem to matter what stood between them; the passion remained. A pain went through him as he thought again of her eyes this afternoon, so sober and steady, sheened with tears as she listened to him read, translating the words back to Analise.

Only their eyes met, and they spoke in the secret language that was contained in his poetry—symbols none but she would know. He had not missed the hurried rise of her breasts as she gazed at him steadily, and he thought it was the first time she had ever heard the poem.

His feet inevitably carried him to her tall house on Piccadilly Street. It was full dark, finally—he could not believe how late the light lingered here—and growing quiet. A dog barked distantly and Basilio heard the clopping of horses followed by the rocking of a carriage not far away. It did not turn his direction, and he looked back to Cassandra's house. He saw no lights in the front.

He stood there, wondering if he ought to simply go to the door and rouse her servant and insist that he be allowed in to speak with her. But no well-trained servant would let him in. And what could he say even if he were allowed in?

In sudden, mad inspiration, he walked to the garden gate and looked at the tree with branches leading to her balcony. He thought of Boccaccio, the story of a man who climbed a tree to his lover's room in the darkness, the first thing Cassandra had read to him that night in his villa.

He tried the gate and found it shamelessly unlocked. Then he was in the dark and cool of her private garden, smelling wallflowers and roses on the night. There was no light from her room, and he imagined himself creeping into the dark to her bed, like Anichino, the lover from Boccaccio—but he would frighten her.

Yet he was here, and his heart was pounding in recklessness and a freedom he had not known since that day she'd left him. Shedding his coat, then shucking his shoes and stockings so he could climb more easily, he leapt into the crotch of the tree and scrambled along the thick branch.

But this was beyond reckless, beyond passion—his love had driven him purely insane. What sort of man allowed his emotions to carry him to such a blatantly dishonorable act? How could he make love to her when he was wed to another? No, that was the act of a man he would loathe.

Feeling heat in his cheeks, he scrambled back down and sat at the base of the tree on the cold damp ground, despair washing through him in vast waves. He would leave London now, return to Italy, attempt to make a life of some beauty with Analise. He did not think desire would ever be part of their union, but perhaps they should both overcome their distaste for sex and indulge enough to have some children. She would be a good mother, devoted and kind.

He saw his life stretching ahead of him, calm and ordinary. He would tend his estates and raise his children to follow after him. He would grow fat like his father, and spend too much time drinking wine on summer nights, remembering a season of great beauty, remembering the poetry that had come from him in that time, spilling out as abundantly as water from a spring.

Perhaps then, this was all. It was not so bad. He had known great love; he had written beautiful poetry. And he would not be going back to poverty or to a shrewish wife who made his life a misery. He was rich and his wife was sweet, and there were many, many men who had never known those blessings. He had been quite blessed.

Still, he wanted to roar out his rage at the loss of the beauty and the words and the love. That politics should have made a mockery of three lives, three passions. It was beyond unfair. It was deepest cruelty.

He stood and bent to pick up his shoes. A noise from above halted him, sent him to hide in the shadows.

Cassandra drifted out onto her balcony. She was cloaked in something white that blew in the soft breeze of the night, and her hair was loose, flowing over her shoulders and arms and back. She came to the railing and rested her elbows on it, her face lifted up to the night. Around her was that profound stillness. Her hands rested together, utterly calm.

A pale wash of moonlight illuminated her face, and Basilio saw that she was weeping silently. The tears streamed over her cheeks, making spikes of her lashes.

He stepped out of the shadows and quietly began to speak. "These are the moments of a poet's heart: a plum, a star, a woman's shoulder, shining in moonlight."

The stillness in her body rippled, and she peered into the darkness. "Basilio?"

It was no accident that he was here. With a swell of joy, he scrambled up the tree again, unquestioning. He nearly ran the length of the branch, feeling it sway dangerously as he reached the end, and he made a leap for the solid footing of her balcony floor. Then he stood there, words gone, only looking at her.

She stared at him for a moment, and he could not tell if she would laugh or scowl. Then suddenly she was flying toward him, and Basilio caught her in his arms tightly, a small cry coming from him as her body, which he had thought never to hold again, pressed hard into him.

And then they were kissing, kissing madly, deeply, both of them weeping, salt on their lips and tongues, their hands touching hair and backs and waists and hips in renewal, in joy, in hunger.

The broke apart, gasping. "I came home and read your poems," she said softly. "I couldn't bear it before, but tonight I couldn't bear not to." Tears welled in her eyes. "They're so beautiful, Basilio."

Basilio touched her face, stroked her skin, drank in the depth of her dark eyes. "And every word is devoted to you, my love."

Her hands went to his face, to his hair. "I know," she whispered. She leaned forward and put her forehead against his neck, and a long, broken sigh came out of her.

It shattered him. Very gently, he kissed the top of her head, stroked the long length of her back, felt her hair slide over his fingers; his body flooded with so much emotion he almost couldn't breathe.

And if that had been all, it might have been enough to appease him. But their embrace grew warmer, and he felt her breasts, free beneath her nightrail, pressing into his ribs, felt her back arching a little under his hands.

Suddenly she stiffened and the face of Analise rose in his mind. She pushed a little against him, and with shame in his heart, he let her go. "Cassandra—"

She shook her head. "We must not sully what was, with something as tawdry as this." Her eyes shone with sorrow. "I do love you, Basilio. But this cannot be."

He bowed his head. "I know." But he could not quite let her go. "I miss your company. There is no one like you in the world, and we do not have to let that go. Can we not just sit here under this moon and talk?"

She wavered.

"I give you my word that I will not touch you again."

She took a breath and smiled softly. "No,

Basilio. Not like this." She moved away, her posture very straight and sure. "Go home, my love, so you do not have shame to haunt you the more."

"She does not love me, Cassandra."

Her smile was sad. "So say all men who have wives, to the mistresses they would take."

Anger rose in him. "You spoke with her. You know I do not lie."

"Yes," she said. "And I know you cannot bear the appearance of lies. If we do this thing, guilt will devour you. And me."

He turned to go, but it gave him a tearing sense of resistance, and he halted. "No. Not this." He backed against the balustrade, his hips firmly anchored to cold metal, and crossed his arms. "You stand there, on the other side. We are friends, Cassandra, no more. We will not indulge our passions."

Sadly, she smiled. "You must be stronger than I, for it will be too difficult for me, too dangerous, to face you under the temptation of a moonlit night." She shook her head. "I am not that honorable."

"Ah." Clambering over the rail, he said, "Then I will go out to this branch, far from your greedy hands, and we can talk that way. Yes?"

She laughed softly. "Very well." When he made his way on to the branch, she made a squelched, terrified noise. "Be careful!"

Settling easily in the dip of the branch, grasping a handhold on a neighboring arm, he said, "So—shall we compose letters?"

"Letters?"

"Yes." He lifted his head, a warmth in his heart, and said, "Dear Cassandra: I have been meaning to write to you about this wonder that is your city. It is not like any place I have ever visited before. It is not a woman, this city," he said with cocked head. "He is a shipshape old colonel, with a thick mustache, who smokes too many cigars."

Her laughter, low and devastatingly alluring, rang out. "Dear Basilio: I had not thought that before about London, but you are right to some measure, though I have glimpsed the woman of London, too. She is mysterious and wise and very old, hiding secrets in her bosom from long ago, letting out only little bits of magic for the odd mystic willing to listen. If you are quiet on Midsummer Night's Eve, you can hear her singing along the river."

"I would like to hear that singing."

"Yes, you would like it." She leaned on her arm, her hair spilling down over the railing. "Dear Basilio," she said quietly, "I have been wanting to write to you about Venice."

He went still, waiting, a little ache in his heart that she had seen it without him.

"When I think of it," she continued, "I remember the red-streaked sky at sunset. The way fire seems to hang in the sky and dance on the water." She made a soft noise. "And you. I think of you when I think of Venice. You were with me every step. Every moment."

He pressed hands into the bark of the tree. "I wish that I had been, that I'd seen her with you the first time."

But he had been at home in Tuscany with his wife. "This is such madness, Basilio."

There was too much tension building between them, and he lightened his voice. "Oh, yes, madness." He laughed softly. "Tonight, I nearly climbed into your bedroom and was halfway up the tree when I stopped, and thought I must have gone insane. And I climbed back down."

"Did you really?"

"I was thinking of Anichino," he said with a rueful laugh. "Do you remember? You read his story to me that first night, in Italian, and you spoke of sex and I was already dizzy with wanting you, but I wanted you to be free to speak of sex, too."

"I remember."

He looked at her. "I sat beneath that tree, and I thought I should go home to Tuscany, hold my memories in my heart, and take up the life of a normal man. And then you came out, with tears on your face—tears I knew were for me. Is that a sign?"

"A sign of our dishonor, perhaps," she said with a broken sigh. "Or that we have been seduced by the devil—because your wife is

God's own. Even I saw that in the course of a single hour."

"She is that. And it weighs on me at times."

"Weighs on you? How so?"

"What if my work was to resist this marriage with her, to stand strong against forces that were not in alignment with God's wishes? What if you were sent to keep me from marrying her, and I was not strong enough to stop it?"

"You did try."

"Not quickly enough. Not when I first knew." It troubled him still. "She missed my letter by only one day."

A soft sigh. "Then she was not meant to have it."

He shrugged.

As if it troubled her, too, Cassandra said more lightly, "Do you know, Basilio, I think you've upset all of London with your passion? Even my brother has an odd gleam in his eye these days, a spark of something that has been missing."

"A season's entertainment," he said dismissively.

"Oh, no. More than that." Earnestly she rose on one elbow. "So much more. I had not read them before this afternoon, it's true. I was afraid. But after I came home, I read them. All of them." A wave of emotion rose in her throat. "They are so beautiful."

"They are all for you, Cassandra," he said.

"I know," she whispered. "You must go now,

Basilio. Good night." She hurried inside, a wraith, a missed destiny, and closed the doors behind her.

He made his way back down, his thoughts bemused. What if his suspicion were correct? That Analise was meant to take her vows and he'd been meant to stand up to their fathers, and that Cassandra had been sent for that purpose?

He put his shoes and coat back on, and let himself out of the gate. If it were so, how could he put things right now?

And how could he ever discover the truth of God's will, with his own desires and selfish needs in the mix?

He walked all night, puzzling it. By morning he knew only that he must try.

Analise, her head covered in a cap, a basket on her elbow, had a pair of scissors with her in the garden. Though a man was paid to tend the place, Analise had asked him to leave the task of cutting the flowers and trimming herbs to her. Every morning, she brought out this basket and rounded the neat beads, cutting off spent blooms and choosing flowers for vases. It was a most pleasant activity and reminded her of the days at the cloister, when she could pause and pray to the saints who stood sentinel around those courtyards. There were none here, but Analise put offerings to St. Catherine at the foot of a fountain. Sometimes she thought the place was under the benevolent eye of St. Francis, for it was filled with birds and little animals who grew brave with her, even if the cat and dog had come with her, which they nearly always did.

She was kneeling to trim a lavender plant into a neat round when a sudden skittering of squirrels told her an intruder lurked. She raised her head to see Basilio come through the garden gate in the golden morning.

A Basilio she had never seen.

His hair fell loose down his back, a wild tumble of extravagant curls, and his coat was flung over his shoulder, held with one careless finger. He did not see her and she didn't call attention to herself, struck by some new aura that surrounded him, as golden as a halo. He moved loosely, slowly, pausing to lift his head to the sunlight, his eyes closed, a benevolence of expression on his beautiful face. Unselfconsciously, he plucked a rose and held it to his nose, his thoughts deep within.

Analise smiled to herself. Here was the Basilio she remembered from childhood. Though he'd outgrown his boyish softness, there was that bemused wonder in his expression, all the more pleasing in contrast to the dark bristles of unshaved beard of his chin.

"Good morning!" she called. "If you like to smell things, come sample this lavender."

She startled him into a different mode, and was immediately sorry. The wonder disappeared under a guarded sobriety. He smiled politely and came toward her, his limbs not so loose now, but stiff with—what? Guilt, perhaps?

It made her smile all the more. Although the world tended to confuse her chosen purity for stupidity, she was not uneducated to the ways of men and women. Animals and birds and humans, all were driven to mate, and she was wise enough to understand that Basilio's expression this morning was one of a man who had been with a lover. Did he think she would mind?

She rose and held out a trio of lavender blossoms. "You looked very happy when you came through those gates, Basilio. I hope I did not chase that contentment away."

He could not quite look at her. Distantly, she admired the cut of his bold nose beneath that broad brow—a striking face. "No, no," he said. "I was—I—" He shrugged. "I walked. All night."

Analise did not allow a chuckle; it would mortally offend him. Instead, she turned her attention to a sturdy stand of rue and broke off a handful of last year's seed pods. "These, too," she said. "Smell them. I love them."

He followed her instruction, holding the crushed pods in his palm. "Very nice."

"It is good to see you less sorrowful, Basilio," she said, smiling.

Guilt—yes it was!—flickered over his eyes. He bowed his head. "I should never have brought you to England."

"Nonsense," she said briskly. "I am learning new things. That is good for me." Picking up her basket, she made her way toward the doors. "Come. I am sure you must be very hungry." This time, she could not help a faintly ribald smile.

Perplexed, he only looked at her for a moment. "You are as puzzling to me now as you were as a child."

She shook her head. "The only puzzle is that there is no mystery, Basilio. I am exactly what I appear to be, and that is most unusual."

"I suppose it is."

"You needn't look for anything more than what is, I promise."

He smiled, and it was a smile that went all the way to his eyes. Slinging one arm around her shoulders like a brother, he said, "Well, I am very hungry, Analise. I want a breakfast big enough for a boar."

Pleased, she said, "That we can do."

Chapter 17

Cassandra slept deeply and without dreams, as if she had not slept in months. When she awakened, it was to full midday sun flooding her chamber. She blinked in surprise. The scent of roses reached her, and she spied the spray of flowers on the pillow just as a knock sounded at her door.

Startled, Cassandra realized a first knock must have wakened her. "Go away!" she called, unwilling to drag herself completely into the world just yet.

The door burst open. "I've traveled a grueling number of miles, and I will not go away."

Cassandra scrambled for her covers, as her sister Adriana sailed in the room, statuesque and buxom. "Riana!" she cried, half-mortified, half-joyful. The joy won out and she reached one arm toward her sister, keeping herself covered with the other.

Riana embraced her, then lifted an eyebrow. "Naked, are you? And your lover has just departed through the doors?" She made a show of going to the window to peek out. "Must be quite a dashing fellow."

She *was* naked, much to her shame. Over-heated and burning with longing for Basilio, she had tossed off her nightrail and slept nude, as she had with him, feeling a delicious sense of wickedness and freedom in the act.

"No lover," she said.

Adriana turned. "Yes, you have." She inclined her head. "I've never seen you look so beautiful, Cassandra. Whoever he is, I like what he's done for you."

A wave of emotion seized Cassandra, and to her horror, she felt as if she might weep and spill everything to her sister. With an act of will, she lowered her eyes and lifted one brow artfully, pressing her thumb into a thorn.

"Not talking, as usual, I see," Adriana said, and there was warmth in her voice. "I'll send your maid and you must come have breakfast. I only have the day."

"What are you doing here?"

Adriana's smile faded. "I've come to take Phoebe with me to Ireland for a little visit. Julian wrote; he's concerned about her."

"I see." She must be very selfish indeed, if she had not realized Phoebe was not doing well. Just younger than Cassandra, Phoebe had taken a fall from a horse a little more than a year ago, and although she'd spent a long time in bed healing a broken leg, Cassandra thought she'd been back to her normal routines for some time now. "Julian said nothing to me." She plucked the coverlet. "I suppose I have not given him an opportunity."

"You mustn't feel guilty," Adriana said. She sailed across the room and settled on the edge of the bed. "Phoebe would not like your life in London, as you know well. Julian only thought of me because Phoebe will love it there so much. You know she will."

Cassandra frowned. "But if she is as stiff as she was the last time I saw her, she won't like the travel at all."

"No, I expect she'll protest." A secret little smile. "Until I tell her there's a baby on the way."

"A baby!" Cassandra cried. "When?"

Riana cast off her cloak, turning sideways to show off the mound of her belly. "I'm very clever at disguising it, but it won't be long. Fall, I expect."

Cassandra laughed and, grasping the coverlet about her body, jumped up to hug her. "Oh, how utterly wonderful, Adriana! I'm sure your husband is beside himself with glee." She suddenly remembered that Tynan had been a twin. "Oh, God! What if you have twins?"

Riana waved a hand. "What will be will be." She laughed and touched Cassandra's bare shoulder. "Now stop scandalizing me"—a wicked lift of her brow, since Adriana had caused enough scandal for ten women—"and come downstair."

"All right."

When Adriana had left her, Cassandra stood in the middle of the room, wrapped only in the coverlet. Sunlight poured in on her from the glass doors, and she remembered another morning, in Basilio's chamber, high in the villa.

She closed her eyes and let the coverlet drop to the floor. Sunlight bathed her naked body and she remembered the love that had poured over her, through her, from her. Last night's single kiss had left the smell of him on her hands, her body, and she did not want to wash it away. Yet it was beyond wickedness not to. It had been wrong to kiss him, and she was shamed this morning at her lack of control. She pinned up her hair, put on her clothes, and left the secret of Basilio carefully in her chamber, where no one could disturb it.

She would not see him again.

The situation was clearly impossible and wrong, and would tear them both to shreds if it was not ended. Perhaps she could go to Ireland with her sisters for a little while, or spend a few weeks at Brighton. Julian had said that running would make her run forever, but the truth was, she had no will to resist Basilio, and no wish to betray Analise. Even the thought of the sweet, earnest child gave her a pang.

She closed her eyes, a hand over her heart.

What a coil! If she were the sort of woman who prayed, she would have asked forgiveness for her weakness the night before, for not being able to make him leave her.

She would depart London this very day, but before she left, she intended to make one thing right. She would teach Analise how to love a man. No, not a man—to love Basilio. Analise was beautiful and kind, and in time, Basilio would forget the headiness of what had transpired during the season they had shared, but it would make Cassandra happy to know he was being well-tended by his wife.

She arranged her face to hide her heart, and went downstairs to join her sister and celebrate the happy news.

Word was sent around to Julian and Gabriel, who joined Cassandra and Adriana for tea in mid-afternoon. The day was mild and sunny, the sky as blue as a length of silk. A white wrought-iron table was set on the lawn. Overhead birds sang cheerfully and bees whirred, and Cassandra discovered that she was quite content, in a sleepy, almost lazy way, to admire the world and everything in it, especially her beautiful siblings.

Julian, his fair good looks given an air of mystery by that air of haunted tragedy lurking behind the gray eyes; Adriana, as blond and radiant as a painting; Gabriel so rakishly dashing with his lush hair and caramel complexion, the green eyes catching color from his emerald green coat.

Cassandra sipped her tea and thought of standing with Basilio on the beach in Italy, water washing over her toes as she told him of her siblings.

Then she thought of the long hours they had spent talking, talking, talking. She missed that now—the long, rambling conversations they'd had. She thought of him crying out in mock outrage as they discussed a particular work of literature, disagreeing exuberantly with her as they ate olives and grapes beneath a soft, star-studded sky.

"Ah, look her," Adriana said. "Do you think our sister is in love?"

Cassandra looked up, aware suddenly that she had been drifting in memory with a soft smile on her face. She straightened and rolled her eyes. "Don't be absurd. I'm not the type."

Gabriel laughed and leaned close to Adriana. "Do you know she arrived at my door at the crack of dawn one day, demanding a book of poetry?"

Cassandra felt heat at the top of her ears and hoped they were not as red as she suspected. "It was hardly the crack of dawn. It was past ten!"

"Poems?" Adriana said. "What poems?"

Cassandra took the offensive. "Basilio de Montevarchi," she said. "An Italian count. He's quite the rage at the moment." She avoided their eyes by plucking a thread off her skirt. "Quite beautiful work, really. I heard him read at Court yesterday."

Only then did she spare a glance at Julian. He gave her the barest nod of encouragement. "I've read them, as well. You'd like them, Riana—they're very much the sort of thing you've always swooned over."

But Riana knew too much. Her eyes brightened. "Is it the same poet you visited in Italy, Cassandra?"

She raised her chin coolly. "Yes. Which is why I was so eager to have a copy of his book when I heard it had been published."

Gabriel leaned back, his hands steepled in front of his mouth. Cassandra was not at all sure if Julian or Adriana had read the travel essays, but she knew Gabriel had. He'd complimented her on it. Now speculation lit his eyes.

Damn. Julian knew, because he'd been with her at the opera when she fell apart.

And this morning Adriana had caught her naked, and though she'd not had her lover there, Adriana would certainly not be convinced of that.

She narrowed her eyes. "Do not," she said. "Do not spin little plays in your head about my life. I will not tolerate it."

Gabriel winked and Adriana chuckled. Only Julian seemed to hear the panic in her voice.

Smoothly, he leaned forward to pluck a tiny sandwich from the plate. "On another subject, Cassandra has been urging me to bring the girls to Court in the fall. What do you think, Riana? Is it time?"

Adriana let herself be distracted. "More than, I'd say."

"Tell him how much work there is to this, Riana. He will not listen to me."

"I have been enquiring," he said. "We will begin next month, I suppose."

"What, exactly," Gabriel said with deceptive laziness, "do you intend to do with Cleo? They cannot be presented as equals, and she will be wounded."

"I have been giving that some thought," Cassandra said. "I believe we shall find her a good husband in your set, brother dear. We'll bring them to my salon, and she will find men of color and good standing there."

"I don't think this is going to be as smooth as you think," he said, and a rare flash of anger tightened his lips. "She has been coddled and treated like a princess her entire life. She'll not easily settle for a tradesman when Ophelia marries a duke or an earl."

"Surely there is someone more suitable than a tradesman," Cassandra protested. "A scholar or a vicar."

Gabriel looked at her. "Cleo, a vicar's wife?"

"Well, perhaps not." She was a vain, pretty

thing, with a taste for clothes. "Then guide us, Gabriel. What shall we do?"

"I don't know," he said, and stood, his back to all of them. "I cannot curse our father for his goodness, but it would have been better if Cleo had been prepared for the life she truly will lead."

Adriana sighed. "We've all known this day would come. Your mother will guide her; Monique is not a fool. We shall heed her advice." She settled her cup. "At any rate, it cannot be avoided. They must find husbands and 'tis better to do it now."

Gabriel nodded, but his mouth still held grimness. "This has been a worry in my heart since our return. I'd not wish on her my own discoveries."

Julian rose. "She has us all, Gabriel. And you." He gestured toward the house. "If we are to arrive at Hartwood Hall before dark, we must be on our way. Are you coming, Cassandra?"

"Not today," she said. "I'll ride down in the morning. There is some business I must attend this evening."

He nodded. As he passed, he put his hand briefly on her shoulder in understanding and strength. Cassandra touched his fingers, just as briefly, in gratitude.

It was not a lie. She did have business. At supper, she donned a dark blue silk cloak that covered her hair, and walked to the address she had gleaned from an acquaintance.

Standing across the street in the shadow of a doorway, she waited patiently until Basilio emerged and climbed into a waiting carriage. After the vehicle was out of sight she moved briskly, tossing off her hood as she crossed the busy thoroughfare.

A servant in red livery opened the door to her. "Good evening," Cassandra said, "I am the Lady Cassandra St. Ives, and I've come to call on the Countess."

He let her into the house, which smelled of oranges and a spice she didn't recognize, and into a small parlor fussily decorated in the Chinese fashion. "Wait here," he said. "I'll see."

As she had expected, it was Analise herself who entered, her face showing her eagerness. "Lady Cassandra!" she cried, coming forward to kiss her on both cheeks. "I am so happy to see you! Would you like some wine, some food? Please, come into the garden."

Until now, Cassandra had managed to keep her guilt and love carefully separated. But now even allowing herself to love Basilio seemed monstrous. Dressed tonight in a modest gown made of gray silk, her hair tucked under her cap, the girl was so painfully young and eager that Cassandra's heart wanted to break.

Somehow she would make this right, and pray

that her perfidy was never discovered. With a bright smile, she took Analise's hand. "I would enjoy that very much."

The courtyard was bricked and neatly lined with beds of flowers, and Cassandra paused a moment. "This is quite Italian, isn't it?"

"Yes! I suspect that is why my husband chose this one. I have spent much time telling him about the gardens at the convent, and this is quite like it."

"He is a very kind man."

They settled and Cassandra accepted a glass of wine. They spoke lightly of gardens and Cassandra's travels in Italy, and a little gossip.

Finally, Cassandra said, "I hope you will not think me too bold, Countess, but I have come with a purpose tonight."

"I suspected that you had." She folded her small hands in her lap. "Please—share what you like. I will not think you bold."

Cassandra took a breath. "I would like to speak to you about your husband."

Analise looked a little surprised, but she inclined her head. "Why?"

"I have been thinking about what you told me," she said. "That he has not . . . required you to attend the marriage bed."

Analise smiled. "But I think has a lover. I . . . felt her this morning when he returned."

Ah, guilt, guilt, guilt. "Oh, surely not."

"I do not mind," Analise said placidly. "Men have needs, no?"

"I suppose." This was not going the way she had expected. "But why not you? Of all the husbands God could have given you, he is quite rare."

The girl frowned, looking at the flowers before them. "His heart is given to another," she said. "I have known that since the beginning, since the first night, when he cut his finger and put blood on the sheets, then spent the whole night writing poetry." Her face was sober as she raised eyes the color of a pansy. "I sometimes sense that he is despairing when he writes like that."

Cassandra swallowed, her heart aching at this vision of Basilio—despairing and sorrowing, thinking of her. Could it be that they were all locked in some monstrous mistake? Some terrible prank by the gods? What if her actions here tonight sent it all careening out of control?

And yet what choice was there? Carefully, she asked, "What do you do at such times—when he is despairing?"

"I leave him alone. If I find him asleep, I cover him with a blanket. Sometimes I take him food."

"I think," Cassandra said quietly, "you must go to him, then. In his grief, he will turn to you."

Analise leapt up. "I cannot!" From a pocket in her skirt, she took out a rosary that she worked between her fingers as she paced, back and forth, in front of the little sparkling fountain. "I do not wish—"

"Does it frighten you?" Cassandra asked. "I was once very frightened of it, too. I learned a gentle man can create beauty from it. Basilio strikes me as gentle."

"No. He is too passionate. I would not like that."

It wasn't fear in her at all, Cassandra realized, but a very different sort of resistance. Stubbornness. Watching the girl pace back and forth, back and forth, she asked suddenly, "Do you mind if I ask why you were so intent to be a nun?"

Analise stopped and turned. "You will not believe me," she said with a faint smile.

"I might."

With an expressive little shrug, Analise said, "When I was a little girl, about four, I saw a vision of Mary. No one believed me, and I learned to never speak of it. Twice more she came to me, and all three times she said that I should go to the island cloister."

Cassandra carefully kept her expression blank. She did not believe in visions.

"The third time, I was six. It was summer," Analise said. She extended her hands, the rosary beads looped around one wrist. Her palms were white and surprisingly strong. "My hands bled for three days. My father was furious, but my mother took me to the priest, who said it was a miracle and they should thank the heavens for my calling."

Stigmata. Cassandra was startled and uneasy. She disbelieved miracles even more than she disbelieved visions. "Weren't you frightened?"

Analise lifted her face, and a radiance came from her. "No. I knew it was a way for the saints to convince my father to let me be a nun. At least it convinced him to let me go to the convent to be schooled."

"But—" Cassandra frowned. "Why you?"

"I don't know," Analise said. "Why is anyone chosen for anything? Why does my husband write such beautiful words? Why does one person sing sweetly and another tend children? We are all called to serve in some way. This is mine."

Cassandra resisted the sense of fate inherent in those words. "But I was not born for anything in particular," she said.

"Of course you were. We all are."

"Men, perhaps," she said. "Not women, Analise. We are at the mercy of men's will."

"But God is greater than men's will." She said it with such assurance that Cassandra was bewildered.

The whole conversation had slipped out of her control. A strange ball of tension and confusion settled in her chest, and she struggled to remember why she had come—to urge Analise to be a proper wife to Basilio. Squaring her shoulders, she said, "If that is so, if God leads you to a marriage He did not prevent, then is it not His will that you should be a wife, not a nun?"

Her eyes grew troubled. "I don't know. I have thought this over many times, and have no answer. If I were meant to be a wife, would not my husband have insisted upon our joining?"

Cassandra's confusion grew. "But if that husband knows you do not wish to indulge him, and he is kind, then how do you know you are not thwarting God's will?" She frowned at the convoluted logic of her words, but could not think how to fix them.

Analise began to pace again. "I want to be dutiful," she said. "But to whom do I owe my highest allegiance?" She halted. "It must be God, but I do not know His will for me in this. So who, then, should I obey? My father? My husband?" She rubbed a thumb over the beads with agitation. "Dare I even choose?"

"You are married, Analise," Cassandra said around the lump in her throat. "God allowed the marriage, and there must be some plan in it. So your allegiance goes to your husband, toward being his wife."

Analise bowed her head. "I had not thought of it that way."

The child made Cassandra feel a million years old, and inutterably jaded. "Think on it," she said. "Speak to a priest."

"I wanted so little," Analise said suddenly, and her voice was fiercer than Cassandra would have expected. "I wanted to spend my days worshipping God. Why could not such a simple thing be granted?"

"I don't know," Cassandra said honestly. She held out a hand. "Come. We'll speak no more of it." Inspiration struck. "I have another matter I'd like to speak of, and I would like your advice. You seem very wise for one so young."

"I will be glad to listen," Analise said. "What is it?"

So Cassandra told her about her sisters, Ophelia and Cleopatra: one blond and more beautiful than any woman in London; the other as beautiful as midnight but of mixed race, and doomed to disappointment on the London social scene.

From there, they moved to other subjects, until darkness forced Cassandra to take her leave, wishing she had met this wise, strange girl in any other way but this.

By morning, it would all be done. To quell the rising grief she felt, she walked briskly, her cloak billowing out behind her. Her actions were guided by love, a love large enough to be unselfish, and she could take some small comfort in that.

Why then did she feel so dirty?

Basilio had been restless all day, trying to think of some answer to his problem. He had to continue his protection of Analise; he could not live with himself if he did not. Which meant that Cassandra could never be his wife.

But he could not believe such a love had been visited upon them only to be taken away. There was an answer, he only had to convince Cassandra it was the right one.

As he walked toward her house, anticipation made his heart light. His blood sang Cassandra's name, his heart sang her song. He felt foolishly lightheaded, and glad to be alive.

A carriage stood before her door, and he saw her come out, dressed for departure in her violet traveling coat. He rushed forward, heedless of how it might look.

"Cassandra!"

She saw him and stiffened. For a long moment she only stood on the step, her face very white in the darkness. She directed the servant to carry her bag to the carriage, then walked with cool purpose toward Basilio. Anger rose in him—how could she turn her emotions on and off this way? Love him, leave him, so easily?

"Where are you running now, Cassandra?" he asked harshly.

"We cannot betray your wife this way, Basilio. I cannot bear the guilt."

"We are betraying nothing! You know this, you heard it from her own lips. I do not lie with her. She has not been wife in any form. I married to protect her, and I will continue to do that. But you"—he took her arm—"you are my true wife, and you know this."

"So what do you suggest, Basilio?"

"You are a widow. I am tied by family to a woman who will never be a wife in truth to me." He slid his hand to hers, then lifted it to his lips. "Ours is so common a situation as to cause no stir anywhere. Who would fault us?"

"You want me to be your mistress."

"I dislike the word—it sounds soiled. And our meeting is not."

She took her hand away, shaking her head. "You knew before you asked it that I would not engage in such an arrangement." He saw the effort she expended to remain cool. "I will not be your mistress, Basilio. And you already know that in your heart."

He closed his eyes. He *had* known it, had known it always.

"Go, Basilio," she said.

"Do not do this. Stay," he pleaded.

"I am not strong enough to only look at you. It is for my own honor that I leave."

Pierced, he stepped back. "There is an answer, Cassandra. There must be."

"Yes," she agreed, tugging on her glove. "You must return to Italy."

Stubbornly, he lifted his chin. "That I will not do."

Without a word, she turned and hurried to the carriage, allowing her man to help her up. When she rode by, she did not look out the window at him.

Chapter 18

He returned to the townhouse, walking to exorcise the twin demons of anger and thwarted passion. By the time he climbed the steps to his own house he was no longer stubbornly angry, only restless, doubting his own sanity again.

From the first, it had been this way with her. A madness in him. A swell of passion and music and beauty that made him heedless, like a youth. He scowled, thinking of his mad run down the hill to kiss her in the orchard that first time.

He thought back even further to the moment he had first seen her on the road below him, her hair glittering in the sunlight, her face so astonishingly beautiful that his heart nearly stopped. In that moment, he had known.

He should have sent her away that first day. Then they would still be writing letters. He would still be smiling when he read them and wrote them. There would have been none of this misery for them if he had been strong enough to send her away that very first day.

But there would have been none of the joy, either. The joy that had made life seem so precious he nearly could not bear it. The joy that had lit her face, and shone from her limbs. Even now he could see that knowing him had transformed her—she was stronger, braver, more alive. He had taken away her demons, given her the courage to reach for true freedom.

So, then, was he only a pawn in some game God played? Had he been only an instrument on her path?

No. For there had also been poetry born of those days. Perhaps that, too, was part of God's plan: to allow him to write beautiful things, to take him farther than he had gone before. Cassandra had been his muse.

But what now? What now?

When he arrived at his townhouse, he saw with surprise that a brace of lights still burned in the sitting room Analise favored. He stopped at the door to find her bent over her sewing in the poor light. Her hair was caught in a long black braid that fell over her shoulder, and it occurred to him that he had never seen the full wealth of that hair. He imagined it was beautiful.

She did not look happy to see him—or perhaps only did not look happy. Her features were pale, and shadows lay under her eyes. "Is something wrong?" he asked.

"No. Should there be?"

He smiled slightly. "It is very poor light for sewing. You'll squint like a witch as an old woman."

"I was only thinking. Sewing helps me to think."

He sat in a chair nearby, relieved to have something else to put his mind on. "Think of what?"

"Many things." She let the sewing drop into her lap. "How I came to be sitting here, instead of my little room at St. Catherine's. How I never dreamed I should speak to a queen." She paused and looked at him intently. "I was wondering, too, what you think of. I never ask you."

A nudging of warning edged into his chest. "Many things. Did you have a subject in mind?"

"The arrangement between us."

He leapt up. "I do not think on that." He crossed to a sideboard, where a decanter of port sat. He poured a measure. "Are you displeased?"

"No." The word was slightly surprised. "I suspect you are."

He drank the liquor, letting it hurt his throat, burn away his guilt. "Perhaps we should return to Italy," he said, and filled the glass again recklessly. "Would you like that?"

"Of course. But are you ready to return so soon?"

"Yes." He would remove himself from temptation. In a year's time, when things had mellowed, when they could bear it, he would begin writing letters to Cassandra again. They did not have to forget everything. He would stay safely in Tuscany and she would remain in England, and their love could transpire entirely on paper.

He closed his eyes. He did not hear Analise move, and he started when she put her hand on his arm. "Basilio?"

There was a note in her voice that he'd not heard. He opened his eyes to look at her, seeing now the hesitant offering in her eyes.

She raised on her toes and pressed a kiss to his mouth. A dry, chaste, cold kiss. The kiss of a child.

And although he felt the wealth of her breasts, the invitation in her small, ripe body, the only emotion it engendered bordered on horror, as if a sibling had kissed him.

He pulled back sharply, and saw the hurt in her eyes. He reached for her, but it was too late. She slid away, humiliation in the bend of her neck. "I'm sorry," she whispered. "I thought I might . . ."

What a beast he was! Urgently, he took her arm and enfolded her body into a tight embrace, resting his head on her hair. "Oh, Analise, it is I who should be forgiven. I did not mean to hurt you."

She began to weep, and it shredded him. "Forgive me."

He put his fingers beneath her chin and raised her face. He thought he should kiss her, but while her lips were pretty and he felt the woman-liness of her form, he could not bear it. He chastely kissed her cheek.

A soft little sound came from her, relief or sorrow, he couldn't tell. She pushed away from him. "No, I am the one who is wrong in this, Basilio. I wish I wanted to, but I do not. It feels horrifying to me." Her blue eyes were bruised and wild looking. "It feels wrong. How can that be?"

"I don't know." He shook his head, turned to pour some port into a glass for her, and gestured for her to sit down. "Listen to me for a little while."

She took the offering, sat straight in her chair and met his gaze. "You are in love with a woman you are denied," she said. "I see it in your eyes. I hear it in your work."

"Is that why—"

"No." With an odd little gesture, she raised her hand and looked at her palm. "No."

Basilio bowed his head. "It is true, what you suspect. But it is an impossible situation. You and I must return home. And soon or late, we must make peace with what our fathers have arranged for us. We need only mate enough to have a child or two."

She only stared at him with those great, blue pansy eyes. "I do not think I can."

He smiled. In this, at least, he knew better. "Do not think on it now. We need not rush."

"Basilio, what of your love?"

Grimly, he looked at the ruby colored liquid in his glass, watching a candle flame shine in the depths. "I cannot speak of that. Not now. Not ever."

Her expression was troubled. "But I wish for you to be happy."

"What is happiness, Analise? And do we not each choose happiness or sorrow?" He lifted a shoulder. "We will find a way to be happy."

Her grave expression did not lift. She nodded, but there was no conviction in it.

At dawn, Analise set out early in the carriage to find a church. All night her conscience had tortured her, and she could not sleep at all. Over and over, she saw herself reaching up to kiss Basilio, saw over and over the horror in his face when she did it, felt again the relief his horror had given her.

Relief, not embarrassment.

Her instincts said there was more here than met the eye. She felt a sense of great urgency about the events that had been building the past few weeks, a warning of some tragedy in the offering, but could not pinpoint where it lay.

Perhaps that was only her own pride again, though; pride in thinking she knew what God

had in mind for her. It was a terrible sin of pride
to aspire to knowing God's wishes, was it not?
Yet if one did not earnestly seek that will, wasn't
that an even greater sin?

Did she simply accept what path had been
given to her, or—as she had begun to suspect in
the depths of night—had she been a coward
when it came to her calling? Perhaps she had
been called to fight for her right to choose to be a
nun, and in doing so, fight for others who might
long for the same path.

All night she thought of the lives of the saints
she most admired: Mary and St. Catherine and
even Magdalena. What would they have done?
Young girls and strong women, all of them. All of
them fighting for their faith.

Analise had not struggled at all; she'd only
given in and fallen to weakness and despair.
Despair, too, was a sin.

Pride, despair, lack of courage. She was rid-
dled with conflict, and could not make her way
through the maze alone.

In the church, she knelt in an empty pew and
began to pray earnestly. Even kneeling there gave
ease. The smell of dust and candles and a faint
lingering hint of incense surrounded her gently,
smoothed away the tightness in her shoulders.
When she heard a step on the stones of the nave,
she raised her head and saw the priest, a slim
man with a head of white hair and a kind face.

She bowed her head again at some inner

prompting, and there came what she thought of as the "Great Opening." She was no longer simply Analise, on her knees in a church in England. Once again she belonged to the great vastness, the great eternity, where there was no beginning and no end. She felt herself filled with light, with love, and she saw again the thing that had drawn her to this when she was only a small, small child: she saw the world, and all the people in it, as shards of that same, great light. Each burning with a rainbow of possibilities, each as perfect as the next.

It was more than she had words to express, and she clung to the sense of peaceful, immeasurable immenseness that was God and His Kingdom, for as long as it was granted to her.

In time, there would be answers.

When the vastness began to fade, Analise raised her head and found the old priest standing by her, a brightness in his blue eyes that she thought might be tears. With a gnarled hand, he touched her head in benediction. "Such a holy light surrounds you, child. Bless you."

Analise smiled, wholly at peace. In some way, she had the power to heal this rift, to prevent whatever tragedy was brewing. She saw clearly that this was a tangle of loves, like a mismatched tangle of flowers in the garden—all beautiful, but none able to thrive until they were properly divided and transplanted.

She had work to do today.

* * *

Basilio had not wakened until late, with a strange, urgent energy in his limbs. He might well be mad—but he could not, would not, give in so easily. And this morning, there seemed a host of possible solutions to the dilemma.

He breakfasted heartily, discovering that Analise had gone early to church and not yet returned, then ordered a horse and took it out on a hard ride, letting the wind blow away the heat of conflict, blow away the cobwebs of his tangled thoughts.

The facts, when examined coldly, were quite simple: Analise required protection. Cassandra would not be his mistress. He would not live his life without her.

So what answer existed that did not betray anyone? The thought gave him a headache. It seemed there had been no other question in his mind for months and months, and he circled it endlessly, finding no answer. The heedless youth in him wanted to annul the marriage posthaste. The man he had become knew it was simply not a possibility. His obligation to his family, to his line and his history, had been washed into his flesh since birth. The line ended with him, and his obligation to that land and that name was too great to turn his back on.

His mother, his brothers, Analise, his obligations, Cassandra. Over and over, with no end.

What did Cassandra want? He believed that

she loved him, but if he were free, would she marry him? Would she wish to tie herself to a man who had nothing but his heart and his pen to offer her? For if he annulled the marriage, he would have nothing. His titles would remain since his father could not take them, but he would be penniless, aside from what he could earn from his writings.

As he rode in the clean sunlight of an English midday, he decided he must find out her heart before he acted rashly.

To do that, he would have to discover where she'd gone.

Cassandra retreated from the giggles and noise and chatter of her sisters by going to her father's old study. She was glad she'd come to Hartwood Hall, but her melancholy mood had already drawn several comments. Brushing them off with pleas of a headache, she had come here.

The room still smelled of her father a little, in a lingering hint of old tobacco in the heavy velvet drapes. His books lined the shelves. A portrait of Cassandra's mother, painted when she was twenty-two and astonishingly beautiful, hung between two long shelves. As a girl, back on English soil after four years in Martinique, Cassandra had often wondered if Monique minded that the portrait hung where James St. Ives could look at it every day.

As she rounded the room, touching the books her father had loved, brushing her fingers over the edge of his heavy desk, she found herself thinking again of Monique, Gabriel and Cleo's mother. She had been the earl's mistress, off and on, for more than twenty years, and had not seemed to mind it. Cassandra had understood from a very young age—even when she was grieving the loss of her mother—that Monique had somehow saved her father. She'd also understood that he loved her.

And in all, they'd appeared quite content with the arrangement, neither of them asking something of society that it simply could not give. Cassandra wondered, broodingly if she were being churlish.

But there had been a difference: Cassandra's father had not had a mistress while his wife still lived. It was true he had loved two women, and loved each of them with the whole of his generous, stalwart heart, but not at the same time. Before he met his wife, he'd loved Monique and given her a son, and he'd granted them both their freedom. When he'd returned to England to take up the title upon the death of his brother, James had given up Monique for Cassandra's mother, his beautiful wife. Only when he'd had to bury that wife, distraught and sorrowing, had he turned again to Monique.

Cassandra flung herself into the leather chair

and stared at the picture of her mother. Ophelia, she thought distractedly, really was a spitting image of her.

A knock came at the door. "Cassandra?" Adriana poked her head. "Are you all right, my dear?"

Cassandra brushed a lock of hair from her face. "Only ill-tempered. I did not wish to mar the day with my poor humor."

"I see. Well, there is someone here to see you."

"Me? Who?"

Only then did she see the gleam in her sister's eye, the mischief and curiosity. A cold hand squeezed her heart before Adriana said, "A very dashing Italian poet."

Cassandra jumped up, looking for escape. Her heart thundered in her chest and her limbs screamed at her to run, but where? "I am not in," she said. "Tell him to go away. I will not see him."

"Too late," he said from behind Riana.

Cassandra bolted. She dashed through the door into the servant's hall, ran past the kitchen, and dashed into the corner stairwell, lifting her skirts to take the winding, old stone steps quickly. At the third level, she dashed into a tiny anteroom, yanked on the door, and found it stuck. With a cry of frustration, she kicked it, yanked again, and it opened into a dark supply room that now sat empty save for a forgotten trunk.

Gasping for breath, her flight instinct burned clean by the vigorous climb, she collapsed on the trunk and leaned her head back against the wall to catch her breath.

It was only then that she realized how insane it was to run from him. And right in front of Riana, who would no doubt have plenty to say about that. She had been acting impulsively quite often since he'd appeared in her life.

Emotion was a woman's downfall. She repeated the litany to herself, thinking how much he'd undermined that resolve in her life. He'd awakened her to the splendor of the senses, given her permission to be as passionate as he was, freed her to do something as wild as run madly through the halls and old passageways of the old castle.

With a little gulp, she started to laugh at her behavior. It began as a little chuckle, but then Basilio appeared, breathing hard, a lock of hair loose on his cheek.

Seeing her, he leaned on the doorway. "Thank God. It would have been rather humiliating to faint dead away in front of your sisters." With a mock gasp, he fell, sprawling on the floor, putting his hands over his heart. "Here, I must only humiliate myself in front of you."

The laughter had crept in deeper and wider, and by the time he fell on the floor Cassandra was howling, her hand over her mouth, the other around her ribs. She had no idea why it slayed her so, but she roared with laughter.

"You looked like a goat, you know," he said from the floor.

"No, no! A sheep!" she cried, and made a baa-ing noise.

He leaned on one elbow, chuckling. "I've never seen a red sheep." He lifted one dark, arched brow lasciviously. "But I would be more than pleased to be wolf to your sheep."

Cassandra caught her breath and sighed, wiping her eyes. "I have no idea why I bolted that way."

"I have that power over women, you know."

"They run, do they?"

"They lose their minds."

"Ah. So I shouldn't be too concerned that I've also lost mine."

Sitting up, he crossed his arms over his knees and looked at her, a straight and honest gaze.

And there he was, her Basilio, so simply, completely himself. She took a breath. "You have no idea how much I missed you. All those months."

"Oh, yes. I do."

"Why did you come here?"

"To chase you." He smiled ever so slightly.

Cassandra stood. "My sisters will be dying of curiosity if we do not go down immediately."

"Let them wait a little," he said. "I will not move from here until you listen to me."

She put a hand on her hip. "It is rather difficult to take you seriously when there are cobwebs in your hair, and I know your bottom is going to be as dusty as a baby's."

"Would you like to help me clean up?"

It felt so normal, so ordinary to be with him. She sank down next to him, shaking her head, and took his long, beautiful hand into her lap, holding it between her own. She touched the half-moon nails one by one, and traced the lines over his palm. "I am only free to be totally myself when I am in your company, Basilio. What accident of fate caused that to happen?"

"I do not know," he said. "In this moment, I am more myself than I have been since you left Tuscany." His mouth quirked. "I have no answers. But when I know you are close enough in the world that I can look into your face, I don't have the strength not to do it."

"And here we are, back to the beginning." That loose curl on his cheek called for her fingers to smooth it into place, but she resisted.

"Not quite. For it came to me that there is no crime in our loving one another as long as we are chaste." His liquid eyes were clear. "In honor, we are free."

"So simple," she said quietly. "And so very difficult."

"I am kissing you now," he said softly. "And you are kissing me in return. Our eyes kiss. And our hands. We know."

Her heart caught. "Yes," she whispered.

"In time, I must return to Italy—but until then, Cassandra, can we not be chaste in body and passionate in spirit? I can't bear to be away from you, to waste these days we do have."

She had not thought it was possible for her to love him more, but the rush inside filled her, making her dizzy. She swallowed. "How much time?"

A wash of regret crossed his face. "Probably only a week or two."

"All right, then. We will not waste it."

He smiled and stood, tugging her to her feet. "Come. It will be better if we do not spend too many minutes in private, tempting places. Introduce me to your beautiful sisters."

"Can you stay the night here?"

He paused to tuck a lock of her hair behind her ear. "No, but we have the afternoon. You can show me your home."

"I'd like that," she said.

"Do you have your seashell collection here?"

She laughed, surprised that he remembered. "I do."

"Then after your sisters have satisfied their curiosity, you can show them to me."

If she had been free, she would have kissed him then. Instead, she only tugged his hand, and they went back the way they had come.

Chapter 19

As she worked in her garden that day, Analise thought and thought how to discover Basilio's secret love and begin to put it together. The key, she suspected, lay in his poetry. But how could she unlock the English when she barely had enough of the language to greet people? Who could translate it for her?

The first and obvious solution was a dead end: Lady Cassandra was not at home. Analise pursed her lips in the carriage, holding Basilio's book of poems in her lap, trying to think what next to do. Surely someone in this city spoke Italian and English, and would not mind translating the poems for her.

The coachman waited patiently for her instruction, and while Analise puzzled over the problem, a man on a horse rode up, tall and swarthy and a little daunting-looking. With him was a man she recognized: Cassandra's brother, Lord Albury, equally severe and straight, his blond hair shining in the low gray day. He leapt easily from his horse and gave the other man his reins, then dashed up the steps to Cassandra's door. Drawn by the stillness she'd glimpsed in him that day at Court, Analise opened the coach door.

"Sir!"

As she climbed down, Lord Albury turned. She was struck by the simple elegance of the movement, and reached inside herself to see what appealed about that. As she approached he did not speak or move, only waited, and she thought perhaps it was the fact that he seemed completely aware—of himself; of the other man, who must surely be his half-brother; of the passersby and the taste of the wind. An unusual quality, particularly in an English lord, most of whom struck her as all too eager to drown away any impression of anything.

Analise struggled for words of English. "Hello," she said. His height and air of lethal grace made him a bit intimidating, and his gray eyes were as still as a pond at dawn. "Do you speak Italian?"

"Very little," he said in that language, but gestured to the other man, who dismounted and came over with an easy expression. And, she thought with an inward smile, some mischief about him. She liked him instantly.

The dark-haired man grinned and gave a short bow. "How may I help you?" he asked in her language.

She showed him the book she carried in her

gloved hands. "I am seeking someone to read me these poems in my own language. Where might I find such a person?"

His expression sharpened. "Are you the poet's wife? The Countess?"

"*Si.*" She smiled. "Do you know his work?"

He nodded slowly, then looked to his brother. Analise had the sense that they were both a little disturbed. "Will he not read it to you?"

"He would, if I asked," she said calmly. "For reasons of my own, I would like to know what they say myself."

"I see. A moment, if you please."

"Of course."

The men went a little way down the walk, their heads bent together. Lord Albury's hands were clasped loosely behind his back, while his brother gestured gracefully with one hand. In form they were much alike, with long limbs and broad shoulders, and she saw a likeness in their high cheekbones and beautifully sculpted mouths, but their coloring made them an extraordinary pair. She smiled. The ladies likely swooned at the sight of them.

At last Lord Albury nodded, and they returned. "Have your driver follow me," the dark-haired brother said. "I know a woman who might help you." He turned to the driver and gave him an address, then turned back to Analise. "Tell her Gabriel St. Ives sent you."

"Thank you." Before he could leave, she asked, "Are you the Lady Cassandra's brother, too?"

"Yes. How did you know?"

"She spoke of you."

A flicker of surprise went across the pale green eyes. "You know her?"

"She and my husband are acquainted," she said. "They are both writers, you know."

"Yes," he said. There was a faint wrinkling of his brow, then all expression was gone. "I do."

And in that short pause, Analise knew. It was so obvious that she felt a fool for not recognizing it before. Who else would Basilio love but a woman who was as passionate as he, who loved words and the world, as he did?

Lifting her chin against the press of emotion in her chest, she managed a smile. "Thank you for your assistance, sir."

He bowed in a courtly fashion. "The pleasure was mine."

The carriage moved, and Analise leaned back against the plushly appointed cushions and probed the emotion in her. Was it betrayal? Sorrow? Jealousy, perhaps?

No, none of those things. It was fear. A new, sharp, and terrible fear. She had been imagining a mild-mannered creature, an Italian beauty from the stage, perhaps, a woman unsuitable to Basilio's station.

She allowed the driver to take her to the address Cassandra's brother had given them, and took the poems inside to the severe-looking middle-aged woman who answered the door. When Analise gave her Gabriel's name the woman fluttered a little, and color touched her sallow cheeks, and Analise could not help but smile.

They sat together in a room that expressed the beauty the woman lacked—appointed in rich reds and lacquered blacks, with touches of brass and gold. It was a very sensual place, and as the woman began to read and translate Basilio's poems, Analise thought it was a perfect back-drop for it.

If there had been any doubt lingering in her mind that Cassandra was indeed the woman who held Basilio's heart, the poems removed it. Every word was drenched in the colors of the woman—the russet and red and gold of her hair, the whiteness of her face. And although not even one line said anything sexual or even anything about women, there was such voluptuousness to their spirit that Analise found her ears hot.

"Oh, my," the woman breathed. "This is extraordinary work."

Analise nodded. "It is, indeed." And all at once, she was filled with an inexpressible sense of joy. Of alignment.

Yes. She loved them. They loved her. They loved each other. Somehow their lives had been entangled, and Analise did not believe in coincidence. There was a reason, and it was left to her to discover it.

Cassandra let everything go for the space of that afternoon—all guilt, all sorrow—and let herself enjoy the company of this man who had so transformed her life. They walked the grounds of Hartwood, up the hills and across green meadows dotted with sheep, and settled on a hilltop beneath an ancient oak that was said to have magic in it. Basilio put his palms against it, whistling in admiration. "I have never seen such a tree!"

"I thought it was alive, when I was a child. That I could hear it speaking." She grinned.

"Like my grandfather chair!" His eyes crinkled at the corners. "And what did it say?"

"Oh, I don't know. Warm things. Fatherly things." She lay back in the thick grass and looked up through the branches. The leaves were so thick they were nearly a roof, with only the smallest chinks of light passing through. "I thought if I ever ran away, I would live here."

Basilio, too, fell back in the grass. His body angled away from hers, but his head was close enough she felt his curls against her ear. "Did you want to run away?"

"Not particularly." She folded her hands over her stomach. "But it did seem an exciting adventure in the novels I read."

"I wanted to run away with gypsies and dance all night long."

Of course he had. "You did not write a poem about gypsies. Now you shall have to."

"Mmm." The word was so lazy, she knew he was as sleepy as she. She closed her eyes. Birds twittered and insects hummed, and she could hear the distant shout of a man, perhaps working in his field.

Moments, Basilio had said. Perfect moments. This would be one she'd save: lying peacefully in the grass with Basilio nearby, his hair against her ear, his simple presence making her feel whole. Impulsively she reached for his hand, and found it coming toward hers. Their fingers twined and fell to rest.

Behind her eyelids, Cassandra saw plums, and then just the color of plums. She was aware of her banked need of him and was oddly content to simply feel it, rising and falling with her breath, pulsing now here, now there, as if looking for some break in the wall so it could come spilling out.

His thumb drifted over her index finger. Hers touched the heart of his palm. Love, pure as morning light, moved through her, and somehow mingled with the color of plums. "I think," she said quietly, her eyes still closed, "that Boccaccio would have liked days like this very much."

There was no answer, and Cassandra turned

her head to see if he'd fallen asleep. He had not. His dark velvet eyes were fixed on her face, steady and deep and full of love.

They moved at once, she scrambling to her feet with a pounding heart, he pulling his hand free, turning away from her. She brushed her skirts, giving him time, and realized with a sinking heart that they could not even allow this small measure of companionship. Danger and temptation lay at every turn. With a pricking of new loss, she turned away, trying to find the words to send him away, finally, for good. She felt him behind her, warm and close but not touching her. His breath wafted over her neck as he spoke. "My love," he whispered softly into her hair, "my love, my love. My only, only love."

"Stop."

"I cannot. It is the truest thing there is to say."

"There is no honor in it."

"Then perhaps I care no more for honor."

She shook her head. "If that were true, I would not love you. And God help me, Basilio, I love you with all my heart."

"Such an ordinary phrase."

A soft, breathy sigh. "She is so kind, so good, so . . . holy." She raised her head. "And she is beautiful, Basilio. Perfection. How can you bear to let her down?"

He met her eyes honestly. "She kissed me last night."

"And?"

"I felt her against me, her breasts and her woman smell. I tried to want to put my hands in her hair, and touch her body—"

"I do not want to know that much."

"But you opened this, and must listen now." He lifted his eyes to hers. "Analise is beautiful, and kind, and"—he frowned—"unique. I like her." His mouth tightened. "But touching her was like kissing a sister. It horrified me."

"It would not always be that way."

"Perhaps it would not. Perhaps I can learn. I want children. I want to do what I must—and if you had not appeared in my world as you did, perhaps it would have been bearable." He shook his head. "But it is not bearable now, and I do not know what to do, Cassandra. I look at it from every direction, and each way leads to trouble for one or the other of us." Slowly, he drew a leaf through his fingers. "We are trapped, all three of us, in a net of the world. I cannot leave her to the wolves who would devour her. Yet I cannot bear to think of my life without you in it."

"I sent her to you," she confessed suddenly. "I went to see her and urged her to be a real wife to you. I told her not to be afraid, that you would be a gentle and good lover to her."

"She did not care for it—the kiss." He looked up at the dappling of gold and green light above them, frowning. "I think that my mother was right to worry over her, and I must wonder why

God made a woman so beautiful who was meant to only serve Him."

"But to God, are we not all beautiful?"

He made a soft sound of laughter. "So we must be." He leaned close to her again. "But Analise was made for the pleasures of men. One man. God must know that, too."

"Perhaps He meant to teach a lesson to men: to stop trading on the physical attributes of women."

His lips turned down in surprise, and Cassandra had to smile. "You had not thought about that," she said.

"No." A faint scowl pulled down his brows. "But perhaps you are correct. And if that be so, what lesson then, for us?" The frown deepened. "For me?"

"I don't know," she said. "But surely if there is a lesson in Analise and her vocation, there must be a lesson to us, too."

"I am not a religious man," he said. "I dislike bowing to lessons or fate."

"But you opened the box," she said, reminding him of his earlier words. "And now must see it through. What lesson to us, Basilio?"

He watched the light play over Cassandra's hair, red and gold, and struggled for answers. He did not want to claim the lesson he thought was being given here—that the world had failed Analise, who wanted to serve only God, so it fell to Basilio to protect one of God's own. "I cannot answer. Were you brought to me so I might compose better work? Because I did. But then, what of you? What did you learn?"

Her face grew radiant. "I learned to be free, Basilio. I learned there are good and kind and honorable men in the world apart from my relatives. I learned there is beauty in moments." She took a breath, her hand fluttering to her throat. "I learned that making love can be beautiful."

"I wish there was some way to make this right, my Cassandra." He sighed. "I fear there is not— that we will spend our lives writing letters, thinking of this moment, and of those other moments we've shared." He tucked his hands behind him to avoid the temptation of touching her. "We will have children with others, and learn to be happy, but there will always be this part that is apart, separate. It makes me so sad to think of it."

"But maybe that's part of our lesson: to accept the moments we are given!"

"I had already learned that lesson."

Suddenly earnest, she stepped forward. "I do not much care for the male sex in general. I do not wish a husband." A faint crease appeared on her brow. "I wish I might have children, though. And you must promise to write to me of yours."

"Are we ending it this way, then? I will go back to Italy with Analise and give her children and write to you on summer nights?"

"I think we both know there is no other answer."

Cassandra stood with him by his horse as afternoon began to slant toward evening. Mindful of the all-too-curious eyes of her sisters that might be watching from the windows, Cassandra kept her hands clasped loosely behind her back. Basilio's mouth was tight with his own misery at this parting. She wanted only to go inside, take him to her bed, and lie there all night with him, making love and eating and talking.

"You must go," she said, taking a step backward to release him. "The road is not safe after dark."

"Cassandra, I do not think I can—"

"Do not say it. We both know you must."

He scowled. "What will anything be worth to me if I lose you? Nothing!"

"And I will mean nothing if you lose your honor," she said patiently. "We have been over this ground too often, my love."

He nodded, but Cassandra saw with a ripple of worry that he did not appear convinced. "Come to see me in London before you go," she said. "Bring Analise and we will have a farewell dinner."

He sighed, and with an obvious effort, changed his expression, lifting his eyebrows in a rueful expression. "How can we both care so much for the woman who stands between us?"

Cassandra smiled her agreement at the irony. "Go. She will worry if you are late."

Finally he mounted his horse and lifted a hand, and rode off down the road. Cassandra watched him, a thudding melancholy mixed with the joy of the hours they'd shared. She watched him until he was out of sight, then turned to the house. A figure stood on the steps, gilded by the long fingers of sunlight: her sister Phoebe, leaning on her cane, her pale brown hair kindly painted with gold by the sun.

Cassandra did not want to break the spell over her senses, and with any of her other sisters, would have stalked toward the house and brooked no question. But Phoebe was different, had always been different. She was the most like their father, and not only in appearance. The same depth of human understanding lived in her, the same kindness. One could not brush her off.

It pained Cassandra to see the lines of effort around Phoebe's mouth as she leaned on the cane, one hand pressed to her lower back. She had taken a nasty spill from a horse and broken her leg quite badly, which caused her still to limp, though the physicians said it would heal completely with time. The more serious and lingering malady was pain in her back, which Cassandra suspected was nearly constant. She could neither sit nor stand for long, but said walking helped her, so she hobbled with her cane and her dogs across the fields whenever the pain grew intense.

"Are you going to walk?" Cassandra asked.

"Yes. I was giving you a little privacy to part with your poet." She smiled, and Cassandra saw their father twinkling from the bright blue eyes. "Very dashing. I nearly swooned. Ophelia is still looking for the smelling salts."

Cassandra chuckled, grateful for the faint mockery in her words. "Ophelia faints over everything. You, on the other hand, have never swooned in all your life." She gestured toward the field. "Would you like a companion?"

"If you do not mind." She took Cassandra's elbow to get down the stairs, letting go when they reached open ground.

"When do you leave with Adriana?"

"Oh, of course, you didn't hear." She smiled happily. "We've had a letter from Leander this afternoon. He's on his way home, so I am not going to go to Ireland."

Leander and Phoebe had been very close as children, and exchanged long, frequent letters. "Phoebe, that's wonderful! When will he arrive?"

"I don't know." A spasm moved through her back, and though she tried to hold a straight face, Cassandra could feel the sudden rigidness in her body. When it passed, she took a breath and added, "He says he knows treatments for this malady that he's learned in India."

They both laughed. Leander was given to wild enthusiasms.

"It will be worth exploring."

"Yes." Phoebe looked at her. "So, do you wish to talk about him, this beautiful poet who is obviously besotted with you?"

Cassandra looked down the road with a pang. "I must marry," she said aloud, realizing the truth of it only as the words came from her mouth.

"Marry your poet?"

"Marry Robert Wicklow. If I do not, Basilio will throw away everything he holds dear, and he will hate himself, then me, and we'll be more miserable than we are now."

Phoebe touched her arm. "I see."

"It would shock you to know what has transpired between us," Cassandra said, an edge of defiance in her voice.

"Would it?" The words were mild. "Do you want me to be shocked?"

Cassandra smiled, caught. "For once in my life, the answer to that is no. I wish it could be honorable, that we could simply embrace one another and love with all our hearts. But it cannot be, and my honor requires that I let him go."

"So you intend to marry."

"Yes."

"But is that fair to the man you intend to marry?"

Cassandra thought of Robert's assurances, then lifted a shoulder. "I will tell him the truth and allow him to decide if he wishes to accept my bargain."

Phoebe was silent for a moment. "And can you be a faithful wife?"

Cassandra took her hand. "I can."

"Then it sounds a very . . . sensible decision, Cassandra. I hope it will make you happy."

A small, bitter smile. "My happiness will flee with Basilio."

"I never thought to see you in love."

"Nor did I," she said softly.

Chapter 20

C assandra returned to London only a half hour behind Basilio, and immediately sent a servant with a note for Robert. She had a bath and changed her clothes, and by the time he arrived, looking perplexed and curious, she was firmly in control.

"What is it, Cassandra? I came as soon as I could. Are you all right?"

"Please sit down," she said. "Would you like port? Tea?"

"Port at this hour, certainly."

Seeing him did not test her resolve—in fact, quite the opposite. He was tall and good-looking in a hale, solid English way that would age well. She enjoyed his company, his wry humor. Bedding him might at first be a little awkward, but she felt quite certain he would not be cruel. She settled across from him and folded her hands. "I have a proposition for you," she said, and laughed. "It's awkward, so I'm simply going to spill it straightaway."

He nodded, puzzlement still on his brow.

"You said the other day that you had hoped I might . . ." It was harder than she thought to do this. Bloody awful, actually. "That you had feelings for me."

A glint of light in his eye. "I believe I hung my heart on my sleeve and more or less asked you to consider marriage." He sipped his port, looking at her carefully. "Dare I hope you might be considering my suit?"

"You also said that you would require no declaration of love from me. Did you mean it?"

"Are you in some sort of trouble?"

She laughed a little. "Not in the way I think you mean. But in another way, trouble looms and I would like to prevent it."

"I see." He placed his glass carefully on the table. "Is it the poet?"

She was startled into honestly. "Yes. How did you know?"

"He looks at you as if he will burst into flames—but it was the way you spoke of him that gave you away. You are in love with him."

"I am," she said quietly. "And I fear tragedy if it is not halted. He is honorable. If you and I are married, he will return to Italy with his wife and we will all be saved."

"And you will be yoked to a man you do not love."

Her spirits plummeted. "I suppose it was

naïve of me to think you would find this appealing." She shook her head. "Forgive me."

"You misunderstand, my lady," he said. "I meant what I said, that I would not require a declaration from you. There is enough comfortable respect between us that the marriage would be sound. But I am stolid enough to require faithfulness in deed. You would not see him again."

"Of course. No, I do not wish to see him."

His chin lifted. "I would require it be a true marriage. You will sleep in my bed."

She smiled gently. "That will not be a hardship."

It pleased him, and he lowered his eyes, as if to hide his pleasure. "Is it possible there will be a child from your lover?"

"No."

"Good. I would have taken it as my own, but the coloring might have given us away."

Bless him. "Are you agreeing?"

A slow grin spread over his wide mouth. "Cassandra, I've been tortured with dreams of you from the moment I first saw you. For the chance to lie naked with you even once, I would leap from London bridge."

She blinked. "Oh! I did not—that is—I—"

"I shocked you."

She laughed, covering her hot cheeks with her hands. "A little. But that is all to the good. I do not wish the bargain to be one sided."

"I think I shall have the best of it, in all."

Nearly dizzy with gratitude, Cassandra resolved he should never have cause to think otherwise. She rose and held out her hand, very sure. "Then sir, you shall lie in my bed tonight."

His eyes burned as he rose. "An honorable man would insist upon waiting."

She smiled, very slowly, and only raised one brow. He took her hand and kissed it, then pulled away. "Ah, no," he said with regret. "I will wait." But he put his hands on her face, gently—and to Cassandra's surprise—trembling slightly. "Tonight I only ask a kiss."

Which she gladly granted. It was not Basilio's kiss, but neither was it her husband's. It was rich and skilled, and she could grow to like it in time. That would be enough.

Life was what one made of it.

Analise believed in signs. Her life had been guided by them, and now she prayed earnestly for an answer to the dilemma that faced all three of them. A dilemma that she had put into motion when she had lacked the courage to stand up to her father.

The world did not put much value on visions or prayers or signs, but Analise knew they were real and important methods of communication.

She remembered, as clearly as if it had happened this morning, the vision she had received as a girl. She had been kneeling in the garden, putting flowers on the feet of the Virgin, when a soft yellow light covered the landscape. Dazzled, Analise raised her head and saw a most beautiful Lady sitting on a rock nearby. She was not at all ghostly—even now, Analise could recall details about her that were as real and solid as the rings on her own fingers. The Lady wore leather san- dals on her slim brown feet, her belt was made of cleverly woven hemp, and a silver ring circled one finger. Her hair flowed to her hips, loose and dark, and the ends lifted in the breeze Analise felt in her own hair. The woman smiled, the gen- tlest, most benevolent smile, and asked if Analise knew who she was.

Analise had known. She was the Mother. The Virgin. Mary. And all those names seemed too small to encompass the wisdom, the power, the joy that had come from her, so she had become simply the Lady.

The Lady said that Analise had been chosen for a special task. There would be tests and trials along the way, and she would need to be very strong, very devout. But if she were true to the callings as they were given, she would serve a great purpose. And all Analise had to do in the beginning was to go to St. Catherine's on Cor- sica. Analise had wept with joy—to be a nun!

When she had encountered resistance, the Lady had made Analise's palms bleed—right in front of the village priest, who saw to it that she could go to the nunnery for her education.

The Lady had done so much for Analise, and

what had Analise done in return? Quailed like a baby in the face of her father's disapproval!

Walking briskly along a busy thoroughfare, Analise probed her heart for the truth of that vision. She was not, as many believed, insane or strange. If she had imagined the vision, it was a very thorough envisioning. No, even all these years later, she believed it was true.

A man stood on a box and bawled out some message Analise could not understand, but the power of his delivery captured her attention, carrying it away from her own troublesome thoughts. She paused, wondering what caused him to be so angry.

A woman, her brown hair bound up in a tight bun at the nape of her neck, pushed a piece of paper into Analise's hand. She shook her head in protest—she could not read it, so it would be a waste—but the woman bustled away, her cape billowing around her shoulders. Absently, Analise looked down at it. Some English words, and then—a bright heat of recognition—the numbers written in a style she recognized, a scripture number.

A sign.

Urgently, she hurried toward home, the paper clutched tight in her hands. *St. John*, it said: *15:13.*

Basilio was restless, unable to settle to any task. He knew he ought to be making plans to return to Italy but could not seem to take that step. He could not keep himself from hoping to see Cassandra—no, not only see her; to touch her, kiss her—one more time. That vain wish kept him in London, hoping that she might appear at the pleasure gardens, at some rout or ball, some dinner party. He did not go so far as to attend her salons, though he was sorely tempted.

Analise seemed strange and distant these past days, as well. He would come upon her and find her staring out the window with a frown, as if troubled by some dark thought, but whenever he asked her, she only gave him that sweet smile and brushed his inquiries away. He did not think she was eating well, either.

One evening, to please her, he accepted an invitation to the opera. She enjoyed the music and the beauty of it, and it was written in Italian, which would please her. Dutifully she wore the gown he'd had made for her, allowed the maid to put up her hair, and even allowed her neck to be draped in a strand of delicate sapphires that glowed against her pearlescent skin. He kissed her hand when she came down. "You're very beautiful tonight, my dear," he said, though he was disturbed by the sharpness of the bones in her face and along her shoulders. The gown gaped a little over breasts that were not as full as they'd been. He frowned. "Are you eating at all, Analise?"

A flutter of one hand. "Of course." She

brushed at the gown. "I am pleased you like it. I wanted you to be proud to be seen with me."

He tucked her small hand into his elbow. "You could wear your oldest rags, Analise, and I would still be proud of you."

Suddenly there was a flash of something in her face. The sorrow disappeared, the vagueness, and her astonishingly blue eyes danced. "So I could."

Puzzled, he led her to the waiting coach.

She seemed to perk up at the opera, leaning forward, engrossed in the drama played out. Basilio could not quite find the same measure of excitement, for he found his eye constantly searching for a headful of flaming red hair, listening for that robust laughter.

At last he found her—ensconced in a box with a man Basilio recognized from the salon, a tall, droll-humored Englishman. He leaned to his companion. "Who is that, with Lady Cassandra?"

James said, "Ah, Robert Wicklow. They've just announced their engagement. A very fine pair, are they not? 'Course, he's only a tradesman, but she has little enough to bring to marriage aside from her beauty."

Basilio only heard *marriage*. He made a soft, dismayed sound, and caught himself quickly. With a perfunctory smile, he nodded. "Very nice."

But Analise felt the wind of his unease, and following his gaze, saw Cassandra with her fiancé. A soft, almost translucent expression of pleasure crossed Analise's face. "There is a poem for the writing," she said to Basilio. "Look how she shines in the darkness."

He looked at his wife, alarmed, but she only lifted those enormous blue eyes to his face, guileless as always. He thought of what she had said to him, that the only mystery about her was that she was exactly what she seemed to be. "You like her, don't you?"

"Yes. She appears to be very strong and unconventional, does she not? And yet she is very gentle and good, too. I think she has not been happy, or maybe only rarely."

Basilio nodded, and forced himself to smile. "What a wise young thing you are." He heard himself add, "That man is her fiancé."

"What?"

"Yes. James just told me they are to be married."

"No." Analise rose. "I do not think so."

Alarmed, he took her hand. "Where are you going?"

With that queer, wise smile, she pulled out of his grip. "Only to powder my nose, sir. Do not fret."

She patted his hand like a much older woman, and left the box, her skirts swishing along the floors. Basilio forced himself to look only at the stage, but the lure of Cassandra was at the edge of his vision. Guilt ate at him, burning in his chest and belly—guilt that Analise was fading right before his eyes and he could not make himself return to Italy, guilt that he had behaved badly all around.

And now, whatever gift of freedom he'd delivered to Cassandra by loving her would be lost, because of his selfishness. Because Cassandra, to ensure that Basilio would not make some grand gesture and spend the rest of his life hating himself over it, was willing to trade her freedom for marriage.

He had to stop her.

In the torchlit hallway behind the boxes, Analise moved silently, praying for guidance, slowing at the curtained entrance to each of the ones she thought might be right until a nudging told her to halt. Brushing the curtain to one side a little, she peeked in and saw the shine of Cassandra's red hair. "Sir," she whispered. "A moment, please."

The Englishman, startled, looked around. Cassandra turned, too, and her eyes widened at the sight of Analise. Afraid Basilio might guess what she was about, Analise scowled and gestured for Cassandra to turn around. With some confusion, the man rose and came out into the hall.

It was only then that Analise realized she had no English to tell him what he must know—that he must not marry this woman. She stared up at him pleadingly, and he politely peered back, waiting patiently.

"Lady Cassandra," she said at last. "Basilio di Montevarchi, the Count." She put her hands up in front of her, palms facing, and then slowly put them together, enfolding her fingers tightly, and raised them to her lips and kissed them. She put her locked hands over her heart.

Understanding cleared his brow. Gently he reached for her hands and smiled, nodding. "Grazie," he said, then turned to go.

"No!" Analise said in a fierce whisper. He only thought he understood. She tugged at his sleeve.

"You," she said and held up one hand, fingers spread. Then held up her right hand. "Lady Cassandra." She shook her head fiercely keeping her hands far apart. "No."

His mouth tightened, and she saw the suspicion that she was crazy. "Yes," he said, and dipped back into the box before she could halt him.

Frustrated but not yet finished, she returned slowly to her place next to Basilio, and gave the man a dark glare across the room. He did not notice.

Basilio's agitation grew with each passing moment. At last, he leaned close to Analise and whispered, "Do you mind if we return home, my dear? I do not wish to stay here."

"Of course not."

Inside the carriage, she asked, "Are you well?"

"I am suddenly weary of this place," he said with a faint smile. "Will you think it too rash if we leave for Italy in the morning?"

He had expected her to blaze with happiness over the prospect, but she only looked at him for a long moment. "I had hoped to bid Lady Cassandra farewell before we left."

"Ah." What did he say to that? "Perhaps then, you may send word to her in the morning. We can wait that long. It will give us both a chance to offer our happiness at her engagement."

"Yes."

There was an odd note to the word, and Basilio looked at her closely. "Do I detect dismay?"

Analise frowned, lowered her eyes. "It is only that she once said something to me. That she did not find marriage to her liking."

Guilt. "Ah. I did not know that."

"Perhaps," she said quietly, "he has changed her mind."

"I'm sure that's it."

Analise's mind whirled with possible actions—perhaps she ought to speak with Cassandra herself, convince her that this engagement was not the right action. It felt terribly wrong somehow, and there was doom in it for all of them.

But it seemed Analise was not the only one

with that thought, for Basilio managed only to stay at the house long enough to think Analise had retired, before he was out again in the dark streets. On some nudging she did not question, Analise slipped out behind him, staying close to the buildings, glad of the soft kid evening shoes she wore that made no noise.

For many days, she had prayed over the sign she had received. Terror burned in her that she might have it wrong, and she was frozen in indecision. When she had looked up the Scripture that was on the piece of paper that woman gave her, it read "Greater love hath no man than this, that a man should lay down his life for his friends."

And Analise had been deeply dismayed. If it were only so simple as to remove herself for all of this to be fixed, she would have done it joyfully. But suicide was a mortal sin, and the one punishment Analise could not bear was to remain apart from God and the Lady for all eternity.

So she had spent many hours in prayer, awaiting a new sign. If the sacrifice were true and honorable and right, then the Lady would intervene with God, and all would be set to rights.

It frightened her very much to make such a large decision. She wished with great regret that she'd had the courage to stand up to her father, and the thought made her scowl. He seemed an easy hurdle, looking back. How much she had grown these past months!

When Basilio neared the townhouse where Cassandra lived, he leaned on the wall beneath a tree that grew in her garden, and looked up at something. The house was dark, and Analise, standing in the shadows herself, could see nothing that might have drawn his attention.

He settled as if to wait, and Analise made herself comfortable, taking the rosary beads from her pocket and running them through her fingers. "Guide me," she whispered. "Show me a sign."

Cassandra returned from the opera with a heavy heart. Robert would tell her nothing of what Analise had said to him, and it left her uneasy.

This was madness—all of it. Everything. It seemed a hundred years since anything in her life had been reliably normal, ordinary. Climbing down from her carriage, she shook off her hood and headed for her stairs. A voice came out of the shadows, as it had once before. "Cassandra."

She braced herself, inhaling a great lungful of air. A servant stepped forward, ready to come to her defense if required, but she saw Basilio, halted in a pool of light thrown by a torch, and she waved her servants away. "I will be all right."

She waited until the carriage moved away, until it was only she and Basilio with the moon shining down on them, lighting his face set in such sober, sorrowful lines.

As if drawn by some force higher and more compelling than themselves, they moved toward each other, halting a foot apart. His eyes were tortured. "Forgive me," he said roughly, "for forcing you to such a dramatic act."

Her hand fluttered up, but she brought it back without putting it into his hair. "I want you to be happy, Basilio. I know it seems mad that this marriage will allow it, but it will. You must trust me."

"You must not make that sacrifice. I leave tomorrow morning. You will be free."

"Leave?"

A somber nod. "We will return to Italy, Cassandra. I will not come back to England, ever. You need not be afraid of our betrayals any longer."

A tightness rose in her throat. "I have already given my word to him."

He took a half step. "If you marry, all that has been gained for you in this will be lost." He took her hand, put it on his face. "You want my happiness," he said. "And I want yours."

Down the street a church bell began to ring, tolling the hours. Cassandra heard it distantly, and heard a second bell start up behind it, a half beat slower, so it always seemed there was one extra hour ringing out. "This is, then, a true love. You must go and take your wife. I must marry Robert and make a new life. It is not disaster, love. It is a choice for life."

He made a soft, pained sound and closed his eyes. "Ah, I am only insane with jealousy."

Impulsively, she touched his hair. "I know," she whispered. Against her will, her hand pressed against his cheek. "I know," she repeated.

With a sharp exhalation he reached for her, and Cassandra found she had no ability to turn away from this last embrace. She flung her arms around his neck, pressed her face into his neck, and felt his strong arms around her back. Tears welled in her eyes. "I do so love you, Basilio."

He tightened his hold, crushing her to him, his breath soft against her neck, his hand against the back of her head. "Never so much as I love you," he said, and lifted his head, his eyes burning in his sculpted face.

For a long, long moment, they only stared at each other, and Cassandra felt a powerful, enveloping light surround her, bind her to him, and he to her. Unbreakable, powerful, eternal. Long before he bent his head, she knew he would kiss her, and her body swelled with the need of it, the need of his taste, his lips, his tongue. Dizzy, she looked at his lips in longing, and accepted their touch. Only their lips touched, but at the moment of joining, the light around them splintered and turned gilded, bathing her heart, her mind, her soul with it. With reverent sweetness, she kissed him back. Then, shaking, she lifted her head.

He pressed his forehead against hers, his hands clasped around her face. "I love you, Cassandra, more than all the world. I will love you always."

The bells rang out the last chime—thirteen, which seemed unlucky somehow—and Cassandra allowed herself to touch his face one last time as she released him. "You must write a thousand poems."

"I will write them all for you." His grip tightened, urgent. "You must write to me of your children."

"I will."

He took a breath, dropped his hands, and stepped back. For another moment they only stood there. Then he said, "Be well."

"And you," she whispered. Then she turned and hurried away from the temptation of calling him back, of begging him to stay with her just this one last time. In honor they had begun. In honor, they would end.

In the shadows, Analise watched as they said their farewells. Every line of their bodies was etched in deepest grief, and they swayed together, resisted, and then fell into an embrace of such power Analise felt tears on her face.

As she watched them, it seemed she could see a golden aura of beauty around them, the same color that made her think of the Lady. They kissed, sweetly and without carnality, and Analise felt something swell inside of her—a hunger for that unity. The unity she would only know with God.

A soft breath of illumination went through her. Only Analise had the power to make this right: to save Cassandra from a marriage that would destroy her spirit, save Basilio from the resignation growing in his eyes, save herself from making further mistakes.

"No greater love . . ." she whispered, and hurried toward home, praying earnestly. Silently, she sent up her prayer, the most earnest prayers of her life, to the Lady for her intervention with God. It seemed suddenly so plain, so very clear. Suicide was a mortal sin, but not if undertaken for the sacrifice of others, surely. Surely the Lady would intervene with God after all Analise had done. Or intervene here on earth, if her purpose was skewed.

And then—oh sweet relief!—she would be in heaven and free of these earthly coils, free to be an angel to guide these two for whom she had discovered such love.

Exuberant, she rushed through the darkened streets, her heart very clear.

Nearly blind with sorrow, Basilio walked back to the townhouse. There was a strange joy in him gilding the sorrow, and he wondered how it was possible to feel such relief in something that had caused so much pain.

But he recognized with a smile that Cassandra had always been correct in this. For both of them, honor was valued more highly than indulgence. It was not written that he could not love her—and love her he would. Always.

Weary, he climbed the stairs to his chamber. At the top he halted, instincts quivering in a strange and powerful way. There was a smell he could not quite place. Frowning, he went to the chamber where Analise had been sleeping and knocked softly on the closed door.

The door burst open, and Analise stood there, her face pale and somehow radiant at once. She wore only a chemise, and her extravagant hair fell down her back, well past her hips. And—oh, God!—a strip of cloth bound her left arm, but already great drips of blood were welling out of it.

"Basilio," she cried, pressing her right hand over her left arm. "I am so glad to see you; I have so much to say!"

"What happened to you?" He grabbed her, pressed his own hand over her arm.

"I thought," she said, and there was a wispy sort of breathiness to the words, "that I was meant to take my life."

A bolt of terror shot through him, and he grabbed her, lifting her arm above her head as she fainted. A drop of blood fell on his coat, and he screamed for a servant. A girl scurried out of an alcove, and yelped when she saw the blood, freezing in her steps.

"Get help! Now!" He turned back. "Analise!"

Her head lolled. In terror, Basilio swept her up in his arms and urgently carried her down the stairs, keeping those gruesome wounds high above her head. She weighed little and he was barely winded when he ran into the garden and plunged her into the ice cold water of the fountain.

It roused her. Blinking, she looked at him. "Did you tell her?"

"Who?" he whispered, touching her face gently. "Tell her what?"

"Cassandra," she said clearly. "My vision was real. The Lady called me to be a nun, and I was too weak to stand up to my father." Her eyes drifted closed, but her breath seemed strong enough. "No greater love than this . . ."

"Oh, God!" he cried, and buried his face against her neck. "Oh, God, forgive us all."

But now she was rousing herself. "No, Basilio, you are not listening." She pushed away from him, then pulled off the cloth. "I am only weak from a fast I undertook to see the truth of this situation." She showed him her arm, the small cut still bleeding but not so much as it had seemed. "See? I had the razor on my arm, and The Lady appeared to tell me it was not so dire as that."

Visions again. He scowled. "What are you talking about, Analise?"

She raised out of the water, and put her hand on his face. "We must go to France and annul the marriage. I have the name of a man who will do it quickly. Then I will find refuge in a convent, and you will come back and claim your love." She splashed out of the fountain in her bare feet, her black hair stuck to her back and hips. "Come, I must eat to regain my strength."

"You have a *name?*" Basilio asked. "From where?"

She looked over her shoulder and spoke slowly, as if to a dim-witted child. "From the Lady, I told you. Mary." Catching his expression, she laughed. "Ah, I forgot. You do not believe in visions. But that does not matter. I do." She paused, very seriously. "We must act quickly, my friend, and there is something very specific you must do in order to secure my safety from my father. Will you trust me?"

He frowned. "I suppose."

"It will not be easy, but we must go tonight."

"But—"

"Trust me, Basilio. Trust the Lady. She has not failed us yet. This is for you, this part."

Chapter 21

In the morning, Robert Wicklow arrived at Cassandra's house very early. She had not even awakened yet, but when Joan told her that he was most insistent about speaking with her, she had him shown to her salon, and quickly dressed.

Concerned, she ordered chocolate to be brought, and hurried in to see him. Her fears were not alleviated when she saw his face, haggard and gray with the mark of no sleep. "God! Who died?"

He turned with a heavy expression. "Sit down, Cassandra," he said. "Your brothers will be here shortly, but first I must apologize to you for my own part in this."

"In what?" Dread built in her chest, spreading to her belly, and she put her hands around herself. "What are you talking about?"

"I cannot marry you," he said. "That was what she was trying to tell me last night, and had I not allowed my pride to intervene, I would have listened."

"Who said? Analise, you mean?"

But there was a commotion just then, and Cassandra knew it was bad news the moment she saw both of her brothers together, early in the morning, their faces grave as they entered the salon. Sunlight streamed in the windows behind them, illuminating the same gray expressions as marked Robert's countenance.

She put a hand to her ribs. "What?" she cried, thinking it must be Phoebe—or perhaps Adriana. A carriage accident, perhaps, or bandits, or—

"Sit down," Gabriel said, not unkindly. "Let me pour you some chocolate."

"No!" She stood her ground. "Tell me! Who is it?"

Julian took her arm and led her to the divan. "Not your sisters," he said.

Her eyes flew to his face, praying—oh, God, not—"Basilio?" she whispered, and was barely able to get the word out.

"No." He swallowed. "His wife. She tried to kill herself last night."

"Analise?" A cold knot formed in her chest. It was nearly worse to hear this. Her hands began to tremble. "But she . . . it is a mortal sin."

"Yes. But she is very young, and she thought—" Julian broke off and looked at Gabriel for help.

Gabriel poured chocolate and pressed the cup

into her hand. "She thought it would be a kindness. She thought she had been wrong in not defying her father and taking her vows, and she believed"—he glanced over his shoulder—"that she had created—"

Robert said, "I did not listen to her."

Cassandra doubled over. "Stop!" she cried, putting her face into her hands. A low, wild sound came from her throat, and even as it appalled her—now they would know, would see the heart of things—she could not stop it. She jumped up, guilt an animal that threatened to devour her whole, and Basilio, too. She put her hands in her loose hair, clutching it away from her face, pacing the floor in an attempt to regain control. "She is alive?"

Gabriel offered the answer. "Yes. He arrived in time, and saved her life."

A tumble of visions swelled over her eyes, and she whirled, resumed pacing.

It did not help. Her mind echoed with ricocheting images—that sweet, beautiful, *innocent* face, pale white, near death. Because of her. Because of Basilio. Because they had—she halted with a moan, pressing the heels of her hands to her eyes. "Oh, God!" she cried. "What have we done?"

And she sank to the floor, consumed by sorrow and guilt, her eyes dry even as she began to tremble from head to toe. She could not think of what to say, how to sweep her emotional storm beneath a carpet this time, and only raised miserable eyes to her brothers. "What have we done?" she whispered.

It was Gabriel who came to her, putting his long arms around her shoulders, pulling her into his gentle, soothing embrace, stroking her hair, her back. "She told him she wanted to be a nun. That if she had been stronger, none of this would have happened, that all of you would have had what you wanted." He pressed a cheek against her hair. "All of you are blaming yourselves for it. And none of you are to blame." Very, very gently, he stroked her hair. "He is worthy of loving, Cassandra. I always knew, when you fell, it would be to some very great passion. You mustn't regret it. He loves you. She loves you. And you love them both."

At that, she crumpled. For the first time in her life, she let another person witness her pain, because it flowed from her in vast, unstoppable waves, grief and sorrow and guilt, all mixed together with relief—she had not died!—and a vast, strange love. Through it Gabriel held her, a rope in the vastness of the uncharted territory of emotions. When she was spent, he led her to bed, rinsed a cloth with cold water, and put it on her eyes.

"You see," he said, holding her hand. "You were honorable, both of you, and it saved her life. If he had not arrived when he did, she would have bled to death."

"I cannot believe she would attempt suicide. She is so devout!"

He smiled sadly, wisdom in his pale green eyes. "She is young. All young girls wish to be martyrs to something."

That brought a fresh wash of tears, and Cassandra clutched his hand tightly. "Oh, what if she had succeeded!"

"She did not."

Cassandra tried to capture a sense of herself, her old self, before this new one had emerged. "I did not ever think to love that way."

"I know. Nor did Julian—and he fell as hard as you."

"And what of you, Gabriel? I thought it would be you."

A flicker crossed his eyes, but was hidden quickly in a smile. "I love them all. Tall and short, blond and brown, white and black, rich and poor. That is my place in the world."

She smiled wanly. "Where is she this morning? Analise, I mean."

"He is taking her home to Italy."

She let go of a breath. "Good." It didn't seem enough, so she repeated it, drifting in the aftermath of her storm. "Good."

Hours later, when the worst of her storm was over, Joan tiptoed into the chamber. "Milady?" she said, and again, more urgently. "Milady, there's a letter for you. It came from his man."

Cassandra sat up and took the note, her hands trembling a little as she broke the seal. But it was not Basilio's hand on the paper. It was written in Italian, in a strong, bold handwriting that was as beautiful and surprising as the young woman who'd written it.

My dearest Cassandra,

Do not listen to the rumors of my attempted suicide. The story is not what it seems, but the world must believe it to be true, for all our sakes. My father must believe it to be absolutely true.

You must not marry. Wait for Basilio, who loves you more than the sun, as you love him, as I love God.

Analise

Gabriel, roused by Cassandra's sharp intake of breath, sat up. He blinked his long eyes like a cat. "Are you all right?"

She folded the letter carefully and tucked it into her bodice, close to her heart. "Yes," she said. "I'm very well."

Part Four

England

I have not a joy but of thy bringing,
And pain itself seems sweet when springing
From thee, thee, only thee.
Like spells that nought on earth can break,
Till lips that know the charm have spoken,
This heart, howe'er the world may wake
Its grief, its scorn, can but be broken
By thee, thee, only thee.

THOMAS MOORE

Chapter 22

Autumn, 1788

Cassandra sat alone in her walled garden, as she had most afternoons through the long autumn. Overhead the leaves fluttered orange and yellow and red; on the ground spread a carpet of the same. Sitting at her white-painted iron table, rocks weighting her papers, she wrote intently, transcribing the exuberant Italian of Boccaccio into equally exuberant English. This fine October day, surrounded with the colors of autumn, she wrote, "The Tenth Day, where tales are told of those who have acted liberally or munificently in Love Affairs or Other Matters." It made her smile.

The translation was nearly complete, and with the help of a powerful admirer of her work, she had procured the interest of a publisher who was willing to present the book as that of a woman. Of Cassandra herself.

She did not allow her mind to dwell upon the

possible reactions of the public to the work. There would be those who were scandalized, and those who scorned the work because it was the efforts of a mere female, and others who would say she had not done it right or according to the standards they would have set, or any number of criticisms which really just meant that Cassandra had not done the translation the way they would have done it.

But she was finally brave enough to do it anyway, to risk the possibility of ridicule on something heartfelt, to risk being honest. Basilio and Analise had given her that.

A cloud passed over the sun, and as if called by the sudden lack of light, a wind whipped through the garden, scattering leaves against the tree trunks and the legs of the table. With a cry, Cassandra held down the sheet upon which she worked. It was time to go in, though she was reluctant to do so.

"Would you like some assistance?"

Cassandra started at her brother's voice. Julian, his cheeks made ruddy by the autumn air, reached for the rock holding her notes in place.

"Thank you. If it's going to gale, I'm afraid I'll have to go inside."

"I've come to whisk you out of your moldy study anyway," he said, gathering the ink pot and a pile of scribblings. "You've been entirely too lacking on the social scene, and they're all asking about you."

Cassandra scowled, but did not answer until they were inside. Depositing the materials on her cluttered desk, she shook her head. "Thank you, Julian, but I find I do not wish to make small talk out in the world. They're all so bloody curious and gossipy."

"Such language!" he said mockingly, and grinned.

Grinned. Julian.

"What are you about today, sir? You've Gabriel's mischievous look about you. Am I to be the butt of a practical joke?"

He laughed softly, taking the pen from her hand. "I have a surprise for you, that's all. Go don your prettiest gown and come with me. Not a word more."

She inclined her head, smiling a little at the spark of the devil in his eyes. She remembered a famous swordsman was due to visit, to duel with the king, and perhaps Gabriel had been matched with him for public sport. Or maybe there was some wicked party she would enjoy.

"Very well," she said. "Anything that can make you grin is worth the viewing. I shall not take long."

Joan hurried her into her favorite green brocade, and helped Cassandra arrange her hair. Donning a cape against the cool wind, she hurried back down. Julian helped her into the waiting coach just as the first long streamers of sunset pinked the edges of the sky. "No hint at all of what we're doing?" she asked.

"No." He patted her hand, and a sudden sense of anticipation caught her chest.

When they halted, Cassandra scowled. "A coffee shop? Isn't this Gabriel's haunt?"

"It is."

And busy, too. She saw through the bow-fronted window that there was a crowd within, men in coats and hats, shoulder to shoulder. "We'll be crushed!"

Gabriel had been watching for them evidently, for he appeared at the door, holding out a hand to draw them forward, his lean figure nearly blazing with excitement. "Hurry. It has already begun!"

"What has?"

"Just come with me." He drew her into the hot, strong smelling throng. Cassandra could see nothing in the smoke and gloom, and whatever might have been visible was blocked by shoulders that all seemed to be at the level of her eyes or above. An approving roar and round of clapping arose as they entered, and Gabriel used the sudden movement to push through the forest of bodies. Julian came behind, smelling of something spicy and sweet, a scent she was grateful for in the press of bodies. A man stepped back onto her toe and she winced, her frustration growing. She halted. "Julian! Is this really—"

He only pushed at her, and at the same moment Gabriel took her arm and pulled her through the last blockade, to an area around a table upon which a man stood, a sheaf of papers in his hand.

She halted, dizzy, and closed her eyes, then opened them again.

It was still Basilio who stood there. Basilio, his hair caught back in an elegant queue that could not entirely tame the wilderness of black curls. Basilio, as beautiful as any sculpture, his long legs and virile shoulders even more dear than they had been upon her first sighting of him. Basilio, his dark eyes shining as he stared at her. She put a hand up to cover her madly pounding heart, and heard the room settle in anticipation as he smiled and lifted the paper and began, in his lilting voice,

> *And now, at last, I speak love freely,*
> *Shout it boldly, whisper it sweetly.*
> *Not hidden in plums or sonnets to light,*
> *Sing it loudly, murmur it deeply,*
> *Not woven in rhyme or the color of night,*
> *My love's name, color of fire,*
> *color of night, color of light, color of all*
> *Cassandra,*

Cassandra,
Cassandra.

Julian pushed her or she would never have moved, horrified that tears were streaming over her face in public, tears of revelation and joy and relief. Yet once moving, she could not stop. He leapt down and ran to her, and all around them was a cheer, clapping, celebration. She halted as he took her hands, his face full of laughter and love and joy, and whispered, "Oh, Basilio, this is so excessive."

"The excess of excessiveness," he agreed, and hauled her into his embrace for a kiss of sweetness and power, of passion.

She allowed it for one moment, then grew aware of the dozens and dozens of eyes fixed upon them. "Please," she protested. "We must retreat to some private corner, or I shall die of the embarrassment."

"Of course," he said, and as if he had prepared for such a reaction, led her to a room near the back.

Cassandra heard Gabriel soothing the hungry crowd. "Only give a moment!"

In the quiet corner, lit dimly with a single tallow against a dark mirror, she looked at him. There was wear on his face, new depth of maturity etched into the hollows of his cheeks, around his mouth. His eyes, dark and beautiful, held a quiet sobriety she had not noticed before. "I wish to ask you first if you can forgive me, Cassandra," he said, touching her fingers with his thumb. "I was not the warrior you deserved, but a boy in search of rescue."

"What . . . how . . . ?"

"In a moment, but I need you to understand that I have grown to a full man now. Not only poet, but warrior. You shall never lack for anything, not love, or honor . . . or husband."

"Analise?"

"I have something for you." From within his coat, he drew out a letter. Cassandra sat down to read it, peering hard at the writing to make it out in the bad light.

My dearest Cassandra,

I have you to thank for granting my heart's desire, for though I do not write to you from my beloved convent in Corsica, I do write from such a haven in France, where I am to take my vows in a matter of months. Here I am free to sing the praises of God from morning until night, and all through my sleep.

I return to you your husband, who kept me chaste and whole for my own marriage to God. My father, in thanks for Basilio saving my life, has persuaded the elder Montevarchi to accept his son's choice of wife, so you shall not be poor and he shall not suffer the loss of his obligation to his family.

*Thank you for allowing him to protect me this
way. May your love bring you the same joy my
own has brought to me.*

Analise

Cassandra raised a shaking hand to her
mouth, and looked at him. It seemed impossible
that after so long, after so much, it should just
be . . . done. "You are not married any longer?"

"No. It was annulled in France. Very quickly."

Still, she could not seem to bring her mind
around the fact that he was standing here,
though her body seemed to recognize it more
quickly than she. A liquid heat moved in her
knees, her hips, tingled over her breasts and
throat and into her lips. She found her gaze on
his mouth, those full-cut and sensual lips. In a
sudden wave of erotic vision, she saw his body
nude, pressed into her own, and she had to take
a breath against the overwhelming lust.

"If your feelings have altered, Cassandra, I
will understand. Either way, I thought you
deserved to know that she is well and happy."

She nodded, her lungs too airless for speech.

"I brought you something," he said, and
pulled out a handful of plums.

Cassandra half-laughed, and tears sprang to
her eyes. "I do not want plums," she said clearly,
and plucked them out of his palms. Clean and
strong, those hands, with their powerful fingers.

With a soft breath, she bent her head and pressed a kiss to the heart of each, imprinting her lips upon the lines of life and heart.

"What do you want, Cassandra?" he whispered.

"You," she said. "Only you, Basilio."

With a cry he came to her, putting his arms around her, kissing her, kissing her face, her mouth. "Oh, God!" he cried. "I have died a thousand times the past few days. I was so afraid that you would not have me after so much."

Cassandra laughed, filled with such giddy happiness it was like gold in her blood. She gave a whoop of purest happiness, like a pirate of her childhood games, and squeezed him to her. "I love you, Basilio. I love you, I love you."

And there he was, suddenly back again, her prince of laughter, her joyous poet. His eyes blazed, and his smile burned brilliantly, and his laughter rolled out into the fire-colored day. "We must marry immediately," he said. "I wish to lie with you, man to wife."

"Oh, yes," she whispered. And suddenly she was weeping, laughing, both of them were, in amazement and relief. She put her head on his shoulder and breathed in the scent of him, and knew there were things that would have to be worked out—Italy and England. Time in both, perhaps.

But just now, none of that mattered. He embraced her tightly. "At last I can write poetry that has your name," he said. "The only name worth speaking is Cassandra, for it is the name of my only love. My wife."

She kissed him, and a wild open sense of perfection filled her suddenly, a sense of seeing all of creation, a world of light, and all the people rainbows within it. *Thank you,* she thought. *Oh, thank you so much.*